OAKDALE
CONFIDENTIAL

OAKDALE
CONFIDENTIAL

ANONYMOUS

POCKET BOOKS
New York London Toronto Sydney

POCKET BOOKS, a division of Simon & Schuster, Inc.
1230 Avenue of the Americas, New York, NY 10020

ISBN-13: 978-1-4165-2481-6
ISBN-10:   1-4165-2481-9

This Pocket Books hardcover edition April 2006

10 9 8 7 6 5 4 3 2 1

Manufactured in the United States of America

For information regarding special discounts for bulk purchases,
please contact Simon & Schuster Special Sales at 1-800-456-6798
or business@simonandschuster.com

OAKDALE
CONFIDENTIAL

Prologue

Katie Peretti chose to panic.

She did not make such a monumental decision in haste.

Prior to determining that panic was the best—indeed, the only—option under the circumstances, Katie reviewed the facts.

Fact #1: Katie was broke. Katie was almost always broke. One would think that between co-owning a gym and a detective agency, she should have at least one stream of income flowing in at any given time. One would be wrong.

Fact #2: To remedy her cash-flow problem, Katie had taken a job helping Oakdale Memorial Hospital's most dynamic board member, Mrs. Nancy Hughes, octogenarian extraordinaire, organize a benefit to honor the Marron family's fifty years of support for the institution.

Fact #3: There were four members of the Marron family. Gregory Marron Sr., who insisted on being called "Gig,"

Gregory Marron Jr., who insisted on being called "Mr. Marron," Gregory Jr.'s wife, Aurora, who'd had the nerve to say, "So what might be considered haute cuisine in Oakdale, these days, Kathryn? Is it still pigs-in-a-blanket, or have you all moved up to smoked salmon on a cracker?" and Gregory Jr.'s twenty-two-year-old stepdaughter, Monica, who told Katie, "Don't pay any attention to my parents, okay? They kind of . . . well, they're snobs." All four were expected to be at the gala.

Fact #4: All four were not at the gala.

Katie had been the first to arrive at the banquet hall, located across the street from Oakdale Memorial Hospital. Her first order of business was to make sure that the botanical centerpieces for all fifty tables were the same size. The last thing she needed was for Barbara Ryan to pitch a public fit about how her roses were a millimeter less open than Emily Stewart's, or for Lucinda Walsh to ask why her view was obstructed when Lisa Grimaldi could see the stage perfectly. Next, Katie checked that the band was set up, that the waiters were all accounted for, that the catering staff was at attention, and that the lights were dimmed to a level that flattered the "women of a certain age" in the room. She also double-checked that a gleaming engraved bronze plaque, thanking the Marron family for all they'd done for Memorial through the years, had been set up in front of the hospital's main entrance. Encircling the plaque was a huge red ribbon for Gig, Gregory, Aurora, and Monica to cut with a pair of oversize scissors.

In anticipation of this spectacle, half of Oakdale was currently waiting in the plaza in front of the hospital. The men were dressed in tuxedos, the women outfitted tastefully in a rainbow of cocktail dresses. Unfortunately at the moment almost everyone's hair was being whipped about by the still-brisk April wind. Simultaneously everyone's hands were darting to keep the variety of French twists, extensions, and chignons from flying off into the blue yonder.

Fact #5: It wasn't supposed to be this way. Katie had originally planned this evening down to the last second. By the time the sun started to set and the wind picked up, all the guests were scheduled to be safely inside, savoring their choice of vegetarian lasagna or filet mignon.

Fact #6: The reason the above had yet to happen (forty-five minutes off schedule and counting), was that while Gig, Aurora, and Monica Marron were already in their appointed spots, standing by the bronze plaque and in front of photographers from both the local papers plus one from a national syndicate, Gregory Marron Jr. was nowhere to be found.

Gig, Aurora, and Monica had all arrived together in one limousine, explaining that Gregory had some business to attend to, but would be following shortly in a different car. They'd assured her there was nothing to worry about.

Still, Katie worried. She worried when Gregory was five minutes late. She worried when the five minutes turned to fifteen. And, when that fifteen crept over the half-hour mark, she allowed herself to panic.

Because she'd be doomed if this gala didn't go off smoothly.

Nancy Hughes had vouched for Katie's competence because Katie had sworn she could handle it, that she would take care of everything and that nothing would go wrong.

But in spite of Nancy's endorsement, the hospital board still hadn't been enthusiastic about hiring her. Before the first meeting began, Katie had overheard bigwig Lucinda Walsh sniping that she wasn't exactly comfortable handing over the gala honoring the institution's biggest donors to "a twenty-something cheerleader Barbie doll."

So Katie had sweetened the deal. In a burst of act-first-think-later exuberance that had gotten her in trouble in the past, Katie told the board members they didn't have to pay her until the benefit had gone off without a single hitch. Katie was that confident she could pull this off.

Confident.

Stupid.

Such a fine line between the two.

The hospital board took Katie up on her offer. Apparently, a twenty-something cheerleader Barbie doll—though Katie preferred to think of herself as petite, perky, and unapologetically enthusiastic—handling the institution's biggest donors was okay as long as it also saved them some money during the planning stages.

Less okay for Katie was the reality that during the four weeks she'd worked with Nancy, putting everything together alongside the Marrons, she'd proceeded to spend her future earnings. Her credit cards were nearly maxed out and the fee she was counting on would only come her way if she pulled off a flawless evening.

But Gregory Marron Jr. was forty-five minutes late for his own party.

Katie looked helplessly into the shivering crowd and, gratefully, caught sight of Nancy standing by the plaque and the ceremonial scissors. She was making polite conversation, trying to placate the increasingly impatient guests in the front row. As they were doctors—there was Nancy's son, Bob, plus his colleagues Susan Stewart, Lynn Michaels, and Ben Harris—they were particularly eager for the ceremonial part of the evening to be over, so they could return to work. If anyone would know what to do in this situation, Katie felt certain, it would be Nancy.

Murmuring "Excuse me" and "pardon me," Katie eased her way through the crowd, trying her best not to step on a dress-train here or snap a tuxedo button there as she passed.

She ended up right next to Nancy and, covering her mouth discreetly with one hand, whispered, "Please, help me, Mrs. Hughes!"

"I'm sorry, Katie," Nancy whispered back, equally discreetly. "But I'm afraid I just don't know what to do in this situation."

Oh, well. Showed how much Katie's certainty was worth.

Once again scanning the crowd in hope of finding a solution, Katie instead caught sight of Carly Snyder. Even within an assembly of over two hundred people, Carly stood out. She was dressed in a strapless silk turquoise ensemble with a full skirt and matching silver-trimmed wrap. On most blondes with her shade of fairer-than-fair skin, the dress would have appeared overwhelming. But Carly wasn't the sort of five-foot-two, blue-eyed blonde who would allow an accident of biology to keep her from wearing the season's hottest color. Carly simply made up for what she lacked in actual melanin with a—how to put it?—colorful personality.

Carly's husband, Jack, a detective with the Oakdale Police

Department, was in attendance, as well. He was moonlighting, doing security for the event. Katie wondered if maybe Jack would consider her plight enough of an emergency to put out one of those all-points bulletins on Gregory Marron and send a police car to escort him to the gala.

Katie also saw . . . no, it couldn't be . . . Henry, her business partner in their less-than-successful gym, would never let his little sister come to a party where alcohol was being served. Still, that sure did look like sixteen-year-old Maddie Coleman loitering there on the sidelines, doing her best to appear sophisticated and give the impression of fitting in. If Henry saw Maddie here, he'd pitch a fit. That's just what Katie needed now. More things to worry about. If Henry found out—

Henry!

Henry, for God's sake!

How could Katie have been so stupid?

Just like Katie needed to grovel for gigs to make ends meet while they waited for the gym to hit it big, so did Henry. Only, in his case, he'd taken a job driving a limo. And he'd driven for the Marrons before. In fact, Henry had even gone so far as to boast that the family, who preferred to use a car service when they didn't feel like driving rather than keep a full-time chauffeur on staff, requested him by name now.

If luck was on her side and Henry was driving Gregory tonight, he could tell her where the heck they were!

And whether or not now was an appropriate time to panic.

Katie pulled out her cell and, within seconds, was patched through to Henry.

"Fear not, Bubbles!" he boomed majestically. "The Mounties always get their man, and so does Henry Coleman! The Marron Baron and I are rounding the corner of Oakdale Memorial, as we speak. So strike up the band, pop the champagne, and let's get this dog-and-pony show on the road!"

Katie allowed herself a little squeak of joy plus a hop of glee. All right, so maybe there was still a bit of the high-school cheerleader left inside her, after all.

She stood on her tiptoes and craned her neck for a clearer look at the end of the block where, as promised, Henry's limo dramatically rounded the corner and pulled to a stop right in front of the hospital's entrance.

Everyone applauded. Out of relief, gratitude and, she suspected, to stay warm.

Henry, with his flair for drama, alighted from the driver's seat just in time to catch the ovation's peak crescendo. He clicked his heels and offered a bow, then walked around to the passenger side door and opened it with a flourish.

Gregory Marron Jr., dressed in a black tux with a cream-colored bow tie and matching cummerbund, fell out of the car, rolling slightly mid-plunge so that he hit the pavement first with his shoulder, then with the back of his head.

Oh.

Wonderful.

Gregory Marron Jr. was drunk.

At his own tribute.

For a moment, the crowd could do no more than gasp and gape, not necessarily in that order (a few may have even nervously giggled). Then, the wire service's shutterbug stepped up to snap a photo and the flash of his camera seemed to galvanize the spectators.

Somebody screamed. Was it Gregory's stepdaughter, Monica? It might have been Monica. As far as Katie could determine, the scream was high-pitched and youthful and seriously freaked out.

Somebody else lunged toward Gregory and as soon as one person began moving, the entire crowd surged forward.

Gig pushed his way toward the car, hollering to no one in particular, "What's going on?" He glared at Katie in passing, as if this was all part of her agenda.

Aurora followed, shoving people aside. She bent over to reach for her husband's arm, seemingly meaning to shake it, but Jack Snyder leaped ahead to stop her.

He stood between Gregory's inert body and the crowd, effectively blocking everyone, except for Ben Harris, who was the first doctor to reach Gregory.

Ben felt for a pulse along Gregory's wrist. Then his fingers moved to the base of Gregory's neck. In retrospect, that was Katie's first clue that maybe there was more than mere public drunkenness going on here. Drunk people, she suspected, still had detectable pulses.

Ben lifted Gregory's eyelids.

Katie suspected that wasn't a very reassuring sign, either.

She expected the good doctor to leap into action. To perform CPR, slam down a cardiac punch, call for backup or a crash cart, maybe even jab a long needle into Gregory's chest.

Unfortunately, when Ben failed to perform any of those life-saving measures, when all he did was sit back on his heels and helplessly look up at Jack Snyder, Katie realized that now finally, was the appropriate time to panic.

Because Gregory Marron Jr. wasn't drunk or even experiencing what the medical establishment referred to as a cardiac or cerebral "incident."

Gregory Marron Jr. was clearly, indisputably dead.

Forgetting about her salary, her reputation, even her personal debt to Nancy, Katie found herself abruptly terrified about something much more important.

If Gregory was dead, and not from obvious natural causes, then Katie was very, very afraid that she knew who'd killed him.

Standing in the crowd, two other women suddenly felt exactly the same way.

1

"I'm not going," Mike had said the day before the gala.

His tone suggested it was the end of the discussion and that if Katie said another word about it he would leave the premises.

Unfortunately for both of them, Mike and Katie were currently in his car. He was driving her to work. Which meant that Mike had nowhere to walk off to and that Katie was faced with a dilemma.

On the one hand, she could press him for an explanation and maybe get an answer. That would clear the air, and their drive to work would end with a passionate kiss hot enough to make even Katie's usually stalk-straight blond hair curl a bit, and perhaps even an explicit promise of more to come once they reunited back home at the end of the day.

That would be good.

On the other hand, if Katie pressed Mike for an explanation, he might only withdraw further. He'd silently steam, while she'd try to hold back her tears. The ride would end with a slammed door and the implicit promise of more silent treatment to come that evening at home.

That would be bad.

Katie knew from past bouts of fighting in the car that she should keep her mouth shut, give Mike some time to cool off, then pursue the topic at another time. It's what any mature woman who knew her man well would do.

So, while Mike drove, Katie bit her tongue and gazed out the Ford's window, desperately looking for something to distract her from the chorus of "But, why, why, why, Mike? Why won't you go to the reception with me tomorrow tonight?" that was echoing in her head. Alas, Oakdale, Illinois, at eight o'clock in the morning was not a bustling metropolis that was up to such a relationship-saving task. The problem with living in a small town was that you weren't likely to see anything at 8 A.M. on Thursday morning that you didn't see at the same time any other day of the week. There was Burt, owner of Burt's Garage, rolling up the groaning metallic door to announce he was now open for business. There was Gwen, the breakfast waitress at Al's Diner, smoking her final, hurried cigarette before reporting for her shift. And there was Gwen's older sister, Carly Snyder, walking down the block from her house, holding her daughter, Sage, with one hand and waving bye to her son, Parker, as he got on the school bus, with the other.

Katie waved to Carly like she usually did, thinking she could have done the same with her eyes closed. The daily route to work was that predictable and offered nothing to distract Katie from her need to mulishly question Mike's terse refusal to attend the reception at Memorial.

Okay. Sixty seconds had passed since Katie had committed to postponing her questions until another time. Sixty seconds later. That was another time. Wasn't it?

Katie asked Mike, "Why not?"

He shrugged, hands on the wheel, eyes on the road. "Just don't feel like it. You go on without me. Have a good time."

"I don't intend to have a good time. I intend to have a successful time and show everybody who doubted me that I can pull off a big function like this without something going catastrophically wrong."

"You do that, then. I'll be rooting for you."

"This is a very big night for me, Mike."

"I thought it was a big night for the Marrons."

"And it's a very big night for Nancy Hughes. This party was her idea and hiring me was her idea — kind of, after I suggested it. Nancy Hughes is one of my best friends in this town. I can't let her down. I owe her."

"Nancy Hughes is a very nice lady, I couldn't agree more."

"You weren't living here a couple of years ago, but there was a time when, well, there's no nice way to put this — everyone hated me."

"So I've heard."

"Well, believe it. Rumors of my pariah-hood were not greatly exaggerated. People enjoyed taking turns telling me what a horrible person I was. And all because I was a woman interested in a career."

"Didn't you poison Molly so you could take over her newscaster job at WOAK?"

"I didn't poison her! I simply stepped in and read her newscast when somebody else did."

"And didn't you make up a stalker for publicity purposes?"

"I did. But then it turned out someone was stalking me after all, and nobody ever gave me any credit for being—"

"Deceitful?"

"Prescient."

"Katie, I already know all this. I'm not sure what the point—"

"The point is, back when everybody and their great-uncle was calling me names and crossing the street so they wouldn't have to be on the same block with me, Nancy Hughes was the only one who believed I could grow and become a good person. And I have, haven't I?"

"Yes, Katie, these days, you're pretty darn swell."

"Well, this hospital benefit is a big deal to Mrs. Hughes. She wants a good turnout for the ribbon-cutting part of it so the Marron family can see how much we appreciate what they've done for Memorial and not think we're all just there for the drinks and dinner afterward. You should really come."

"Katie, give it up. I told you I'm not going."

"You haven't told me why, though."

"Because I don't want to. These black-tie affairs aren't my thing. I'm always nervous I'll eat my dessert with a salad fork and trigger a scandal or something."

"Yeah, right."

He turned the wheel more abruptly than he needed to, to make the turn. "Have it your way."

"Mike, you've been to plenty of black-tie functions and not once did I catch you drinking from the finger bowls."

"That's because I kept my little problem under wraps until now."

"Since when do you care what other people think about your manners, or anything else?"

"You're making too big of a deal about this."

"Only because you won't tell me what's really going on."

Mike shrugged. It was his "end of the line" shrug. The one that, in a mere twitch of the shoulders, managed to convey obstinacy, indifference, and resolve.

They rode the rest of the way in silence. When Mike pulled up in front of Katie's health club, he didn't turn off the engine or lean over to kiss her good-bye.

He didn't even wave as he drove away.

Or promise to see her at home, later.

Yup. This was bad.

Katie Peretti fell in love with Mike Kasnoff because he was the exact opposite of her ex-husband, Simon.

Sure, both men had that tall, dark, and handsome thing going for them, except that Simon's appeal was of the devil-may-care, Australian variety, while Mike's was all-American, God-and-country. Both men had equally disciplined abdominal muscles, smooth pectorals, and also a way of looking at a woman so intensely that it made her insides turn into a pit of warm chocolate pudding. That's where the similarities between the two men ended, though.

The first time Katie and Simon had sex, they were drunk and bitter. Both had been thrown out of a Roaring 20s Halloween bash. Katie had looked at Simon, Simon had looked at Katie. He'd held out his hand. The next thing they knew, they were at Burt's Garage, in the backseat of a gold convertible Simon was supposed to be repairing, drinking beer and making-out hard enough to prove to all of Oakdale that Simon Frasier and Katie Peretti didn't give a rat's hindquarters about their silly costume party. It was the beginning of a beautiful friendship. At least for a little while.

On the other hand, the first time Katie and Mike had sex, they almost didn't because Mike was too much of a gentleman. He was staying at her cottage while his own home was being remodeled, sleeping in the guest room right down the hall from Katie's.

Mike knew he wanted Katie. But Mike wasn't sure if Katie was ready for him to make the first move. So Mike waited politely for her to do it. As they sat on her living room floor, surrounded by empty Chinese food containers, sharing a final fortune cookie, Katie coyly asked, "So, what do you want to do next?"

Mike bit his lip and replied, "Whatever you want to do."

Later that night, as Katie lay frustrated in her double bed across the hall, she called out to an equally awake Mike, "Are you warm enough? I can turn up the heat." He'd called back, "Don't worry about what I want. What about you?"

And when she asked him to keep the doors between them

open, so that, if Mike needed anything in the middle of the night, she'd be able to hear him easily, he obliged. "Whatever you want."

"Why does he keep saying that?" Katie wondered out loud.

Finally, when she couldn't stand playing games any longer, Katie called in her ultimate weapon: a fluffy white rabbit named Snickers who somehow, mysteriously, managed to get out of his cage and escape into Mike's room.

Naturally Katie had to follow him. And naturally, once the poor little lost rabbit was rescued, she and Mike ended up sitting inches apart, face to face, mouth to mouth, on his rumpled, warm, and inviting bed.

"You are so beautiful," Mike said.

Katie smiled with relief.

"But I can't," Mike said.

"Why not?" she asked more harshly then she intended.

"Because. I want what comes next to be what you want, too. You know I love you. I obviously want to be with you. But if you have even the slightest hesitation—"

Katie grabbed Mike's face between her hands, the slight stubble of his beard tickling her palms, and laid a kiss on him strong enough to push them both down on the bed. Whereupon Katie did what she wanted. Several times.

When Simon had agreed to marry Katie (yes, agreed; she had had to do the proposing) it was because there were immigration officers standing outside the door, threatening to deport him back to Australia.

When Mike had asked Katie to marry him, he strewed

rose petals on the floor of the Lakeview Hotel and dropped down on one knee—right in front of the hotel staff.

"I don't care if the whole world sees us," he said. "The only person I care about right now is you. I've waited my whole life for you. To fall in love and know it was so absolutely perfect that no one could ever take it away from me. You are that love. And I want to marry you. Will you do me the honor of becoming my wife?"

Katie fell in love with Mike because he was considerate, romantic, and, most important, because he didn't lie to her.

Except that now, after his unexplained brush-off that morning, Katie could not shake the feeling that currently he was doing just that.

Of course, she understood that not telling her something she wanted to know did not technically constitute lying. But it sure did feel the same.

Just like it felt depressingly familiar to come home from work that evening with a feeling of dread. When she was married to Simon, Katie got that feeling a lot. Because she never knew what might come jumping out at her from behind the door. The brother of a man Simon had murdered? The sister of a woman Simon had married for her money then dumped? An evil look-alike? Katie had dealt with all that and more during her marriage. And, truly, she was over the whole "surprises are fun" thing.

Except for when the surprise proved to be dimmed lights, softly playing jazz, a table set for two, complete with freshly lit candles, folded linen napkins, a single rose in a long-necked vase and Mike standing sheepishly next to it all. His hands were behind his back, his head cocked to the side, and a half-smile was begging to burst into a full one as soon as he'd cleared up how Katie felt about his little presentation.

She squealed, dropping her purse on the couch, and ran across the living room, leaping into Mike's embrace, throwing her arms around his neck and kissing him hard. "You like it?" he asked.

"I love it!" Katie hopped back down to the ground. She ran her index finger along the flower's fragile stem to convince herself that this perfect scene wasn't a hallucination. "But, Mike. I—Why? Why did you do this?"

Mike looked at his fingernails. As a contractor, he was self-conscious about his hands being rough or unkempt. "My way of apologizing."

"For what?" Katie asked. It may have sounded as if she were playing dumb, but, in fact, she was merely hoping that her analysis of what he did wrong matched Mike's analysis.

"For the way I acted earlier."

"You mean, when I asked why you didn't want to come to the Marron benefit with me?"

"You have every right to be mad at me. I was a total jerk."

"I'm not mad at you," Katie lied. Now that she'd sort of gotten her way, there was no sense in fanning the flames. "I'm just confused. I thought we could talk about anything. But your getting so upset about a silly reception at the hospital . . ."

"It had nothing to do with the reception. It had to do with who the reception was honoring."

"The Marron family?"

"The Marron family."

"What about them?"

Mike said, "I used to work for the Marron family."

"Really? Doing what? Construction?"

"No. No, this was before I got into construction. This was when I was a kid, still in high school. Right after I dropped out, actually."

A few months earlier, they'd gone to a Halloween party, the theme of which was Come as Who You Were in High School. Mike wore a green-and-white number-nine football jersey, complete with gargantuan shoulder pads and adorably tight pants. Ever since then, Katie thought of her guy as the Big Man on Oakdale High's campus. She'd actually forgotten he ended up dropping out to go to work.

"The Marrons," Mike said. "They have this huge house about thirty miles outside of town, practically in the woods."

"I know," she said. "Nancy and I went out there a few times to get pictures and things for the benefit's program. Their estate is huge. And gorgeous. Wow, I had no idea you worked there when you were a kid. Lucky you."

"Yeah. Lucky me." Mike scratched the back of his neck, right at the point where his haircut ended and Katie always thought was so adorable. He said, "I didn't exactly work in the house. I don't know if you ever saw it, but they have a private garage behind the main building, with a load of classic cars, real beauties, Cadillacs, Rolls-Royces, even a World War Two Mercedes-Benz. They keep them in mint condition by never actually driving them off the property. Anyway, I worked helping the full-time mechanic. Which was cool. Until one of their cars turned up missing. The Benz, as a matter of fact. The cops were at my door first thing in the morning, locking me in handcuffs and then taking me down to the station for a chat."

"They thought you stole the car . . ."

"Yeah. They asked the Marrons who they thought might have done it and—what do you know—every finger just automatically pointed in my direction. Didn't matter that there wasn't any physical evidence."

"But didn't your lawyer—"

"My lawyer." Mike rolled his eyes. "My lawyer was the one who told me to plead guilty. She said the Marrons—Gregory Marron, in particular—were hell-bent on seeing me pay for my crime and that they'd called enough important people to make sure it would happen, one way or the other, evidence or no evidence. She said if I pled guilty, I might end up with a lighter sentence. That the judge would admire my honesty and my willingness to take responsibility for my actions."

"Did he?" Katie was afraid to hear his answer.

"How the hell should I know? Besides, what did it matter if the judge thought I was swell? This was a felony charge. And I was over eighteen so no juvenile leniencies to make things easier. I went to prison for two years because Gregory Marron Jr. insisted the state throw the book at me."

"Oh, Mike . . ."

"These last few weeks, when you were working for him and talking about being around him, and I had to keep my mouth shut, I thought the top of my head would blow off, Katie. I can't go to some ritzy party honoring Gregory Marron. I can't even be in the same room with the bastard. I'm afraid if I so much as lay eyes on him again, I'm going to lose it and bash his brains in."

*   *   *

Twenty-four hours later, as Katie watched Gregory Marron's body tumble out of Henry's limo and smack the ground with its dead weight, she did her best to cling to the observation that Gregory's brains did not, on the surface, seem to have been bashed in.

But that detail, in and of itself, wasn't exactly reassuring.

2

As Gregory Marron's limousine rounded the corner, the only person not craning her neck for a peek at the late arrival was Madeline Coleman. Maddie, as a matter of fact, was hiding from it.

The driver of the limo, her older brother, Henry, had told her in no uncertain terms that she was not allowed to attend this shindig. No, he would not ask Nancy Hughes for an invitation. No, she couldn't ask Katie for a VIP pass. No, she could not ride in the limo with him. No, she could not crash it, either. Because she was only sixteen. And alcohol would be served there. And thus potential drunken debauchery.

Maddie dutifully nodded her head, and sat, hands folded in her lap to look as innocent as possible. Until Henry left to pick up his fare. Then Maddie unfolded her hands, grabbed her oversize handbag, and tore out the door.

At the hospital, Maddie asked a security guard where

waitresses were supposed to change their clothes before the party. She did not, at any point, actually tell him that she was a waitress hired to work at this event. Was it her fault the guard gave her directions, then waved her through?

Maddie followed the path he'd indicated until she rounded a corner. Then she ducked into the ladies' room and, from her oversize handbag, pulled out a little black dress the saleswoman back home in Louisiana swore was perfect for any occasion. And didn't wrinkle much.

Maddie put on the dress, changed shoes, stuffed her jeans, T-shirt, and sneakers into the bag, and stepped out of the ladies' room, looking both ways to make sure no one noticed the suspicious transformation. She continued walking down the hallway until she found another security guard.

"Excuse me," Maddie said cocking her head. "I think I'm lost. Where is the reception for the Marron family supposed to be?"

She did not, at any point, tell him that she was an invited guest.

If her brother hadn't so unreasonably forbidden her attending the reception, Maddie was certain Henry would feel awfully proud of her initiative. Because he was the one who'd taught her the lying-without-actually-lying trick.

Once upon a time, Henry had taught Maddie a lot of useful tricks.

Her whole life, Henry was the only member of their family who ever took any real interest in Maddie. Fifteen years apart in age, with five sisters in between them, Henry and Madeline Coleman should have been virtual strangers to each other, siblings in name only, without a single common interest or any reason to do more than wave while passing each other in the hallway. But, when Maddie was less than a year old, their dad, never the most steady and reliable of fellows to begin with, took off. After that, their mother viewed Maddie as simply another needy mouth to feed. To her sisters, she was a tag-along inconvenience, not worth paying attention to. To Henry, however, little Maddie was his chance to mold an original character from scratch. And he took the project very seriously.

Every afternoon after school, while their sisters were flipping the pages of fashion magazines, haunting department store counters for free makeovers, and making lists of the boys in their classes in descending order of coolness, Henry and Maddie sat in front of the TV, inhaling a world that was far removed from their chaotic home life in a four-bedroom tract house across the road next to a congested highway.

It wasn't cartoons that they watched with such fascination. It wasn't even those wholesome family sitcoms where everyone loved each other very much and Mom and Dad were always solving problems with a freshly baked, chocolate-chip homily. No, Henry and Maddie were glued to *The Three Thirty Movie*, where, every afternoon, they were allowed to enter the homes of chic sophisticates, who lapped up mixed drinks, drove around in vintage cars, and dropped witty bons mots like anvils on the heads of anyone who might dare question their lifestyle, gaiety, or general classiness.

It was from *The Thin Man* that Maddie and Henry learned to make martinis. It was from Addison DeWitt gossiping *All About Eve* that they learned to make snarky comments to cover up any emotion or embarrassing sentiment they didn't want the rest of the world to be privy to. And it was from Bob Hope and Bing Crosby that they were inspired to go *On the Road* and look for all the humor and good-natured zaniness that seemed to be tragically missing from their everyday lives.

But, while Maddie and Henry may have been equally inspired to hop on a boxcar and see the world, only Henry was old enough to legally walk out the front door. So he set off to seek his fortune first in Chicago, then in Rockford, and finally in bucolic Oakdale, while Maddie was left behind. Eleven years old, lonely, and very, very weird.

She started junior high the year Henry left and, with her after-school buddy gone, Maddie tried to make friends.

Of course, there was a problem. Thanks to her daily diet of *Three Thirty* movies, Maddie may not have been as up to date on pop-culture as her fellow students would have liked. When they said "boy bands," Maddie thought Benny Goodman. When they said "movie-star hairstyle," Maddie could only conceive of Veronica Lake with that cool swath of silver-blond hair hanging down her face. And when chatter switched to Harry Potter, Maddie got the distinct feeling that talking about the Dorothy Parker poems and Dashiell Hammett mysteries she loved wouldn't interest her classmates.

So the great friend-making experiment of junior high school was a big bust.

And social matters didn't improve much in high school. It didn't matter that, by objective standards, Maddie was a pretty girl. Well, at least cute, if not drop-dead gorgeous. She had a heart-shaped face, with large brown eyes and a smile that could be either sweet or mischievous, but often somehow ended up as both. Her ginger hair had long proven itself impervious to any curling iron, so Maddie merely kept it neatly swept back off her face and called it a day. Her biggest flaw was that she was skinny and didn't need a bra. In high school this was a huge problem. But, Maddie felt pretty confident that even if she woke up one morning looking like Jane Russell, it still wouldn't have been enough to make up for her reputation. Which was, Maddie Coleman: Brainy. Mouthy. Weird.

Maddie missed Henry, even if it was all his fault that she'd turned out like this. Because Henry understood her. And so, during a summer vacation between her sophomore and junior year, Maddie called her brother and told him she was coming for a visit. And when she got there, she told him she was there to stay.

He sputtered a bit. He stammered and queried and hedged. Then he realized that Maddie wasn't asking him, she was informing him, and so promptly made peace with the situation.

Of course, for Henry, an out-of-the-blue roommate meant making a few small lifestyle changes.

It turned out that Maddie's getaway landed right in the middle of a small, financial downturn for her brother. The health club he and Katie Peretti owned was seriously in the red. He'd moved out of the house they shared because Henry realized that while he would always love his best friend, Katie had eyes only for Mike. And three—when two couldn't keep their hands off each other—was definitely a crowd. So the limo became both Henry's source of income and his bachelor pad. When Maddie announced her plans to move in, this became something of a problem.

Her brother, however, stepped up to the plate. He asked for more driving shifts. He got them an apartment. He enrolled Maddie in the best private school in Oakdale and told her to make him proud.

What he didn't tell Maddie was how he was paying for it all.

When Henry was visibly worried about making ends meet, Maddie was worried right along with him. But when Henry stopped acting worried and returned to whistling a happy tune, that's when Maddie truly got scared.

She'd cornered him at the breakfast table the morning of the Marrons' reception. "What's going on, Henry?"

"Life, Madeline, is good." He was wearing his chauffeur uniform and popped his brimmed hat jauntily onto his head to emphasize his point. If there was one thing they learned from all those afternoons watching classic movies, it was how to don caps jauntily. "The birds are singing, the bees are buzzing, and the Dow, I'm happy to say, is jonesing."

"So that's it! I should have known. You're playing the stock market again. Henry, don't you remember what happened the last time you thought you had a sure thing? You lost your shirt."

"Little sister, you will be happy to hear that I am no longer playing the market."

"So then you're gambling. Even better. What is it this time? Cards? Roulette? Slots? Football? Greyhounds? It's horses, isn't it? You could never stay away from the horses."

"No, no, no. Henry Coleman no longer runs with the ponies. They kept winning. It's not good for the self-esteem."

"Then where has all this money come from lately? A couple of months ago you were practically homeless—"

"I wasn't homeless. I was living in my car."

"And now we've got this great apartment and you're sending me to school and—"

"The world turns in mysterious ways, Maddie." He stood up to leave, but the way their breakfast table was kitty-cornered, his only way out was past Maddie. And she wasn't budging.

"Tell me what's going on."

"Nothing is going on."

Maddie crossed her arms and raised an eyebrow. She stared at Henry very hard.

"Nothing at all."

She added an impatient foot-tap.

"Nothing for you to be concerned about, anyway."

She pursed her lips.

"I borrowed some money," Henry blurted out. "Damn, you're good."

"I owe it all to you." Maddie planted her hands on Henry's chest and pushed him steadily backward until he fell into his seat. "Spill it, Coleman. What have you gotten us into?"

"Nothing. A little business transaction. Grown-up stuff. You wouldn't be interested."

"I'm interested in anything that might get you into trouble. When Henry Coleman has money to burn—"

"Barely a flicker."

"Where did you borrow this money from? The bank?"

"Not exactly."

"How not exactly?"

"Not at all?" Henry raised both of his arms, wrists crossed, head ducked into his shoulders, shielding his face from the expected Wrath of Maddie.

"Don't tell me you went to a loan shark!"

"Absolutely not! What do you take me for?"

"Then where did the money come from?"

"A friend."

"None of your friends have money."

"A business acquaintance?"

"Ditto."

He lowered his arms. "A client."

"What client?"

"Someone I've been chauffeuring around. Gregory Marron. You know, the guy I'm driving to his coronation tonight. He's rich, I'm needy, it was a match made in heaven."

"How much did you borrow?"

"A couple of bucks."

"As in enough for a cup of coffee, or a trip to Colombia?"

"Maybe British Columbia . . ."

"How much, Henry?"

"Twenty thousand dollars."

He wasn't quick enough. Maddie's punch hit him right in the jaw. "Are you out of your mind? Why do you do things like this? We can't pay back that kind of loan!"

"Ow!" He rubbed his face with one hand while using the other to fend Maddie off. "That right hook of yours has improved over the last few years."

"When did you promise to pay him back?"

"A couple of weeks—"

"Weeks?"

"—Ago."

She didn't say anything to him after that. Instead, Maddie turned to address the refrigerator. "Doomed," she told it conversationally. "We're doomed."

"We are not doomed," Henry insisted. "In fact, things are looking up."

"We used to just be broke. Now we're in debt. How's that looking up?"

"Oh, ye of little height." Henry flung his arm around Maddie's shoulder. Though he did keep the rest of his body angled a good distance away, lest she decide to come out swinging again. "Don't you know by now that your big brother always has a plan?"

"That's what I'm afraid of."

"Maddie, my dear, do try keeping your youthful cynicism at bay and believe me: After tonight, you and I aren't going to have a thing to worry about."

Trying to keep out of Henry's line of vision, Maddie didn't see him open the limo door. By the time she heard the horrified gasp of the crowd and managed to push herself to the front for a closer look, Gregory Marron was on the ground being swamped by a host of Oakdale professionals, mostly doctors and police, but there were a few tycoon types as well.

Because Gregory was on the ground and everyone else was bent over him, the dominant figure on the horizon proved to be Henry. He was still standing by the car door, frozen in place, staring not so much at the body, as at the scurrying taking place at his feet. Maddie tried calling his name, no longer caring if he knew that she'd disobeyed him, but the scene was too frenetic for Henry to hear her.

He did, however, hear Margo Hughes telling him to come with her, the Oakdale P.D. had a few questions they needed to ask him.

Henry nodded and mutely followed Margo inside the hospital building.

So did Maddie.

"Sorry, Maddie, you can't talk to Henry now, this is police business." Detective Margo Hughes attempted to shut the door in Maddie's face. Over her shoulder, Maddie could see Henry sitting on a couch in some doctor's office.

"Is Henry under arrest?" Maddie demanded.

"No, we're just asking him a few questions."

"Then why can't I come in? Look at him, Margo, he's all messed up. He needs some support. He doesn't need you beating him with a rubber hose or whatever it is that passes for interrogation techniques here in Oakdale."

Margo asked Maddie, "You watch a lot of old movies, don't you?"

"Can't I just come in and sit next to him? I won't say a word. I promise."

Margo glanced over at Henry, who looked a little green around the gills and thoroughly stunned.

Maddie was counting on Margo, who was Katie Peretti's older sister, to realize that having a friendly face around would help Henry pull himself together so he could answer questions. Margo wasn't stupid. In fact, Maddie kind of admired Margo. Because she was an original. She was the only female high-ranking cop on the force, for one thing. She'd even been acting police chief for a while. She wore her red hair short, dressed in comfortable jeans and simple blouses, and loved to eat junk food and talk about old cases. In short, she wasn't your typical Oakdale girlie-girl. Margo also had a husband who was crazy about her, and a son who wasn't totally the lamest guy Maddie had met at her new school. And if he were to ask her out she wouldn't say no right away. So Margo was cool. And someone Maddie strongly suspected she might turn out to resemble someday. If she was lucky.

Margo sighed. "Okay, Maddie." She moved aside to let the girl pass. "Go on in. But not a word, you hear me?"

"Not a word," Maddie promised.

"Henry," Margo said slowly, settling down in the chair across from him. "Did you know something was wrong with Gregory Marron as you were pulling up to the hospital? Was he sick or—"

"No. I didn't know anything. We've got that partition between us. I can't hear him unless he wants to talk to me, and he didn't say anything, didn't even try to push the button, the whole ride over."

"Did he usually talk to you during a ride?"

"No."

"Not ever?"

"No, just not often."

"You picked him up at home?"

"Yes. At seven on the dot. On the dot, that's the key to a happy customer."

"How did Mr. Marron seem? Did he look all right?"

"He looked fine, downright dapper and brimming with health."

"So Gregory Marron Jr. walked out of his home and got into your limo perfectly fine, but arrived here . . . dead?" Margo laid out a scenario that seemed to be missing an act.

"Yes! I guess so. I don't know. What do you want me to say? Can I plead the Fifth? Am I under oath?"

"Calm down, Henry," Margo said. "You're not under oath. I'm just trying to get a timeline of events. For instance, did you stop off anywhere along the way?"

"Absolutely not. Straight here. A prompt customer is a happy customer."

"But Gregory Marron wasn't prompt. He was, in fact, late for his own party."

"I arrived at his house on time. He's the one who kept me waiting for forty-five minutes. We bill for that, you know. Gregory doesn't care. He doesn't care about the cost of anything. He's got money to burn. It's not fair, you know, the rest of us . . ."

Maddie inhaled sharply. Which caught Margo's attention. She turned to look at Maddie, seemingly poised to chastise her.

But, just as Maddie tried to summon up a valid excuse for her blunder, Margo turned back to Henry, prompting him with, "The rest of us, what?"

Maddie feared that Henry was about to tell Margo about

the money he owed Mr. Marron. Didn't he realize he might as well paint a big MOTIVE FOR MURDER on his forehead?

Thankfully, rather than telling Margo about the money, Henry only said, "The rest of us . . . don't."

Margo stared at Henry. Henry stared at Margo.

Maddie stared at both of them.

Finally, Margo said, "You're free to go, Henry. But after we get the coroner's report and figure out the cause of death, we might have a few other questions for you, so no disappearing acts, all right?"

At that, Henry's face, which had regained its normal color, turned green again.

And he clutched Maddie's hand as if for dear life.

3

While Margo was questioning Henry, Detective Jack Snyder attempted to control the situation on the street. As soon as Ben Harris officially pronounced Gregory Marron dead, Jack arranged for the body to be carried inside the hospital to the morgue.

He directed two of his policemen to lead the family inside the hospital to a private office. But as soon as the first officer approached Aurora, she flung his arm off her elbow and tried to follow the gurney carrying Gregory's body. When deferentially informed that she couldn't follow it to the morgue, she turned to Gig, grabbed his arm, and demanded that he do something. Gig, however, was no help at all. After making a mad dash to his prostrate son, the senior Marron had all but frozen in place. The only words he managed to get out as Monica urged both her mother and grandfather to do what the policeman said, were, "I just don't understand this. How could this happen? How could this happen to us?"

Jack's wife, Carly, trapped amid the curious throng craning their necks over the joined arms of the half-dozen patrolmen who were attempting a combination of crowd control and witness sequestering, was the only person not straining for a look at either the body or the newly bereaved. Carly's eyes were glued to one man, and that was Jack.

To be fair, Carly's eyes, no matter what the occasion, were always on her dark-haired, muscular husband. It had been that way since the first day they met. Even during those times when they'd both wished that they could ignore each other, forget the other, move on, their eyes had still always been on each other.

Except that right now, Carly's gaze wasn't tracking her husband's every move because of the incredible chemistry between them. She was doing it out of fear.

Carly watched Jack taking charge of this latest professional emergency in exactly the same manner as he did all others, calmly and confidently. Even out of uniform, dressed in a black tuxedo with only his gold shield that he'd briefly flashed at the Marron family to identify his official position, there was no mistaking Jack's authority, or the confidence that he radiated. As soon as Jack jumped into any fray, others stepped back to give him room. They understood, even if only instinctively, that this was a man they could turn to, a man who could straighten everything out.

Jack looked over his shoulder, caught sight of Carly, and froze. Even if he hadn't expected to see her there because she'd told him earlier she didn't plan to attend, Carly had hoped to receive one of his lopsided grins. The ones that Jack saved only for her. The ones that told Carly, even in the middle of a crisis, that their particular world was still turning.

This time, however, there was no private smile, no raised eyebrows, barely an acknowledgment. Instead, as quickly as he'd spotted Carly, Jack looked away from her.

Unfortunately, he didn't look away fast enough. Because, in that split second when their eyes met, all Carly saw gazing back at her was terror.

Before Carly met Jack, she'd made a lot of mistakes.

Actually, after Carly met Jack, she'd made a mountain of mistakes, too. Love, after all, could make a girl very, very stupid.

The difference was, after Carly met Jack, she had someone to fix her mistakes.

When Carly had tried to frame a rival by drugging her water bottle, Jack covered up the evidence—and was suspended from the Oakdale P.D. When no one in town was speaking to Carly because of a scam she'd pulled to get Jack's friend, Hal, to marry her, Jack was the only one who offered her a hand in friendship and a chance to put her life back together. And, when Carly ran home to Montana because she wasn't sure who'd fathered her unborn baby, Jack had followed her, pledged his devotion, and even single-handedly delivered her daughter. Then Jack had married Carly—even before a blood test thankfully proved that Sage was his own little girl.

That was how their relationship went. Carly made a mess,

and Jack cleaned it up. But she'd never dreamed that her past might one day drive Jack to commit an act that wasn't so easily forgotten. Or forgiven.

She never dreamed that her past might drive Jack to murder.

To be fair, Carly knew that he was capable of killing. He was a policeman, after all, and in the course of executing his duties, he'd had to fire his gun. But those killings were all connected to a confirmed crime and occurred only after Jack had done his best to prevent the fatality, often at the risk of his own safety. It wasn't the same as committing a murder in cold blood. And yet, after the Snyders' accidental encounter with Gregory Marron Jr. the previous afternoon, Carly couldn't shake the feeling that her husband had been pushed too far.

They'd run into Gregory outside their pediatrician's office at the hospital, of all places. Sage was due for her three-year checkup, so Carly had also scheduled an appointment for her son Parker to get his camp health forms filled out. She coerced Jack to come along with the promise that he could stay outside the examining room at all times. Because while Jack Snyder could dangle from a collapsed bridge by the tips of his fingers and survive a plunge into the frigid river below, or go head-to-head with a criminal mastermind any day of the week—a weeping toddler or a fearful eight-year-old boy trying to resist a shot was more than he could handle.

All four of them managed to survive the visit relatively trauma-free, however. For Sage, a lollipop did the trick, for Parker it was a new cartridge for his Game Boy, and for Jack it was permission to leave the waiting room and go bring the car around to the main entrance while Carly juggled insurance cards and copays.

Except that, once Carly and the kids stepped outside, Jack's car was nowhere to be found.

He wasn't by the revolving door, like he said he'd be. He wasn't even pulling up to the semicircle drive. It took Carly a few minutes, but finally she spotted him. Jack was still half a lot away, standing beside their parked car.

But he wasn't alone.

The well-dressed, blond man standing with him was Gregory Marron Jr.

Carly felt the name before she actually thought it. Her first reaction was visceral. Seeing Gregory again was like an open-handed blow to the side of her head. Clutching both handles of Sage's fold-up stroller was the only thing that kept her upright. Needing to remain calm for both kids' sake was what prevented her from gasping.

Gregory Marron Jr.

Gregory Marron Jr. had returned from New York.

Gregory Marron Jr. was back in Oakdale.

Gregory Marron Jr. was back in her life.

Gregory Marron Jr. was talking to Jack.

She'd thought it would never happen.

She'd prayed it would never happen.

But it was happening. Right here, right now, right in front of her children.

A part of her wanted to run toward Jack, to force herself between him and Gregory, to try to stop the inevitable disaster. Another part of her wanted to grab the kids and run the other way, leave Oakdale if she had to, anything to keep from seeing the crushing disappointment she knew would be in Jack's eyes after Gregory got through with him.

She ended up doing neither.

To be honest, she ended up unable to do either.

Because, aside from the way her body was shaking, Carly couldn't move a muscle.

She was rooted to the spot, watching, as if it were a silent movie, Jack and Gregory's conversation which went from the body language of Jack politely responding to the greeting of a total stranger, to his tensing up in response to whatever it was Gregory said to him, to Jack grabbing Gregory by the shoulders, spinning him around, and shoving him, face down, onto the hood of the car.

"Jack!" Carly screamed.

Jack froze. He looked up and saw her and the kids.

Caught, he jerked Gregory back onto his feet, setting him upright, though still shoving Gregory away from himself with all his might.

Gregory stumbled a bit but quickly regained his footing. He winced and rubbed his left shoulder, the one that had absorbed the bulk of Jack's slamming him against the hood. But he also smiled. Right at Carly.

Gregory said something else to Jack, and for a split second Carly was afraid Jack might go after him again. But a quick look in her direction as she and the kids approached effectively squelched that impulse. Jack merely turned his back on Gregory, visibly struggling to catch both his breath and his temper.

Gregory dusted himself off, brushed both hands one against the other, and headed toward the hospital entrance.

When he passed Carly, he blew her a kiss.

The kids, of course, were full of questions on the drive home. Jack, to Carly's eternal gratitude, neither blew off their concerns nor made too big a deal out of it. When Parker wanted to know who that man was and what he wanted and why Jack hit him like that, Jack, sitting in the front seat and making eye contact with Parker through the rearview mirror, though pointedly ignoring Carly who was sitting right next to him, calmly explained that the man had come up to Jack and said some things that made him angry. But he also stressed that his reaction had been out of proportion and that he was deeply sorry for having lost his temper like that.

"What did he say?" Parker wanted to know.

"That's not important. What's important is that I set a bad example for you guys today. You should only try to solve problems with violence if it's absolutely, positively your last option. You got that, pal?"

"Got it."

"Good boy," Jack said.

"What did he say?" Carly repeated Parker's words to Jack later when Sage was napping upstairs and Parker had gone next door to play with a friend.

"It's not important," Jack repeated in turn.

"Did Gregory tell you—"

"Yes."

"I'm sorry."

"Whatever."

"I wanted to be the one to tell you," she said, realizing even as she did that it wasn't the truth. "Or maybe I didn't. I don't know."

Jack shrugged. He didn't seem all that interested in pursuing the issue but, still he said, "The floor is all yours."

She swore. "It all just seemed so irrelevant to the life we're leading now . . . Telling you . . . I didn't see the point."

He sighed. "Start at the beginning." He sank down on the couch in their living room, arms raised and draped over the back cushions to show he wasn't going anywhere. "And don't leave out any details, please."

Carly wanted to sit down next to Jack. She wanted to curl up against him, rest her head on his shoulder, and bury her face in his chest so she wouldn't have to look at him while she spilled the whole sordid tale. But Carly knew that from there, she'd still be able to feel his heart race, his muscles tighten, his jaw clench. Carly had engendered that reaction in Jack so many times before, and she really dreaded going through it all again.

And yet, she knew she had to, if she wanted to be honest. And Carly did want to be honest with Jack. She just didn't want to look at him when she revealed the truth.

So she kept her back to him, looking instead at the family pictures hanging on the wall. There was Jack with Sage at their wedding. There was Parker with his biological dad, Hal Munson, and his "other dad," Jack, on either side of him, grinning like the double-blessed kid he knew he was. There were all four of them next to the tree at Christmastime, and at the Fourth of July picnic, and at Parker's last birthday.

"When I was younger, I didn't know what I wanted," Carly began. "I mean, I thought I did. Growing up on a farm in Montana, the one thing I was pretty darn sure of was that I didn't want to spend my life on a farm in Montana. You know what my father and stepmother were like. They were the pits, nobody will argue that. But it wasn't just them I was aching to get away from. It was the whole dirt-poor, dirt-covered, dirt-everything scene. And when I finally found out what happened to my mother, that she'd dumped us to trade up for a millionaire, well, I figured—what's good for the mother is good for the daughter, right?"

Jack didn't respond. Sure, she'd asked a rhetorical question, but still, why the hell didn't he respond? Carly wanted to turn around and see his expression to gauge how he was feeling about all this, but another part of her was afraid to find out.

So she pressed on. "Problem was, Mom didn't leave a manual on how to marry rich. So I had to go with my instincts. When this rich man passing through town on business asked if I'd like to head on out with him, I leaped at the opportunity. I thought it was the only one I'd ever get." Carly admitted, "I knew he was married, of course. I wasn't naïve. It's not that I didn't understand what he was offering or what I was getting into. But he took me to New York. I'd always wanted to go to New York. He set me up with an apartment. Gregory did a lot of business in New York, he was out there a couple of times a month. And my job was to be available."

Carly couldn't take it anymore. She had to see how Jack was processing all this. She turned around. He was still sitting on the couch. Looking straight ahead, nodding at nothing in particular. And curling his fists in and out, in and out, tightly.

Carly said, "He treated me pretty badly. Nothing criminal, I guess. I don't know, actually. He . . . hurt me. He liked to hit me and . . . some other things. I put up with it because . . . because, like I said, I thought it was my only chance to live the good life. What I thought was the good life. Before I knew what that really meant."

Jack's fists had clenched all the way. The artery running down the side of his forehead to his neck throbbed. And still, he didn't say a word.

"So I did whatever he wanted," Carly admitted. "But, in the end, he dumped me anyway, after six months, not even a whole year. I suppose he found me boring. Or maybe I got too demanding. I kept telling him I wanted to get into the design business. I asked him to help me get started, introduce me to some people. I guess it was more than he bargained for. He threw me out. No cash, no place to live. I didn't even get to hang on to any of the clothes he bought me. I tried to make a go of it in New York on my own, at first, but I was in over my head. I ended up going back to Montana, back to the farm. So much for my grand plan."

"Is that why you came to Oakdale originally?" Jack asked. "To try and hook up with Gregory Marron again?"

"No!" The suggestion was so ludicrous Carly practically laughed out loud. "No, if anything, it was the opposite. I knew Gregory's family lived around here, so I almost chickened out of coming to Oakdale. My first few months in town, I used to walk around every corner thinking, What if he's there? What if I bump into him? What will he say? What should I say? Or worse, what if it's Aurora I end up face to face with?"

"Did you?" Jack wanted to know. "Ever run into him, I mean."

"No. In retrospect, I'm not surprised. We hardly spin in the same social circles. And anyway, I think Oakdale is just sort of a home base for the Marrons. They keep a house here, but they spend most of their lives in more, well, cosmopolitan places. After a while, I even sort of forgot they were around. But then I fell in love with you, Jack."

"I see . . ." he said. Though he didn't sound as if he saw, at all.

"Before you, I was afraid of running into Gregory or Aurora because I thought he would be his usual nasty self, or that she would make some scene and call me names in public, trivial nonsense like that. But, after I met you, I was scared . . . I was scared that Gregory might say something that would make you . . . make you feel differently about me, Jack. And I couldn't bear the thought of that."

She trailed off. Her unspoken question hanging in the air.

Carly didn't have the guts to inquire directly, so she went with a softer query. She asked Jack, "In the parking lot, how did Gregory know who you were?"

Jack turned over his right arm, his fist still tightened, and looked at the cut between his fourth and fifth knuckles from where he'd scraped it against the hood of the car. "You and Gregory may not run in the same social circles," he said, his voice strangely devoid of inflection. "But he did mention that he'd seen our wedding picture in the newspaper a few years back. 'Hero Cop Jack Snyder.' That's what he called me. 'Well, well, well. If it isn't Hero Cop Jack Snyder,' he said."

"I'm sorry, Jack."

He shrugged, but neither accepted nor refused her apology.

"What did Gregory say about me?"

"Nothing I didn't already know, honey."

She wasn't sure how to take that.

"I do know you, Carly. Very, very well," Jack said, looking deeply into her eyes.

"I should have told you about—"

"Why? What good would it have done? I knew you had a past."

"Then why did you hit—"

"Because. Carly. Nobody talks about my wife that way. Even if it is true."

"Oh." She asked, "Are you mad?"

"I am not mad."

"Then what . . . what are you?"

"I don't know," Jack admitted.

And Carly believed him. However, Jack's lack of visible rancor didn't mean that she necessarily felt the same way.

Now that she'd gotten the full story out and Jack wasn't standing at the door, bags packed, a terse good-bye letter in his pocket, Carly's own anger at what had transpired in the parking lot spilled out with a fury she hadn't even realized she'd been suppressing.

"Where does that son of a bitch get off, coming up to you like that? And in front of the kids, Jack! Our kids! What if they'd been there? What if they'd heard—"

"They didn't, Carly. You guys were too far away. I'm certain Parker and Sage didn't hear a word."

"Today!" she exploded. "They didn't hear a word today! But what about tomorrow? What about the next time we all round a corner and, this time, Gregory actually is standing there?" She calmed down long enough to muse, "You know, so much time has passed, I assumed he'd forgotten all about me . . ."

"Oh, no," Jack said. "He remembers. Some things in very picturesque detail."

"Damn it!" Carly was shaking again. Shaking as badly as she had back outside the hospital. This was her worst nightmare. And it hadn't even happened yet. "What if he says something to Parker and Sage? How am I going to explain it to them? What are they going to think about me? Oh, God, Jack, they'll hate me. If he talks to them like he did to you . . . he'll make my kids hate me. I can't let that happen. I won't lose my kids. Especially not over someone like him. I'd rather—"

Jack stood up abruptly. He walked over to Carly and wrapped both of his arms around her. When she rested her head on his chest, Jack's heart was beating as steadily as if they had just been discussing what to have for lunch or whether it might rain later in the afternoon and should they remind Parker to bring his bike in.

Jack said, "Don't worry, Carly. I'll take care of this for you. You don't have to worry about a thing."

Nevertheless, Carly worried.

Jack acted as if nothing had happened. When Parker came home, Jack announced he was taking the whole family out for dinner as a reward for the kids being so brave at the doctor's office. They went to Al's Diner, where Jack made small talk with the waitresses and ordered chili-cheese-dogs "with extra chili, extra cheese, and extra dog." He helped Sage sip her milkshake without spilling it and showed Parker how to cover the top of a drinking straw with your finger to keep the liquid from spilling out when you raised it. Jack kept on talking about nothing in particular all through their meal, and during the drive home, and even as he and Carly were drifting off to sleep later.

The only thing he didn't do, even once that evening, was look Carly in the eye.

Late the next afternoon, however, he called her from the station to say, "Don't wait up for me, honey, I'm going to have to work late tonight."

"Doing what?" she asked.

There was a pause. A pause much longer than warranted by her simple question.

Finally, Jack said, "Nancy Hughes asked me to handle security for her benefit tonight. I couldn't say no. You know what a sucker I am for that lady."

"The Marron family benefit," Carly said. She'd known about it for weeks. When Nancy had offered her an invitation, she'd said, "No, thank you," and nothing more.

"It's no major deal," Jack said. She wasn't sure if he was trying to convince her, or himself. "Gives me a chance to kill two birds with one stone."

"Oh . . ." Carly said.

He hung up before she could ask him what he meant, leaving Carly standing in the middle of her living room, a dead receiver in her hand. Jack was going to work security for the Marron benefit? How could he, after everything that had happened yesterday? Why would he want to pour salt into his wounds like that? Why would he want to . . .

Carly hung up the phone, picked it up again, and quickly dialed Jack's direct extension at the police station. There was no answer. She tried Margo Hughes, who picked up right away, but told her that Jack wasn't at work.

"What do you mean?" Carly asked. "Where else could he be?"

"I don't know," Margo said. "He took the afternoon off. Said he had some personal business to take care of."

Maybe Carly was imagining it, but it sure did sound like Margo was insinuating that, if Jack's business was personal, then shouldn't his wife know about it?

Carly tried Jack's cell phone. No answer there, either. She considered leaving a message asking him to please, please call back and tell her where he was and what was going on, but then changed her mind.

Carly called her sister, Gwen, and asked if she could possibly watch Parker and Sage for a few hours this evening. Carly needed to be somewhere, ASAP.

Carly arrived at the ribbon cutting early, figuring this part of the event didn't need an invitation and she could worry about wrangling a seat at the actual benefit later. She'd dressed as if she belonged, in a teal, floor-length gown trimmed with silver thread and shoes dyed to match. The right clothes, Carly knew, would go a long way toward helping her blend in with the crowd and get swept along, invitation or not. Besides, it wouldn't hurt if, while she was keeping an eye on Jack, Carly also happened to cross Gregory's field of vision. The previous day, she'd been wearing her mom outfit. Jeans, purple T-shirt, hair held back with a headband, sneakers with a dollop of baby food ground into the laces. It wouldn't hurt her ego if Gregory saw her in a "Carly Snyder Original."

But first, Carly wanted to find Jack. She didn't see him anywhere. Which didn't mean a thing. Jack didn't need to be out front, he could be coordinating security from inside the hospital. But Carly thought she'd feel better if she could just lay eyes on him. Just to see how he was doing. And where he was.

But Carly didn't see Jack until she heard the screaming and the mad rush forward started. She first sighted him hovering over a prostrate Gregory on the sidewalk. After ensuring that his officers had the crowd under control and away from Gregory, Jack got down on his knees and pressed both hands along Gregory's chest, practically frisking every one of his pockets, including the internal ones. Jack said something to Ben Harris, who shrugged in reply, then nodded. Jack bent over farther, his face only a few inches from Gregory's. After a moment, he straightened up and called out to a nearby uniform. That's when the energy of the scene shifted.

It was a small change, subtle, probably only noticeable to the officers at the site—and one officer's wife. Because Carly saw that, after Jack examined Gregory, he put on a pair of clear gloves, and gestured for the patrolmen taking his body away to do the same. She saw that only after he'd examined him did Jack order the area to be cordoned off with yellow police tape, and that he sent another cop into the limo with an evidence kit. If Jack thought Gregory's death was due to natural causes, he wouldn't have taken all of those precautions. Jack must have figured that Gregory could have been murdered, and so he was taking great care to protect what might well be a crime scene.

Meanwhile, all Carly could think of was the promise Jack made to her earlier. "Don't worry, Carly. I'll take care of this for you. You don't have to worry about a thing."

When Carly got close enough to speak to Jack, instead of his expressing surprise or asking what she was doing there, Jack simply grouped Carly in with a bunch of other possible eyewitnesses and advised, "You folks better head home. Nothing to see here. Someone from the department will be in touch if we've any more questions."

And then he disappeared under his newly drawn crime tape without so much as a look back at her.

Carly did as he asked. She went home, thanked Gwen for watching the kids, changed out of her clothes, and then sat down to wait for her husband.

Except that he wasn't home by midnight.

Or by 1 A.M.

By two, Carly was itching to get dressed again, call another sitter, and head down to the police station. She got as far as taking fresh clothes out of her bedroom closet, before she was able to successfully suppress the impulse.

And so Carly waited. She didn't call Jack at work, even after the kids woke up and asked where Daddy was. She didn't call him all the next day, even after she'd put the kids to bed again and had nothing but free time on her hands to wonder . . . and worry.

By the time Jack did come home, it was over twenty-four hours since she'd last seen him. He was still dressed in the white shirt and black pants of his tuxedo, although he'd long since ditched the tie. It was almost 5 A.M. Carly was in the kitchen, having woken up half an hour earlier and decided to get a jump on the kid's breakfast when she heard the front door opening.

Carly walked into the living room and saw Jack taking off his shoes in the dark, probably hoping not to disturb them.

When she turned on the light, Jack winced and held up his hand, looking vaguely disoriented.

He caught sight of Carly standing there, and he slowly lowered his arm.

She looked at him and didn't say a word.

Jack looked right back at her, meeting Carly's eyes for the first time in what felt like an eternity. She wanted to ask him where he'd been and what had happened. Not so much at the hospital or at the precinct, but between the two of them in the hours since she'd told him about her past with Gregory, and Gregory had ended up dead. She wanted Jack to tell her what he was thinking and what he was feeling and — oh, God — what he had done as part of his promise to protect Carly from Gregory Marron.

But before she could start in on any of that, Jack said, "Your friends the Marrons certainly know how to get things done, don't they?"

"Jack . . ."

"Most people who die in a town this size, their families need to wait three, four days, sometimes longer for the coroner's report. The guy has to do the actual autopsy, plus run a whole bunch of tests, toxicology screens, you name it — our guy likes to be thorough. Gregory Marron, though? He got a twenty-four-hour turnaround. Seems his daddy made a few calls, woke a few people up. Those folks, in turn, woke a few other people up. Including, more or less, the entire Oakdale P.D., not to mention the honchos at the state crime lab. You know what we've all been doing over the last God-knows-how-long-it's-been? Every last one of us was working on the Gregory Marron Jr. murder case. Detective Jack Snyder at the lead."

"So Gregory was definitely murdered?" Carly didn't so much say the words, as exhale them, along with all the tension she'd been holding in and trying to keep from Parker and Sage. She'd suspected it, she'd feared it, but now she knew it. And knowing made everything so much worse.

"It looks that way," Jack replied. "Also looks like you just might know our prime suspect."

4

Katie suspected that Jack Snyder's turning up on their doorstop at 7 A.M. two days after the hospital fiasco was not a social call. Or good news of any kind.

She'd been in the kitchen, watching the coffee percolate and waiting for Mike to come downstairs from the shower, when Katie heard the doorbell ring. She hoped it was the paperboy, but, deep down, she knew who it was.

"Hey, Katie, morning. Can I talk to Mike?" Jack didn't ask if he could come in. He just did. He glanced around the living room and up the stairs.

"What's going on?" Katie asked, trying to pretend she had no clue about why he was there.

"I need to talk to Mike, Katie," he said.

"So talk." Mike came down the stairs. He must have heard the doorbell ringing, because he'd only had the chance to throw on jeans and a T-shirt. His hair was still wet, he was barefoot and hadn't yet shaved. He looked young, vulnerable, and, Katie thought, as if he needed someone to protect him.

Jack said, "Hi, Mike. You heard about the murder at the hospital Friday night?"

"Katie told me when she got home."

Katie had run home nearly hysterical, and somehow eventually got across the point that Gregory Marron Jr. was dead.

Mike's only reaction? "Couldn't have happened to a nicer guy."

And then he'd rolled over and gone back to sleep. Every time Katie had tried to tiptoe around the subject the following day, Mike had cut her off.

Now Jack asked Mike, "Think you can find some time to come down to the station and answer a couple of questions for us?"

"Sure." Mike shrugged. "I'll stop by tomorrow morning."

"This morning would be better."

"Sorry. I've got plans for today. And, now that I think about it, weekdays aren't good for me at all. Got a lot of work to do. Can't put up a building in the dark, right? Maybe tomorrow evening, I'll stop by." Mike might have been joking, but he certainly wasn't smiling.

Katie looked from one man to the other. Both were standing there as casual as could be.

"Maybe it would be better if you took a ride with me right now," Jack said. "We'll get some things sorted out. . . ."

"I don't think so." Mike walked over to where Katie was

standing and gave her a wink. She wasn't sure what it was supposed to mean. She wasn't sure what any of this meant. "I don't have the time for this, Detective. And I know my rights. I don't have to come in for questioning. You want me down at the station, you're going to have to go ahead and arrest me."

"All right, then," Jack said. Katie let out an audible sigh of relief. Obviously this thing wasn't all that serious if Jack was willing to back down so easily. "Mike Kasnoff," he said, "you're under arrest."

Jack allowed Mike to go upstairs and finish getting dressed before taking him to the station. He didn't, however, allow Katie to go up there with him, despite her rather loud argument that it was her house and she wasn't under arrest, was she? Jack strongly advised Katie not to, and pointed out there wasn't a limit to how many arrests he could make in one day. Obstruction of justice was a legitimate charge.

When Mike came down, he was wearing jeans, a blue denim workshirt, shoes, socks, and was drying his hair with a towel. When Mike finished, a few errant, ebony spikes of hair still stuck straight up in the air. Katie reached to smooth them down, but Mike shook his head and pulled away.

"I'm all yours," he said to Jack.

Katie grabbed Mike's arm. She realized this was her moment to say something reassuring. Something that Mike could hold on to as he fought this unfair arrest, something that would tell him that Katie was solidly in his corner.

But all Katie could think to say as Jack led him out the door was, "I'll call a lawyer!"

Which, in retrospect, she realized wasn't exactly the battle cry of a woman who thought her guy was innocent.

No sooner had Jack, with Mike in the backseat, pulled his car out of their driveway and onto the main road, than Katie was in her car, following them to the police station. When her car ended up alongside Jack's at a red light, Katie waved to Mike. He kept staring straight ahead.

Katie figured he hadn't seen her.

He was so still. Almost frozen, really. That's what Katie didn't get. If she were in Mike's place, she'd be trying to explain to Jack why this was all a misunderstanding and how he should just turn the car around and admit he'd made a mistake. But Mike wasn't even bothering to answer the few questions she could see Jack was tossing over his shoulder. Katie supposed she shouldn't blame Mike. After all, didn't the police always tell the people they arrested, "Anything you say can and will be held against you?" Mike was probably just being cautious. Not cagey.

Ruefully, Katie reminded herself that Mike had been to jail before.

Gripping the steering wheel with one hand, Katie picked up her cell phone with the other and called her brother-in-law, Tom Hughes, Margo's husband. She begged him to come in and represent Mike before Jack threw the book at him. Tom sighed and reminded Katie that he was the district attorney of Oakdale now. Which meant he was no longer available to bail Katie out of trouble.

"Not even this one time? Please. . . . I promise I'll never ask you for another favor again as long as I live!"

This was unlikely, and they both knew it. But Tom didn't even bother commenting on her proposal. He suggested Katie call Jessica Griffin, his predecessor at the D.A.'s office and his former law partner.

Katie mumbled something about how blood was supposed to be thicker than legal technicalities, but she quickly called Jessica and begged for help.

Jessica promised to meet them at the station and warned Katie to tell Mike not to say anything until she got there. That actually made Katie feel a touch better. If Jessica said keeping quiet was the absolutely right thing to do now, then Katie could stop reading sinister implications into Mike's keeping silent with Jack, and with her.

Inside the police station, Katie tried to follow Mike and Jack into the interrogation room, but Margo grabbed her by the arm and guided Katie to the waiting area.

"What's going on, Margo? What do the police have on Mike? How come they want to talk to him? Why does Jack think he would have killed Gregory Marron? Can I talk to Jack?"

"Jack is on a conference call with the mayor. And Gig Marron. In case you haven't heard, this case has been ac-

corded top priority. A lot of very important people are pushing to have it solved as soon as possible."

"Does that mean they're going to charge Mike with murder? They can't do that, can they? Mike is innocent. Come
on, you know him. You know what a good guy he is. Mike
could never—"

"Katie?"

"What?"

"Take a deep breath."

"Okay."

"And Katie?"

"What?"

"Wait."

Katie didn't like waiting.

But she did it. For Mike's sake. The last thing Katie
wanted to do was to make things worse for him, and she figured if Jessica warned Mike not to say anything until she got
there, then, to be double-safe, Katie better keep her mouth
shut while she was at the station, too.

When Jessica arrived, she spoke to the officer at the front
desk, said a quick hello to Katie, and headed for the interrogation room.

Okay, good, Katie thought. Now they would finally get
somewhere.

Fifteen minutes later, Jessica reappeared. She exchanged
a few words with Margo, then briskly crossed the officers'
bull pen to the waiting area.

In response to Katie's barrage of questions, she said, "I'm
sorry, but Mike won't be out today."

"Why not?"

Jessica hesitated.

"Jessica, talk to me," Katie prodded anxiously. "I'm the one who hired you."

"You're the one who called me, Katie. Mike is the one who can hire me. And unfortunately, against my advice, he's refused my services."

"What? Are you kidding? Why?"

"I am not kidding. And I am sorry. But there's nothing more I can do." Jessica gave Katie an apologetic look and walked out of the station, leaving Katie feeling even more lost than before.

"What the heck is going on here?" Katie's words reached Margo's desk even before Katie herself did.

"It's okay, Katie," Margo said gently.

"What's okay? Why doesn't Mike want Jessica to represent him?"

"Apparently, Jessica and Mike have worked together before."

"They have?"

"Fifteen years ago—" Margo began, but Katie connected the dots before her sister had a chance to elaborate.

"Jessica was Mike's attorney when he went to prison? Jessica Griffin?"

"She was working for Legal Aid. Mike was a pro bono client."

"She's the one who told Mike to plead guilty to stealing the Marron's car! Well, no wonder he won't talk to her. Please, Margo, you have to call Tom. I'll do anything—"

"Katie, Tom is the D.A. He can't defend your boyfriend."

"So I'll call another lawyer. Ask Tom to recommend someone else."

"No, Katie."

"What do you mean no? Mike's entitled to an attorney. I know how it goes."

"Mike has waived his rights. Not just to Jessica, but to hiring any lawyer."

"But . . . but . . . that's . . . it's so stupid!"

"I agree with you."

"Mike isn't stupid."

"I agree with you on that, too."

"You have to let me talk to him, Margo. I know it's probably against your rules or something, but it's not like I'm going to slip him a file. I've got to find out what's going on. Please. Please, let me see him."

Margo sat silently for a moment, then stood up and warned, "If you ever let on that I did this, I'm telling Mama on you." She led Katie to the interrogation room clearly labeled POLICE PERSONNEL ONLY.

"You are the best sister in the world!" Katie gave Margo a hug.

"And what kind of pension does that position provide?" Margo asked dryly, then added, "Five minutes, that's it. I am not risking Jack getting off his call and finding you in here."

"Thanks, Margo," Katie said as her sister closed the door. "I appreciate it."

"Well, I don't," Mike said loudly. "What are you doing here, Katie?"

She turned around. Mike was sitting on a metal chair behind a matching table, drumming his fingers. He wasn't handcuffed, and he was wearing the same clothes he'd left the house in. Yet Katie couldn't help thinking that he looked different. Maybe it was just the unflattering fluorescent light, but all of a sudden he seemed menacing. Hostile. Unreliable.

Words that, twenty-four hours ago, she would have never associated with Mike Kasnoff.

Unsure of how to respond in the face of his unmistakable antagonism, Katie tried to lighten the mood. "Hey, whatever happened to the guy who said he's always happy to see me?"

Mike slowly turned his head so that he looked from one side of the room to the other, then back at Katie. He didn't need to say anything. The message was clear. These were not circumstances under which he was happy to see her.

"Margo says you waived your rights to an attorney."

"Yup."

"Why would you do something like that? I mean, I get it about Jessica. She's the one who did such a lousy job defending you before. If I'd known, I'd never have called her. But why don't you want any lawyer at all to help you?"

"That's my business."

"Excuse me?"

"This is my problem, Katie. Let me handle it my way."

"You don't think your being arrested is *our* problem?"

Mike shook his head. "This doesn't concern you, Katie. This deal went down a long, long time ago. I've watched this movie before. I know how it ends."

*　　　*　　　*

Katie left the interrogation room and headed straight for her sister. Margo was on the phone and gestured for Katie to wait a second. But Katie was tired of waiting. She bounced up and down impatiently until her sister cut her call short and frowned up at Katie. "What?"

"Mike wasn't just brought down for questioning. Jack arrested him. That means you guys must have some solid evidence that connects him to Gregory's murder. I need to know what that is." Her sister said nothing. "Margo, my world has been turned upside down! The man I love has been arrested for murder! If you don't tell me why, I swear I'll find out some other way."

Margo rolled her eyes again in exasperation. "You're not going to leave me alone until I tell you, are you?"

"Actually, I'm probably not going to leave you alone until I've found out what's really going on, cleared Mike's name, and set the world back to rights again," Katie said vehemently. "I can do it, you know. I do own a detective agency . . . of sorts."

"Keep your voice down," Margo said as she stood. "And follow me."

"So this is where the *CSI* happens, huh?" Katie and Margo stood outside and just to the left of the door labeled FORENSICS. They watched the white-coated technicians operating inside through a rectangular, glass partition.

"No," Margo said slowly. "*CSI* happens on television. Forensic investigation is what happens in that room."

"Yeah. That's what I meant." Katie looked around. "So what have you got in there that puts Mike at the scene of the crime, much less makes him a suspect? I mean, Mike didn't even want to go to the benefit, that's how hard he was trying to keep away from Gregory Marron."

"You do know about their past together, right?" Margo asked cautiously.

"Yeah, sure, of course." Katie faked a nonchalance she most certainly didn't feel. "Mike and I have no secrets from each other. But that mess with the stolen car happened over fifteen years ago. Mike did his time. He paid his debt to society. It's not fair for you guys to drag up ancient history in order to railroad an innocent man into—"

"Look on the counter over there." Margo pointed to a Formica slab directly across from them. "Do you see a wine bottle, Katie?"

Katie most certainly did. It sat in a large plastic bag. Its label read CHÂTEAU PETRUS 1947. The whole thing was covered in a white powder.

Margo said, "Gregory Marron drank from this wine bottle during his drive to the hospital. We know he opened it himself. He brought his own corkscrew and his prints were the only ones we found on it. Unfortunately for him, the red wine inside was poisoned. Gregory's killer used cherry laurel berries. They're native to this area, you can find them almost anywhere we have woods. They grow wild and are highly toxic. In fact, they release cyanide when ingested. Gregory's killer boiled the berries to extract their juice, then injected the poison into the wine. We found a microscopic prick in the cork that was most likely made by a syringe."

"Okay, fine. Good for you for figuring all that out. Isn't the Oakdale P.D. clever? But you still haven't told me what this has to do with Mike. Why in the world would you think he played any part in this?"

"Because. Katie. When we dusted the wine bottle for prints, we found three sets. Gregory's, of course. Henry's, because we assume he stocked the limousine's bar—I'll be checking in with him about it later. And Mike Kasnoff's."

5

Sunday morning Henry refused to get out of bed. He propped his pillows up against the wall, pulled the blanket to his chin, turned on the TV to *AMC Movie Classics*, and announced that he was taking a mental-health day.

Maddie had a feeling he was going to continue to blow off any questions she might pose to him about why he'd been so nervous the night Gregory Marron had died, just as he'd done yesterday. When she approached him, he said, "Not now, Maddie. We're almost at the end of *The Longest Day*. I want to see how it ends."

"I'm pretty sure our side wins."

"So the history books would lead you to believe. I'm checking the cinematic evidence, just to be on the safe side."

The doorbell rang.

Henry didn't budge.

Maddie asked, "Don't you want to get that?"

"Nah, probably just Jehovah's Witnesses."

When no one responded, the ring turned to an insistent knocking.

"I'm going to get it," Maddie said, standing up from where she'd been perched at the foot of Henry's bed.

"Suit yourself."

Margo Hughes was standing on their doorstep.

"Is Henry around?" Margo asked Maddie.

"No," Maddie said, refusing to open the apartment door any wider or let Margo in. "Do you have a warrant, Detective Hughes?"

"No," Margo said, and she shoved the door open.

Henry, hurriedly tying a bathrobe sash around his waist, approached the door, hissing, "For God's sake, Maddie, let her in."

"Fine," Maddie said. "Come in. But you can't stay long."

"Maddie!" Henry frowned at his sister, then smiled brightly at Margo. "I'm so sorry. Maddie isn't herself today. She's hypoglycemic. She hasn't eaten enough fruit."

"Remember when I said I might have a few follow-up questions, Henry? Well, guess what? I'm a woman of my word."

"Henry won't be making any statements to the police without a lawyer present." Maddie stood in front of the couch, lest Margo get any ideas about making herself comfortable.

"You know, Henry," Margo mused, "they have some lovely finishing schools. On the other side of the country. Perhaps you want to consider getting your sister a few lessons in etiquette. Or maybe just a class on respecting your elders."

"Maddie," Henry said, "go have some fruit."

"I'm not going anywhere," she said.

"Fine. Then sit down and be quiet," Margo advised. "This isn't a game, and cute doesn't earn bonus points."

Maddie opened her mouth to reply. Henry interrupted by saying, "This is the part where we go: Yes, Detective Hughes."

"Yes, Detective Hughes," Maddie mumbled. And sat down on the couch next to Henry.

"All right, Henry," Margo began. "There are just a couple of details I need to get straight. The wine that Gregory Marron was drinking . . ."

"Château Petrus, 1947. It was his all-time favorite. The company would have it flown in special from Europe, then add the cost to his bill. It made for a hell of a pricey ride, but a tipsy customer is a happy customer."

"Okay. So take me through the process, step by step. Tell me exactly how that particular bottle of wine got from Europe to Gregory Marron's glass."

"Well, let me see . . ." Henry rubbed his chin. "I think this particular bottle came in last Wednesday. It stayed in the company safe until Friday morning, when I signed for it and put it in the car."

"The sheet shows that you signed it out at eight thirty-five A.M. Why so early for a bottle you weren't planning on serving until seven P.M.?"

"I had a full day of customers booked, back to back. No time to return to the dispatcher's and get it between jobs."

"So you had a five-hundred-dollar—"

"Five hundred and fifty, actually. That Château Petrus is pricey stuff. Some vintages go for up to a thousand."

"You had a five-hundred-and-fifty-dollar bottle of red wine just sloshing around in the backseat of your car for almost twelve hours?"

"No sloshing. There was definitely no sloshing involved. There's a compartment in the backseat built just for wine bottles. Keeps them steady and safe."

"Still, after a day of being driven around town . . ."

"Okay, look, here's the thing about Gregory Marron. He liked to come off as this ultimate wine connoisseur, *I only drink the best vintages from the best wineries.* But, fact was, he could barely differentiate red wine from white, much less be able to tell when his precious, five-hundred-and-fifty-dollar bottle had been jostled around a little bit before opening. I'd done it before, and he never knew the difference."

"So you had the bottle with you all day?"

"You betcha. The garage would have taken it out of my personal pocket if it'd gone missing, and ol' Gregory would have taken it out of my hide. In case you haven't heard, he wasn't a peach of a guy." Maddie, horrified, stomped Henry's foot hard. He looked at her quizzically. Then, understanding dawning, Henry politely added, "May he rest in peace."

Margo said, "I checked your schedule for this Friday, you made all your pickups and drop-offs on time."

"A prompt customer—"

"Is a happy customer. Yes, so I've heard. But are you telling me you're such a dedicated driver that you don't even take bathroom breaks?"

"Well, um, this is a very delicate subject, Margo."

"I won't faint if you won't."

"Certainly, I take bathroom breaks. Only human, after all. But I make a point of locking the car each and every time I leave it."

"So except for bathroom breaks, was the bottle ever out of your sight that day?"

"Well, I couldn't see it when it was in the back, but I kept checking on it. And, before you ask, I even ate lunch in my car that day. I didn't have a lot of time to kick back, so I bravely chowed down a sandwich and kept right on limoing."

"Who put the wine in the safe when it first arrived?"

"I did. It was for my customer, so I took care of it."

"And you never took it out, maybe just to show to somebody?"

"That would be rather lame, wouldn't it, Margo? Believe me, even the classic 'Come on up to see my etchings' line works better with the ladies than 'Hey, babe, want to check out a really overpriced bottle of wine?' "

Henry was talking a lot. Henry always talked a lot, Maddie realized, but he really seemed to be pouring it on for Margo. Which meant he had something to hide.

"Why all the questions about the wine bottle?" he continued.

"That's classified police information."

"Marron was poisoned wasn't he?" Henry guessed.

Margo didn't reply.

"Don't dick a private dick, Detective Hughes. That's it, isn't it? Gregory Marron's wine was poisoned. That's what killed him and that's why you're so curious about who might have had access to it."

Margo still didn't say yes. But she also didn't say no.

So Maddie took it upon herself to fill the silence.

"It wasn't Henry!" Maddie blurted out. "You have no right accusing—"

Now it was Henry's turn to all but stomp on Maddie's foot to get her to stop talking.

Margo waited for the brother and sister act to reach its Three Stooges–like conclusion before asking, almost as an afterthought. "By any chance, Henry, did you happen to see Mike Kasnoff the day Gregory died?"

Henry paused. Maddie didn't understand why he needed to pause. Or why he answered Margo with another question.

"Why would I have seen Mike Kasnoff the day Gregory died?"

"I don't know, why *would* you have seen Mike Kasnoff the day Gregory died?" Her expression made it clear that Margo could play this game as long as Henry.

"I had no reason to see Mike," Henry agreed.

"Okay," Margo said, utterly unamused. "You had no reason to. Now answer my original question. Did you?"

"No! No, I didn't. But what does Mike Kasnoff have to do with—"

"Thank you, Henry," Margo said as she stood to leave.

"This is great news!" Maddie exclaimed as soon as Margo was out the door.

"No, it isn't." Henry thoughtfully waved his finger in the

air. "Her questions about Mike, those weren't random, you know."

"I kind of figured."

"They must have some kind of evidence that ties Mike to Gregory's death."

"I kind of figured that, too. Which is why—rewind and play—I said, Great news!"

"Do you think the cops have actually arrested Mike?"

"Who cares?"

"I care! Mike is my friend."

"Mike stole Katie from you."

"Madeline Coleman, for the last time, would you listen to me: Mike did not steal Katie from me."

"Oh, I'm sorry. I missed my SAT prep course this morning. What's the correct vocabulary word for when you're married to a girl and another guy sleeps with that girl, and the girl then divorces you and shacks up with him?"

"That's not how it happened."

"It's a matter of public record."

"Only if you go by the facts."

"Fact: Mike Kasnoff stole your wife. Fact: Getting back at him for it would be a case of just desserts."

"And what would that do to Katie?"

"Teach her a lesson, too. You don't mess with the Colemans."

"Maddie, I told you before. I knew what I was getting into when I married Katie. I knew she didn't love me. I mean, she did, but only as a friend. Katie and I have been best friends ever since she came to work at WOAK when I was the station manager."

"Oh, yeah. Wasn't that when she poisoned the anchor-woman—"

"She didn't poison Molly. She just took advantage of the situation."

"And made up that a stalker was after her—"

"Actually, I'm sort of responsible for that debacle."

"And didn't your supposedly good friend, Katie, abandon you on a deserted island after she dragged you out there to look for some lost jewel?"

"Technically, the island wasn't deserted. It had a hermit living on it."

"I guess when you put it that way, dumping you for Mike was probably the least of Katie's sins."

"Once again, Maddie—" Henry waved his arms as if conducting an orchestra and prompting her to repeat after him. "She didn't dump me for Mike. I dumped her."

"You're lying. I see the way you look at her. You're still in love with her."

"I love Katie," Henry said. "I have always loved Katie. But when I asked her to marry me, I knew she was still in love with Mike. Those two would have gotten together a long time ago, if Katie weren't still dealing with the mess Simon left behind."

"Oh, yeah. Simon. She was married to him, too. I remember."

"Simon did such a number on Katie's head she didn't know what she wanted out of a relationship or if she could even have a normal one. So she left town for a few months to get her head together. In the meantime, Mike took up with another woman. I told Katie the best way to get Mike back was to make him jealous. And I suggested she do that by pretending she was going to marry me."

"Pretending? No way, Henry, you guys were really married. I saw the wedding album. White dress, tux, minister, flowers, big gloppy cake, the works."

"That was kind of . . . an accident."

"How do you get married accidentally?"

"Katie kept thinking Mike was going to stop the wedding. First, she thought he'd stop it when we announced our engagement. Then she thought he'd stop it when I asked Mike to be my best man."

"Some best man!"

"She thought he'd stop it when he asked to talk to her before the wedding, and she thought he'd stop it when we were saying our vows, and she was sure he'd stop it when the minister said that part about 'does anyone here have reason why this couple shouldn't be united in holy matrimony.' "

"But, he didn't."

"He didn't. So it was 'I do,' and 'She does,' and, there we were, legally married by the State of Illinois."

"But you really loved her."

"And Katie loved me. She just loved Mike more," Henry said. "She tried to make our marriage work, she really did. But every time she looked at Mike I could see that he was the one she wanted to be with. So I let her go. I broke up with her, not the other way around."

"Henry."

"Yeah?"

"You're an idiot."

He bowed deeply. "Thank you, Maddie."

She patted his shoulder. "I only harangue you because I care, you know."

Henry changed course. "Poor Katie must be going out of her mind."

"You know, if you're worried, you could go over and comfort her . . ."

"Maddie!"

"Sorry. But, you know, it's just so obvious you've still got it bad for her."

"I do not! I will have you know, young lady, that my social life is doing perfectly fine without Katie Peretti in the picture."

"The last girl you went out with was named Sadie. She was petite, had blond hair, and even had a pet rabbit. Oh, yeah, you are so over Katie."

"Sadie's rabbit was a girl. Katie's is a boy. Totally different. And, anyway, Sadie was a terrific person in her own right."

"Then why aren't you still seeing this terrific person?"

"Because, I, well, she may have kind of dumped me for someone else."

"Someone who saw her as an individual and not just as a clone of his ex-wife?"

"Okay, so it might have been something like that. But, anyhow, I ran into her a few weeks ago, and her life is going gang-busters. She's got this great new guy, and the rabbit is crazy about him and, you know how it goes, everything works out for the best, no crying over spilled milk, all's well that end's well, etc. . . . etc. . . . ."

"Whatever you say, Henry."

"That's the spirit. That's what we need a little more of around here. 'Anything you say, Henry.' Yeah! I like the sound of that! Anything I say!"

"Will you at least call Katie and find out why the police think Mike would have a reason to kill Gregory Marron? I want to be sure Mike's motive is nice and solid, and that you're totally in the clear so we don't have to worry about any more surprise visits from Detective Hughes."

"I am not going to pump Katie for details about Mike to cover my own backside."

"I didn't say that. Just make it a friendly call. You're friends. Pals. Amigos."

Henry looked at his cell laying on top of the television and mused, "Okay. Yeah. Maybe I'll do that."

"Cool."

"But, I'd like a little privacy, if you don't mind."

"What for? Seeing if there's still a spark in the old flame . . ."

"Maddie!"

"Sorry." She turned toward her room. "Just pretend I'm not here."

"That is extremely likely to happen."

Maddie closed her bedroom door. And pressed her ear tightly against it.

She didn't care what Henry said. Her brother was still in love with Katie. It was obvious from the way he looked at her, like a hungry puppy dog. Henry's blatant love for Katie was why, when Maddie first came to town, she did little things to try to reunite the former Mr. and Mrs. Coleman. Like convincing Henry to pretend he'd thrown his back out so he had reason to continue living with Katie. And e-mailing Katie's high-school boyfriend claiming to be Katie so the guy would go after her again and anger Mike in the process. Unfortunately, none of those brilliant schemes managed to get the job done—and the latter almost got all four of them killed when said ex-boyfriend proved to be a present-day nut-job. Still, total and repetitive failure didn't mean Maddie had to give up.

Henry and Katie belonged together. The three of them, Henry, Katie, and Maddie, could be the perfect family if they were just given a chance. Henry and Katie could even have a baby and Maddie would help to take care of it, and then Maddie wouldn't have to stress about Henry all of a sudden changing his mind and sending her back home because he and Katie would realize how indispensable she was and how much they loved having her around. Then Maddie could relax and settle in to school and make some friends and have a sort of normal senior year where she could be elected homecoming queen and student body president and all that other stuff that seemed important to other girls so maybe Maddie should at least give it a try once and see if it was all it's cracked up to be.

But none of it, she was certain, ever could or would happen without Henry and Katie reuniting. And God knew, that wasn't going to happen all on its own. Henry was totally clueless about such things. He needed Maddie's guidance.

Which was, of course, the one and only reason Maddie currently had her right ear pressed to the door.

Maddie expected Henry to make the call right away.

When she didn't hear him talking, she assumed Katie hadn't picked up her phone.

But then she heard the phone ring. Was Katie calling him back? Straining her ears, Maddie heard Henry say, "It's me. . . . Yeah, yeah. . . . It's okay. I handled it. You don't have to worry about me. I didn't say a word to the police."

6

"You have to do something about your husband." Katie swept into Carly's living room, past Sage sitting in her playpen, without so much as a "Hello" or a "May I come in?"

"Excuse me?"

Though, to be honest, Carly did have a pretty good idea of what Katie was talking about. Jack had called home an hour ago and explained about Mike's arrest, claiming that Kasnoff had pretty much given him no choice in the matter. Jack also told Carly about Katie's pledge at the police station to find out what was really going on and to clear Mike's name.

"What's his problem?" Katie demanded. "Why is Jack after Mike?"

"Maybe because the evidence points in his direction," Carly suggested.

"Has he looked for any other evidence? I don't think so. Seems to me Jack wants an open-and-shut case so he can be home by dinnertime, and to hell with little things like due process and civil rights and being innocent until proven guilty."

"Do you have any idea what any of those words mean, Katie?"

"They mean that Mike is being railroaded into prison for life all because of a bunch of coincidences!"

"It's a coincidence that, for no reason he can explain, Mike's fingerprints are on a bottle of wine used to poison Gregory?"

"Jack just has it in for Mike, that's what this is about."

"Don't be ridiculous. What would Jack—"

"Sage," Katie said.

Carly looked at her daughter, then back at Katie, dumbfounded. "Sage?"

"It's obvious. Jack is still steamed about what happened with Sage. How you weren't sure whether Jack or Mike fathered her. He's been waiting, biding his time in that cop way of his, and now he's going to frame Mike for this crime because he wants revenge."

"Don't be silly," Carly snapped.

"Oh, you can think of another reason why he's so gung-ho to convict Mike?"

Carly didn't say anything. All she could think of was Jack's blithely telling her he was going to work security at Nancy Hughes's benefit . . . so that he could kill two birds with one stone.

"You're being ridiculous, Katie." Her words sounded so confident. Carly wished with all her might that she could believe them.

"So prove it to me. Please. Get Jack to back off. At least convince him he needs to follow a few other leads. Gregory Marron was a filthy-rich guy with a father, a wife, and a daughter who couldn't even ride in the same limousine with him. Come on, don't tell me there aren't other people who had a motive to kill him."

"You're making your case to the wrong person," Carly insisted. "I don't tell Jack how to do his job."

"Not officially. But Jack is crazy about you, Carly. He got suspended from the force last year because he covered up for you. He'd do anything if you asked it. And I know you and Mike are still friends. Don't you want to help a friend?"

"No. No, Katie. You said it yourself. Jack has already gotten into trouble over something I asked him to do. I am not going to put him in that position again."

"This isn't the same thing."

"I don't care. Your priority is Mike? Well, mine is Jack. I am not going to ask him to risk his job—"

"How is actually investigating the case, instead of jumping to conclusions, risking his job? Heck, Carly, you'd be helping him."

"I said no."

"You're just feeling guilty."

"About what?" Carly practically yelped. Sage heard the odd tone in her mother's voice and began to whimper.

Katie watched her pick the little girl up from the playpen.

"Isn't it obvious?" She gestured toward them both. "You can't ask Jack for a favor to help Mike, because you know I'm right. His Inspector Javert routine is all about that sweet little girl and the nine months of hell you put him through when Jack was afraid she would turn out to be Mike's."

Carly looked at Katie for a long moment. She clutched her daughter tighter, considering all of her possible responses. And then she said, "Okay. Fine, Katie, you got me. You're exactly right. That's exactly what I'm feeling so guilty about. Now do me a favor and get out of my house."

Unfortunately, shoving Katie out of her sight did very little to drive her accusations out of Carly's mind. They spun around in there like loose ribbons of cotton candy, growing bigger and bigger with each pass until she could literally think of nothing else. After several hours of trying to distract herself by playing with Sage, reading a magazine, and sketching an entire new line of clothes that no one would be caught dead wearing, Carly finally realized that the only way to drive the suspicions from her mind would be by getting to the bottom of what exactly had happened to Gregory.

For one thing, Carly couldn't bear not knowing and imagining the worst. And for another, if her worst fears were confirmed and Jack had killed Gregory for her—and framed Mike Kasnoff for the crime—then Carly needed to know about it. So that she could protect her husband.

Carly owed Jack that much. She owed him that and a lot more. Because Jack Snyder had, no ifs, ands, or buts, saved her life.

Mainly by saving her from herself.

Jack Snyder had turned Carly from a woman who'd been

willing to do anything for money, even getting pregnant by the first available guy because she knew it would make her baby eligible for a fifty-million-dollar trust fund, to a woman who would now do anything, really, truly anything, to protect the family they'd built together.

Finding out who killed Gregory would be for Parker. It would be for Sage. And it would be for Jack. Most of all, though, it would be for her. Carly knew that, if her suspicions were correct, she was the one who'd driven Jack to do something so extreme. Carly was always the one driving Jack to extremes.

But now she would finally get her chance to rescue him.

When he got home that night, Jack certainly looked in need of a rescue. He could barely keep his eyes open. Which was probably the only reason why he didn't kiss Carly hello like he always did.

Instead, Jack said hello to the kids and waved away Carly's offer of dinner by saying they'd ordered sandwiches down at the station so he wasn't hungry. In response to her second offer, that he take a shower, change his clothes, and finally get a few hours of sleep, he told Carly, "Nah, I've got work to do. I'm going upstairs."

And then Jack showed her a manila folder containing the case file he intended to read over. The green tag on the side clearly said GREGORY MARRON JR.

It was all Carly could do to keep from tackling him on the spot.

Instead, she waited. She fed the kids dinner, looked over Parker's homework, bathed Sage, and put both to bed. Then, Carly went in to check on Jack.

To see if he needed anything.

To see if he wanted to talk about . . . anything.

But Jack had fallen asleep with the lights on, the file by his side.

The file lay open, beckoning her. It was potentially full of all sorts of confidential information that could make Carly's life either easier or harder, but either way a lot less uncertain.

She couldn't avoid it any longer. It was showtime. Time for Carly to see just what the Oakdale P.D. had on Mike Kasnoff. And, by association, on Jack, too.

Carly grabbed the file, sat down, and started reading it.

Hoping to get to the relevant details as soon as possible, she hurriedly skimmed through the bulk of the file, casting aside for later a half-dozen reports itemizing the contents of the limo, Gregory's wallet, and other inanimate objects, and headed straight for the transcript of Jack's interview with Mike. Or, rather, the monologue Jack performed for him, since Mike, apparently, had refused to answer any questions. All he'd said to Jack was, "You're going to think whatever you want to think no matter what I say. I'm not gonna help you lock me up."

Which was a rather odd thing for Mike to say.

Katie was right about one thing, earlier. Carly and Mike had remained friends since the mess with Sage's paternity was straightened out, so she knew that this kind of monosyllabic hostility was out of character for him. Mike wasn't the macho man who clammed up and communicated through grunts and smoke signals. He was the sensitive guy who always intuited the right thing to say to a woman. It was one of the reasons Carly had fallen in love with him. Well, fell in what—during her days before Jack—she'd believed was love. In all honesty, what Carly really had been in then, was shock. Through a twist of fate, she'd stumbled upon a noble man who'd loved her sister, Rosanna, exactly the way Carly had always wished someone would love her. She'd just put Gregory Marron behind her, so she'd been pretty raw and emotionally messed up at the time. Carly had resolved that she needed to get the exact kind of relationship for herself. Same kind of love. Same kind of man . . . Why not the same man?

So Carly seduced Mike. And then made sure Rosanna found out about it. On her wedding day. Which didn't end with a marriage.

It had taken many years and many apologies from Carly before Carly and Rosanna were able to reconcile. And it had taken even longer for her and Mike to go from one-night stands to seething enemies to polite enemies to genuine friends.

But having seen Mike from several different sides of the interpersonal equation, Carly felt pretty confident that she knew the man. And the man that she knew was not one who would so stubbornly and illogically refuse to defend himself.

Carly liked Mike a lot. In the abstract, she hoped that he would beat this rap, go on to live a long, full life, get married, even to Katie, if that's what he wanted, and raise a family of fluffy, self-centered dandelions just like their mother.

But in the here and now, Carly also had to admit that she was hoping Mike's odd reluctance to proclaim his innocence was because he was guilty.

If Mike was guilty, then Jack was innocent.

And right now, Jack was all that mattered.

Carly kept leafing through the file, looking for that one piece of evidence that would prove once and for all, in her mind if not legally, that Mike was responsible for Gregory's death. She soon realized, though, that there was simply too much information here for her to go through while sitting on the floor, ears peeled for the smallest sound that might indicate Jack was waking up. What Carly needed was her own copy of the file, so she could study it thoroughly. But in order to get that, she would have to take a risk. She'd have to sneak out of the house, drive to the twenty-four-hour copy store six blocks away, run off her own set of documents, then return the originals to Jack. All without his noticing.

Sure. Why not?

This was hardly the most drastic plan Carly had ever concocted. Why shouldn't it work?

Well, for one thing, because, while Carly managed to painstakingly ease most of the papers out of Jack's file (she left a few of the less interesting ones pointedly sticking out, so that if Jack woke up he might, in his groggy state, not notice the theft right away), and managed to silently steal out to the car, drive to the copy shop, make duplicates, lock them in the trunk of her car so Jack wouldn't inadvertently trip over them at home, roll the originals into a tight tube she could fit into her raincoat pocket, and return to the house . . . the one wrinkle she hadn't counted on was Jack sitting in the living room when she walked through the door.

"Hey, Carly." He smiled warmly at his wife for what felt like the first time in days. "Where have you been, honey?"

7

Katie wondered why she'd ever thought Carly Snyder was going to be any help to Mike. Carly Snyder may have been floating around town these days acting all Alpha-Mom, but Katie should have remembered that, at the bitter core, she was still the same Carly Tenney who had once covered up her hit-and-run of Jack's former girlfriend, stolen fifty thousand dollars from a nightclub safe, and induced labor so that her son could be born in time to meet the deadline for his fifty-million-dollar trust fund. In other words, Carly's only concern, now and forever, was Carly. If there was nothing in it for her, she wasn't interested.

But there was something in this for Katie. Her and Mike's entire relationship was on the line. And not just because it would be tricky to have one if he had to serve a life sentence. Katie was looking at more than that. Even if, no, *when* Mike was eventually cleared and released with the Oakdale P.D.'s most heartfelt apology, Katie would still feel disturbed by his behavior during his arrest. The Mike Kasnoff currently sitting in a jail cell, refusing to say a word in his defense, was not the man that Katie knew, much less the one she'd fallen in love with.

It was ironic, actually, but, when Katie thought about it, she had to admit that she and Mike might never have gotten together, if it hadn't been for Carly and her selfishness.

Nine months after Carly and Mike slept together, and her baby was due at any minute, Carly was too stressed out to deal with whether Mike or Jack was the biological father, so she ran off to her family's isolated farm in Montana. Jack being Jack and Mike being Mike, they followed her. Mike invited Katie to come with him. As a friend. For support. But then Carly, being Carly, decided she only wanted Jack, not Mike, to be there for the baby's birth. She asked Katie if she could keep Mike occupied while Carly was in labor. And Katie, who was interested in more than a mere friendship with Mike, agreed. She asked Mike to drive her to a store a few miles away from the farm to buy some milk. On the way back they ran out of gas.

Mike couldn't understand it. He peered under the chassis, demanding, "How could we run out of gas when we had a full tank?"

"Maybe we sprang a leak?" Katie suggested.

"I just checked. Dry as a bone." Mike furiously kicked the nearest tire. "Damn it. We'll never make it now. I'm going to miss my own daughter's birth."

"I know you love your daughter," Katie reassured him.

"It'll be fine. You'll hold her, you'll be together. But for right now, Jack and Carly need a little breathing room."

"Jack!" Suddenly, Mike had it all figured out. "He did this! He siphoned gas out of the car so I'd get stranded and miss everything!"

"Umm . . ." Katie searched for a way to be honest without technically telling the truth. "Not exactly."

He looked at Katie for a long moment. And now, Mike had everything figured out all over again. "You knew about this?"

"Look, Mike, here's the thing. When a woman has a baby, she needs what she needs." Katie, who had worked as a nurse's aide for several months, was suddenly an expert on all matters obstetrical. "And right now, Carly needs Jack."

"You sabotaged my car?"

"The car's fine, it's just empty."

"You had no right, Katie. I'm going to miss the birth!"

"So what?" She stepped closer to Mike, forcing him to look at her. "Mike, if you were the father of my baby, and you came halfway across the country to make sure I was okay and to say hello to your new daughter, do you know what I'd do? You have no idea what that means—that a man is committed, that he cares, that he shows up. You know what I would do, if you did that? I'd kiss you to death—and then thank God my child had you for a father."

It was the word *kiss* that did it. Up to that point, they'd just been Katie and Mike, two pals sharing a road trip. He was all wrapped up in an ex-flame who might be having his child, she was still mourning a husband who just left her one day without so much as a kiss good-bye. But that night in Montana, it was like the ghosts of Carly and Simon, the ones that were always there on the outskirts, hovering, flickering, so that Katie felt like if she just whipped around quickly enough, she'd actually see them—those ghosts melted away. And now that there were no longer four of them, the two that were left had nowhere to look but directly at each other.

Katie had looked at Mike hundreds of times. Hadn't she? Then why hadn't she noticed the way the grooved laugh lines around his mouth turned into this cute little heart with every grin?

She thought they might kiss. They were so close, every breath Mike took, Katie took along with him. They were so close that she could see the line of sweat working its way down his throat into the open V of his shirt. They were so close, the only thing they could do was kiss.

They didn't.

That came later and was even sweeter than she could have ever imagined. When Mike and Katie finally did kiss for the first time, she felt certain that not only was this right and good and, well, hot, but also that it was different. That, for the first time, Katie was with a man she didn't have to kiss with one eye open, always on the lookout for the lies and secrets that were bound to spring from the shadows. Katie believed she was kissing a future untainted by the past.

Katie, obviously, had been dead wrong.

Based on everything she'd learned from her disastrous first marriage, Katie knew she should walk away from Mike and never look back.

But she also knew that she couldn't do that.

Because while her mind couldn't shake the image of Mike at the Oakdale police station, refusing to tell her what the hell was going on here, her heart clung to the image of the Mike she'd almost kissed in Montana. The one she could so easily imagine being the father of her children.

And besides, Katie wasn't a quitter.

She'd promised herself—and Margo, and half the Oakdale P.D.—that she would get to the bottom of Gregory Marron's death. And she intended to do just that.

To that end, Katie resolved to do precisely what Jack Snyder was not doing. She was going to explore other leads, other possibilities, for the role of killer. And she was going to start with the man who should have known the victim best—or at least the longest. His father, Gregory Marron Sr.

Katie supposed she could simply pick up the phone, call his corporate office, and ask for an appointment. They knew her from the benefit, so they might pass the message on. And Gig might reply. And he might schedule some time in the future when he'd be willing to speak to her.

Or, to make everyone's life easier, Katie could turn to Oakdale's ultimate secret weapon. The woman who knew all and saw all. Katie could call Nancy Hughes.

Nancy answered her phone with a chipper, "Why, hello there, Katie. Tom and Margo just bought me this telephone that tells you who is calling before you even pick up the receiver. Isn't it marvelous?"

"Yes, Mrs. Hughes, but—"

"Oh, and I did mean to ring you earlier—the hospital board met yesterday and they decided that, in spite of what happened, they are going to pay you your agreed-upon fee for planning the benefit. The tragic events we all witnessed, after all, they weren't your fault, now were they?"

How odd to think that, only three days ago, whether or not she got paid was Katie's greatest worry. Now, she'd completely forgotten about it. "Oh. I—Thanks, Mrs. Hughes."

"Why, whatever is the matter, Katie? I thought you'd be pleased."

"No. Yes, yes, I am. Thank you very much. Really. I'm sure you had quite a bit to do with—"

"I merely reminded the board members of a few pertinent facts. Such as the sort of bad publicity we might reap if it looked like we were holding you responsible for something that so clearly was out of your hands."

"I'm sorry. I don't mean to sound ungrateful. But, see, since then, something else has come up that I could really use your help with . . ."

Nancy Hughes was a paragon of decorum and propriety, and one of Katie's favorite people in the world. She loved talking to Nancy, but she always feared she would say something stupid and inadvertently offend her. That's exactly what Katie was risking now. Considering how courteous Nancy was, Katie didn't think she would appreciate being asked to set Katie up on an appointment with a man whose son had been murdered not even forty-eight hours ago. It didn't seem exactly . . . respectful.

Still, Katie reminded herself that she was doing this for

Mike and for their future. A bit of bad manners was worth it if it would help guide Katie to the truth.

"Mrs. Hughes . . ." she hesitated.

"Yes, Katie?"

"Mrs. Hughes, I— Mike was arrested for Gregory Marron's murder."

"Yes, yes, I read about that in the newspaper."

"It's in the newspaper already? So fast?"

"Well, the on-line version. I like to begin my day with a quick Google around the globe. I like to be informed."

"Wow. That's really cool, Mrs. Hughes."

"Thank you, dear. Now then, the short item I read alluded to a past connection between Mike and the Marrons. A car theft, was it?"

"Yes. Mike went to jail for stealing Gregory Marron's car. But that was a million years ago. He would never—"

"I agree. Mike Kasnoff is not a murderer. I have been thinking about this matter a great deal since it happened and surely, there must be more to young Gregory's death than first meets the eye."

"You really think so?"

"Why, Katie, do *you* think Mike was responsible?" Nancy queried.

"I . . . I want to find out the truth." Katie realized she wasn't answering the question and she hoped that Nancy wouldn't realize it, too.

"Absolutely," Nancy said. "It's your duty."

Katie hadn't been expecting Nancy to encourage her to go forth and meddle. Feeling empowered, she continued.

"The thing is, I think Mr. Marron Sr. might be able to point me in a direction the police haven't considered."

"Hmmm . . ." Nancy considered her suggestion. "Well, Jack Snyder did interview him right after the murder, I do know that."

"Yeah." Katie sighed. "Jack . . . Jack's got his ideas about how everything went down, and I've got mine."

"So you do think that Mike is innocent, then?"

Here was a question Katie could answer directly and truthfully. "I really need him to be, Mrs. Hughes."

Nancy said, "I understand. I will call Gig and schedule a lunch date for noon tomorrow at the Lakeview. I'll say I want to express my sympathies over Gregory's death. Gig has been asking me out ever since we began working on this project for the hospital together. I suspect he'll accept, even under the circumstances."

"Why, Mrs. Hughes!"

"Is that surprise I hear in your voice, Katie?"

"No, ma'am. It's genuine admiration."

"Life doesn't end at twenty-five. You young women today would do well to remember that."

"That's actually very reassuring, Mrs. Hughes."

"I meant it to be," Nancy said cryptically.

Then she told Katie to just drop by the hotel a few minutes after noon and stop at Gig Marron's table. Nancy would take care of everything.

Katie did as she was told. With Mrs. Hughes, you always did as you were told.

She spotted the couple across the Lakeview Hotel's dining room and made her way over to them past the perfect, circular arrangement of white-cloth-covered tables. Sterling silver cutlery reflected the dangling crystals woven into the chandeliers, and each floral centerpiece of miniature sunflowers complimented the overall chocolate-and-tan color scheme.

Nancy was sitting with her back to Katie, but even from that angle, there was no mistaking her for anyone else. She wore a cream silk blouse, the collar so crisp it served as an upright frame for the gentle waves in her impeccably styled, chin-length gray hair. The blouse had long sweeping sleeves, pinned at both wrists with four neat pearl buttons. Katie noticed that, when Nancy reached for her water glass to take a dainty sip, neither of the sleeves so much as brushed the table, much less landed in the butter dish or snagged on the breadbasket the way Katie's would have. That, Katie comprehended with dismay, was a kind of class no amount of money or even diligent practice could achieve. Nancy simply had it.

Gig Marron obviously understood what a treasure was perched in front of him, because his attention was squarely focused on Nancy. He appeared to be hanging upon her every word. They made an unusual-looking couple: Nancy regal and refined, Gig, kind of Santa Claus–like.

Although he was wearing a conservative three-piece gray suit with a white shirt, a red tie, and a matching pocket handkerchief, the Santa Claus resemblance came from the fringe of snow-white hair atop his otherwise bald head, and the identically colored eyebrow tufts.

"Why, Katie, hello." Nancy dabbed her lips and smiled brightly at her approach. "Gig, look who's here! It's Katie!"

Katie, who knew nothing of Nancy's plan beyond the promise to take care of everything, had no idea what was expected of her next. So, while gentlemanly Gig stood at Katie's arrival, Katie said, "Good afternoon. Hi, Mrs. Hughes, Mr. Marron . . . I . . . um . . . I'm very sorry about your loss, Mr. Marron."

He nodded his thanks, sitting back down.

Nancy then added, "Katie's young man, Michael Kasnoff, is currently under investigation for the murder of your son."

Okay. Did Nancy really think this was going to endear Katie to Mr. Marron Sr.? *What in the world was the woman up to?*

Gig Marron looked at Katie with renewed interest.

"Is that so?" he asked with no particular inflection.

Katie sneaked a peek at Nancy who gently nodded her head and indicated that Katie should do the same. So Katie nodded her own baffled head obediently.

Nancy said, "Gig, would you excuse me for a moment? I'm afraid I need to powder my nose. Katie, would you do me the favor of keeping Mr. Marron company until I get back?"

"Sure . . ." Katie began. But Nancy was already gone.

Gig gestured to the empty chair Mrs. Hughes had been sitting in. "Take a seat."

Katie sat.

"Would you like something to drink?" Gig buttered his bread.

"No, thank you."

He set down the knife on the edge of his plate. "So what's the story?"

"Story?"

"Why you're here."

"Oh. You mean Mike?"

"Mike," Gig repeated. He chewed his bread, swallowed, and said, "I'm not going to pretend I knew the kid well back when he worked for us. It was only a couple of months and he answered to Gregory more than me—those vintage autos were his passion, not mine. I have more important matters to concern myself with. I did go to Mike's trial, though. Sentencing, too. Kid got a tough deal. That was Gregory's doing. Said he wanted to send a message. Don't mess with the Marrons and expect a slap on the wrist. He kept saying how we needed to show the world we're no soft touch. But, you know, to be honest, I have to say, I understand what drove Mike to steal our automobile. Boy like that, no money at home, no education, he comes out to our place and not only do we have the house, the grounds, the clothes, but then we've also got that stunning garage of cars that we don't even drive. What's a kid from a disadvantaged background supposed to think that's all about?"

Katie assumed the question to be rhetorical and did her best to remain silent.

"See, I encounter kids like him every day. You know how much charity work the family does. Well, no, let me amend that: *I* do a ton of charity work. I, and nobody else, though Monica's starting to take an interest now, she's a good kid. Gregory thought philanthropy was claptrap. 'It's our money,' he said to me. 'Our ancestors raped the land and sullied the environment—' "

"Did they really?" Katie couldn't help asking.

"They chopped down entire forests and built substandard housing that they then turned around and charged exorbitant rents for, so . . . yes. Gregory liked to suggest, 'If those Bolshevik peasants want to live like us, let them go out and find their own resources to exploit.' " Gig chuckled. "Some interesting worldview my boy cultivated, wouldn't you say?"

Was he still being rhetorical? Katie certainly hoped so. Because she had nothing to say in response to that.

"Now me, I'm with Andrew Carnegie. You know Andrew Carnegie? Talk about exploiting resources. Carnegie Steel Company. Richest man in the world. But he gave it away. Said the rich should consider their money as a trust fund to be distributed for the benefit of their community. Isn't that inspirational? I may not have Carnegie's wealth, but I can try to emulate his spirit. That's why the fifty years of support for Memorial. That's why I give so much money. It killed Gregory that there was nothing he could do to stop me. Family money is mine to do with as I please until I kick the ol' bucket. Rock-solid trust. Irrevocable. Way it's set up, I kept Gregory on an allowance. I keep all of them, Aurora and Monica, too, on a monthly stipend. They can buy anything they want with it. And boy, do they ever! Gregory in particular loved flaunting his nonsense purchases every time I turned around. He knew it drove me crazy. The money he wasted on wine alone could have fed countless villages in Africa or bought a computer for every schoolkid in the inner city. Which is why I couldn't blame Mike."

"Mike?" Katie felt like she'd been woken from a trance.

"If it made me sick to see how Gregory wasted his money, what was a fellow like Mike Kasnoff supposed to think? Hell, if I were in his place, I'd probably have done the same thing. Stolen the car, sold it to some other collector, set myself up for life without an iota of guilt. Mike didn't know better. He probably figured we wouldn't even notice it was missing, what with all the other models we had just sitting around, spinning their wheels. Literally."

Katie trod carefully. "So you're certain that Mike was guilty? Fifteen years ago, I mean."

"He was the only one with opportunity—his boss, our regular guy, had been with us for years and besides, the night the car disappeared, he was out of town at an auction with Gregory, shopping for yet another acquisition. Also, Mike pled guilty. Can't beat that for certainty."

"What about now?" Katie asked. "It's a long way from auto theft to murder. Do you think Mike killed your son?"

Gig paused to consider the question. His bushy white brows furrowed. Finally, he said, "I have to tell you, Katie, I've been around a long time. And I've been involved in many different projects. Hospitals, community centers, schools, halfway houses, even jails. I funded the first prison-based job skills program in Illinois. I wanted to give those poor fellows a second chance, give them the skills to make something of themselves. But, you know what I've learned after half a century in the business of giving out second chances? Most folks just make the same mistakes over and over again. I see it in my cardiac units—guy has a heart attack, lives through a bypass, goes right back to shoveling junk food into his mouth and clogging his arteries. I see it in the schools—give a kid a little extra tutoring and his test scores go up. Leave him on his own to apply what he's learned, and his grades fall again. Ex-cons are the worst. Most of them don't make it six months on the outside. I can pour all the money I want into any project I want—and I'll keep doing it, don't get me wrong, my enthusiasm is still as high as ever. But fact is, I end up helping maybe a fraction of one percent of the poor souls who take part in my programs. And it's not their fault. Believe me, the last thing I would ever want to do is blame the victim. Fact simply is, when people are hard-wired to act a certain way, there is precious little you or I can do to change it."

"And that's why you think Mike . . ."

"Murder is not as long a stretch from car theft as you may want to believe, Katie. Especially not after a simple boy has spent some time in jail, picked up all sorts of new skills, if you know what I mean."

"But, Mike's been straight for almost fifteen years. He turned his life around, he started his own business, he's got me . . ."

"Then what," Gig asked quite reasonably, "are his prints doing on the bottle of wine that poisoned my son?"

"I don't know," Katie admitted. "But I intend to find out. Mike isn't a killer."

"You're sure of this?"

"I—yes," she scooched up a bit taller in her chair, hoping to radiate nothing but uncompromising certainty. "Yes, I am."

"That good a judge of character are you?"

"Well . . ."

"Nobody ever pulled the wool over your eyes? Never misrepresented himself or got you to fall for a lie?"

Well. . . .

"I'm a pretty good judge of character, yes," Katie told Gig. Only she wasn't sitting nearly as straight now.

He shrugged. "Well, I like to think I am, too. And I've seen a bit more of the real world than you have, young lady. If only I'd known you were Mike Kasnoff's girl from the start, chances are I could have prevented this whole tragedy. See, put yourself in Mike's shoes, would you? Fifteen years ago, he gets a gander at our place, and it makes him so angry and frustrated, he's got to lash out by stealing one of our cars. Then, Gregory sees to it that Mike does the maximum in prison. That's going to make anyone bitter. But the final straw is your coming to work on the gala honoring us. How do you think it made Mike feel, knowing that his girl is helping tell the world what great humanitarians the Marrons are?"

"Well, Mike and I didn't actually talk about the job all that much . . ." In fact, Mike hadn't said a word about it until right before the banquet. When he told Katie he couldn't go with her. For fear of being tempted to bash Gregory's brains in.

"But he did know about it, didn't he?"

"Yes . . ."

"And you must have mentioned, even in passing, how much money everything was costing, and how there'd be toasts and plaques from the mayor and all the usual hullabaloo that comes with these things?"

"I—maybe. Probably. I'm sure I said something or other."

"And there you go. That poor guy. Even in his own house, from his own girl, he couldn't get away from the Marrons and all of our excesses. It drove him over the edge. Not that I blame him, of course. Like I said, some people can't help being who they are. We more fortunate types have no right demanding that anyone change his fundamental nature. Even"—his eyes twinkled at Katie—"for a beautiful girl."

Katie knew Nancy expected her to stay and talk to Gig until she came back from the ladies' room. But Katie just couldn't do it. She felt like she was about to start sobbing at any moment. She needed to get away before she made a total fool of herself.

Katie ran into Nancy just outside the restroom door. "Well, how did it go, dear?" Nancy asked. Katie responded by breaking into tears. It took a few minutes before Nancy could make out her gasps of, "He—he—Mr. Marron thinks Mike is guilty!"

"Well, of course he does, Katie. Otherwise he'd never have talked to you."

"What?" asked Katie.

"I told you, dear, Gig and I have known each other for years and I understand him fairly well. I suspected that the best way to get him to speak openly to you about Gregory would be if he knew you were Mike's girl. Gig holds Mike responsible for the theft and the murder because, well, how can I explain this—it's how people like him think."

"People like him? You mean, rich people?"

"No. I mean people who practice Gig's particular brand of philanthropy. Take, for instance, his most recent contribution to the hospital. He wished to fund a unit specifically for unwed teenage mothers. Now, goodness knows those young women and their poor children can use the help, and we were very grateful for it. But Gig only wanted to provide certain services. Prenatal care, delivery, follow-up exams, birth control. All well and good and needed. However, when I suggested we might consider adding classes on taking care of your child or even academic courses to help the girls get their high-school diplomas, he wasn't interested. He said, 'These poor girls are already in way over their heads. Why do you want to add to their load? We should be sympathetic to their plight, offer them support, not add pressures they obviously can't handle.' Well, I don't know what that's called where Mr. Marron comes from, but, in my world, that's called lowered expectations at best, and patronization at worst. These young women need help putting their lives together, they don't need to be patted on the head and told that everyone understands why they did what they did, and no one expected any different. What good does that do them?"

Finally, Katie connected the dots. "Mr. Marron told me that he understood what drove Mike to steal. And kill."

"Exactly. If you had militantly proclaimed Mike's innocence to Gig, he would not have given you the time of day. He needed the opportunity to pontificate and to appear magnanimous."

"It was just so hard, Mrs. Hughes. Having to sit there and

listen to him explain why he was certain that Mike was capable of murder. Not to mention so weird, how he doesn't act upset at all about Gregory's death."

"Gig Marron is a very complicated man. Don't assume that what you see on the surface is necessarily what is really going on inside."

"I figured he'd at least be furious with Mike, but he was so . . . so . . ."

"Magnanimous, precisely. You pegged it right the first time. That's exactly how Gig wishes to be perceived."

"But he thinks Mike killed his son!"

"Oh, goodness, Katie, didn't your mother ever teach you that 'Sticks and stones may break my bones, but names will never hurt me?' Who cares one whit what that old fogey thinks? What matters is, did he give you any information that you can use to clear Mike's name?"

"I don't know," Katie confessed. "After hearing Mr. Marron describe this Mike that I've never seen, I don't know what I'm supposed to think about anything, anymore."

"Why, that's excellent," Nancy said. "My dear, I've always found that realizing you know nothing is the very best place to start accumulating knowledge."

Driving home from her encounter with Gig, Katie wished she could be even a fraction as optimistic about her ignorance as Mrs. Hughes seemed to be. Katie felt that she couldn't even trust herself to judge whether to make a right or left turn, much less Mike's innocence or guilt. Who was she to think she could make heads or tails of anything?

Heck, apparently, Katie couldn't even be trusted to lock her own front door.

When she got home she found it ajar, and when she stepped into her cottage and looked around the sunken living room, she realized that, while she'd been out playing detective, her home had been thoroughly ransacked.

And, judging from the footsteps she heard coming from the direction of her kitchen, whoever did it was still in the house.

8

"It's okay. I handled it," Henry had hissed into his cell phone. "You don't have to worry about me. I didn't say a word to the police."

It went without saying that Maddie had to find out whom he was talking to. Her best bet was to get the phone away from Henry, check his phone log, hit redial, and ask whomever answered, "Who the hell is this and what have you gotten my brother into?"

The first part of her plan failed immediately, when Maddie asked Henry to borrow his cell phone, and he ordered, "Use the landline, phone company hasn't cut us off, yet. Oh, wait a minute." He crossed to check, picking up the receiver. "Nope. Still hearing a dial tone. See, what did I tell you, baby sister? Final notice never means final."

"The thing is, I wanted to call long-distance. And it costs

so much from a landline, but on your cell phone plan, week-end long-distance is free, right?"

"Who'd you want to call that's long-distance?"

"Mom."

If Maddie had said she wanted to call Santa Claus, Henry would have told her, "Say hi to the Jolly Red Giant for me." If Maddie had stated her desire to call up Tom Cruise he'd have warned her to beware the Scientology tent, and if she'd said she wanted to ring the man on the moon he'd have pointed out that it was the middle of the day.

But her intention to call their mother seemed to have left him speechless. He merely stared at Maddie for a bit, then inquired, "Come again?"

"I know, I know, it's totally out of the blue. I've barely mentioned her since I got here, and she's never called me even once to check on how we're doing. But, see, the thing is, with all the, you know, drama that's been going on the last couple of days, I've been feeling, well, I—Henry, I've been feeling like I need to talk to Mommy." Maddie widened her already large brown eyes. "I'll be quick."

"Um . . . okay . . ." Henry handed the phone over re-luctantly.

Maddie grabbed it, darted into her room, and hit redial. The cell phone made its connection and began to ring.

On the thirty-third ring, she heard the hollow click that meant either the line was disconnecting, or she'd finally reached voice mail. What she got, instead, was a honest-to-goodness live voice. She hadn't been expecting that.

"Hello?" a female voice said. Maddie wondered frantically if the phone she reached was equipped with Caller I.D. If so, the mystery voice might have recognized Henry's number and was annoyed to be hearing from him.

"Hi!" Maddie chirped.

"Who is this?"

"Who's this?"

"You have reached a public pay phone in the Lakeview Hotel. Goodness, you have some staying power, young lady. My guests were about to be driven crazy by that infernal ringing."

"A pay phone?" Maddie's hopes curled up into a little ball and fell to the pit of her stomach. "Oh."

"If you are trying to reach a guest, please go through the front desk. Otherwise, don't call here again."

Maddie promised she wouldn't.

But first thing after school on Monday, Maddie was in the lobby of the Lakeview Hotel to see what she might discover right on the premises. She'd asked to see the manager and was directed to the front desk, where Mrs. Lisa Grimaldi, the Lakeview's owner, and a woman whom Maddie once overheard Henry refer to as "the Elizabeth Taylor of Oakdale" was standing. While Lisa was still as tightly well preserved as any movie star, Maddie knew Henry had actually been referring to her much married status, and her full legal name of Lisa Miller Hughes Eldridge Shea Colman (no relation, as far as Maddie knew) McColl Mitchell Grimaldi.

"I'd like to apply for a job please," Maddie said politely, having decided that the easiest way for her to snoop around and ask questions without attracting any undue attention was to secure herself a job at the Lakeview. She figured she could stand being a chambermaid for a day. She'd probably look cute in the uniform, too.

Lisa reached for the job applications she kept beneath the desk, but stopped mid-gesture. She asked, "Wait a moment. How old are you?"

"Sixteen," Maddie said, recognizing the woman's voice. It had been Lisa Grimaldi who'd answered the pay phone yesterday.

"Oh, honey, then why in the world do you want a job?"

She'd been expecting a yes or a no. Not this. "Excuse me?"

"What has happened to the young women of today? Why, when I was sixteen years old, I certainly wasn't concerning myself with trying to get any old job. I was concerned about parties and clothes and makeup—"

Oh . . . now Maddie got it. This was to be one of those, "When I was your age" lectures. Good thing Maddie knew how to handle those. She got them from Henry all the time.

"Exactly," she chimed in. "That's exactly why I want a job. So I can buy myself clothes and makeup. To wear to parties. That's it exactly, Mrs. Grimaldi, you hit the nail right on the head."

"Well, your wardrobe certainly could use some sprucing up." Lisa all but wrinkled her nose at the jeans and red-hooded sweatshirt Maddie had thrown on that morning without so much as a glance in the mirror. "But, darling, don't you know?"

"Know what?"

"That's what young men are for!"

Maddie was officially lost, again. She thought she was doing so well and could see where this was going, and then—*What were they talking about, again?*

Lisa noted, "Aren't you a friend of my grandson, Casey Hughes?"

"We go to Oakdale Latin together."

"Then there you have it, Madeline. Casey is a lovely boy. I'm sure if you smiled at him in just the right way, flashed those dimples and those big brown eyes, why he would take you to any party you like. Casey's a very popular young man at that school of yours. Takes after his grandmother, you know."

Maddie's mouth dropped open, but not before she managed to sputter out, "Mrs. Grimaldi, are you suggesting that I 'be nice' to your grandson so that he—"

"Oh, my goodness, not when you say it that way. Gracious me, young people today, you've all become so ... so ... forthright. So literal. I'm not so old I don't know that nowadays, when a young woman says 'be nice' to a boy she means something ... well, something not very nice. I ask you, where has the ability to flirt gone? Why, in my day, all a girl needed was a sweet demeanor and maybe a flash of skin here and there, and every boy within city limits was hers for the taking. I remember with my first husband, Bob Hughes, perhaps you've met him, he's a very important doctor at Oakdale Memorial, why he and I never so much as even attempted—not before marriage, anyway. And still he adored me. When will you young women realize that all this body-part piercing and cursing like a sailor only strips away the—"

Maddie thought that Lisa's lecture might be a major revelation to some other girl. But to Maddie, weaned on black-and-white movies where witty repartee meant a couple was falling in love and a kiss to a blackout meant happily ever after, there was nothing here that she didn't already know or agree with.

As Lisa continued her tirade about contemporary young women, Maddie spotted Monica Marron, Gregory's step-daughter, stepping through the door of the Lakeview's exclusive boutique, Fashions. Realizing that this might be her only chance to dig up information on Gregory's murder from an actual member of the family, Maddie hurriedly said, "Excuse me, Mrs. Grimaldi, but I just realized you're right. I'm too young to be tying myself down to a job. I should be having fun and flirting and wearing nicer clothes so that boys will like me better. In fact, I think I'll get right on that now. Maybe I'll pop into Fashions and check out the latest styles."

Lisa beamed. "We carry an excellent line of young people's couture. I insisted on it. If there is one thing I cannot stand, it's teenagers dressing like sixty-year-old women."

Maddie briefly looked Lisa up and down, noting that Casey's grandmother was decked out in a black leather miniskirt, three-inch heels, and a hot-pink blouse. In a show of remarkable self-control, Maddie managed to keep from replying, "And vice versa."

Instead, she merely bid Lisa adieu, and ducked into Fashions, keeping a sound enough distance from Monica Marron to not make her interest obvious, yet close enough that she could monitor her every move.

Gregory Marron's stepdaughter was deeply ensconced in the petite department. With good reason. She stood barely five feet tall and was small-boned, with elfin features so precious she might, in dim lighting, have passed for a freckled fourteen-year-old—or an extra-cute Muppet. She wore her brown hair off her face with a pair of coral combs, and a pair of green cotton slacks that had clearly been hemmed. Standing at the blouse rack, Monica whipped through each selection with the pace of a customer who knows exactly what she's looking for and has no intention of settling for close enough.

Briefly, Maddie wondered: If her stepfather were murdered on a Friday night, would she be out shopping on a Monday afternoon? Probably depended on what kind of stepfather—and overall human being—he'd been. Which was exactly what Maddie intended to find out.

Monica glanced over her shoulder and, with a look of determination, began walking in Maddie's direction. Maddie hoped she hadn't noticed her.

"You're staring at me," Monica accused. So, all right. So she'd noticed her. And she didn't appear flattered. "Can I help you?"

Maddie was either busted, or she needed to come up with an excuse on the spot.

Maddie refused to be busted.

"Actually," she said, "I was wondering how I could help you. I see you're having no luck in our petite department— there's nothing in there that's hip enough for you, I totally agree. Have you considered taking a look at our selections for juniors? We carry an excellent line of young people's couture. Lisa Grimaldi insisted on it. If there is one thing she cannot stand, it's teenagers dressing like sixty-year-old women."

"You work here?" Monica asked.

"I'm new. It's part of our attempt to reach out to the youth-ful customer. And a well-dressed customer is a happy cus-tomer, that's our motto here."

There was a split second there when Monica didn't look utterly convinced. But then she smiled at Maddie, "Well, okay, then. Show me what you've got in juniors."

At that point, Maddie would have been happy if she just knew where the junior section was. Luckily, a sign on the wall closest to the changing rooms clued her in, and she was able to lead Monica there.

"The great thing about your coloring," Maddie said, warming to her new role, "is that you can wear any shade. I bet everything looks good on you."

Monica smiled shyly and headed straight for a multicol-ored array of designer T-shirts. She picked up first a violet, then a copper one, and turned to face the full-length mirror, tucking one option followed by the other beneath her chin, several times. "You really think so?"

"Totally."

Monica said, "I wish I was more confident about stuff like this. My mother, she has a phenomenal sense of style. And an equally phenomenal need to tell other people that they don't. I think every single outfit I picked out for myself from the age of three on was greeted by my mother going, 'Do you really think those colors go together?' She got me to a point where I absolutely have no faith in my instincts."

"Hey, at least your mom noticed you were in the clothes," Maddie said honestly. "I've got five older sisters; everything I had was a hand-me-down. My mom, she never looked at who was actually in an outfit. She just called me by the name of the sister she originally bought it for."

Monica stopped posing with the T-shirts. "You're kidding me."

"Nope."

"That really sucks."

"It's okay. I don't mean to make her sound all bad. She had it rough. My dad walked out and left her with seven kids to support on her own. She had more important things on her mind."

"Wow," Monica said. "Small world. My real dad walked out on us, too. True, there was only me and my mother—not the entire Von Trapp ensemble." Monica grinned at Maddie. "But I guess even one kid was more than he could handle."

Maddie took a gamble. She said, "But aren't you Gregory Marron's daughter? I'm sorry to be so nosy, but I read in the paper about him and—"

"Stepdaughter," Monica said. "Gregory was my stepfather. He married my mother when I was four and he adopted me, too. Though God knows why, he certainly had no interest in playing Papa." She grinned ruefully, putting down all the shirts. "So I guess that makes me two for two in deadbeat dads, huh?"

"I'm sorry about what happened to him," Maddie said softly. "It must have been horrible for you, seeing him lying there like that. Do the police know what happened?"

"Some pissed-off former auto mechanic poisoned his wine. Can you believe it? Gregory spends his life annoying captains of industry and government officials, not to mention every single member of his own family, and who murders him—some guy he probably hasn't thought about in fifteen years."

"You think somebody in your own family hated him enough to kill him?" In order to keep Monica from wondering why a salesgirl was so interested in this subject, Maddie tried to keep her busy by handing her another bunch of T-shirts.

"Somebody? Try everybody." Monica took the proffered shirts and, once again, held one up under her chin. "Sometimes I think our entire family fortune comes from the family getting a nickel every time one member threatens to kill another in some obscure and diabolic fashion. It's like a tradition with us. Some families play board games together, others go ice-skating, mine gets creative with threats."

"But you don't think anybody would ever actually, you know, carry out a—"

"I wouldn't put it past them." Monica gave Maddie the shirts she didn't like. "In fact, as soon as I saw Gregory tumble out of his car the other night, the first thing I thought was—"

"Madeline Coleman!"

There was that voice again. The voice on the pay phone. The voice that thought Maddie should really be dressing better. The voice of Lisa Grimaldi.

She materialized behind Maddie like the shark from *Jaws* beneath a bikini-clad piece of chum and demanded, "Just what precisely do you think you're doing here?"

9

By late Monday morning, Carly felt as if every nerve ending along her neck and shoulders had been ridden by a cheese grinder. First, there was the shock of trying to sneak back inside the house with her pilfered file, only to be caught by a suddenly wide-awake Jack.

"Where you been, honey?" His words certainly didn't sound particularly ominous on the surface. But Carly's guilty conscience was happy to fill in the blanks.

Her chilled fingers tightened around the tube of illicit documents hidden in her pocket while she forced herself to sound as normal as possible under the circumstances and chirp, "Outside. I was outside."

"Why?" Jack didn't budge from where he was sitting on the couch, arms swung over either side, watching Carly closely.

"Parker," Carly said.

"Parker is upstairs asleep. I checked on both kids before I came down. They're fine."

"Exactly," Carly agreed, peeling off her raincoat and draping it over one arm, the pocket with the documents neatly hidden in the folds. "I checked on them, too. They were both sleeping so soundly. But Parker left his bike on the lawn and I had to bring it in."

"Parker left his bike on the lawn again? I didn't see—"

"He did. Even after you told him a million times, he still did. And it looks like it's starting to rain. I know I should have probably left it as is and taught him a lesson. Let it rust and then he wouldn't have a bike anymore, right?"

"Parker's bike," Jack repeated slowly, as if allowing the excuse to float around a bit before deciding whether or not to accept it.

"Oh, Jack, I'm so sorry, did my slamming the door wake you up?"

"I don't know what woke me up, actually. I opened my eyes, saw the time, saw that you weren't in bed, and came downstairs looking for you. Was worried that maybe one of the kids was sick."

"They're fine. I'm fine. But, Jack, you must be exhausted. Let's go upstairs. You can take a shower, I'll make you a sandwich or something, and then you can lie down and get a few solid hours of sleep. I insist on it. Come on." Carly held out her hand. For a moment, Jack just looked at it. It was all Carly could do to keep her hand from trembling. "Please, Jack," she said softly, no longer quite certain what she was begging him for.

What she got was his hand tucked into hers.

It felt colder than usual.

And he only held her hand for a moment before unexpectedly letting go and heading for the stairs. "Shower sounds good," he said. "And I'll take that sandwich, too."

Carly waited for the water to pound steadily against the shower curtain before she dared sneaking a peek at the remnants of Jack's file on the floor by the bed. It appeared that he hadn't touched it since waking up. Which meant Carly should be able to return her contraband without triggering his suspicions. She stuffed the originals back in the file and went downstairs to the kitchen, where she hid the copies in a plastic bag behind the dishwashing powder under the sink. Because while Jack was a hands-on father, a terrific husband, and an amazing lover, Carly could rest peacefully in the knowledge that he would never spontaneously assume responsibility for their plates and cutlery by deciding to load the dishwasher himself.

Now, at last, with Jack at work, Parker at school, and Sage out for a walk with the sitter, Carly was able to hole up in her bedroom and study all the papers in the Gregory Marron file. She spread all of the sheets out in front of her, in an attempt to make heads or tails out of the question mark that was Gregory Marron Jr.'s murder.

First, by deciphering the autopsy notes, she learned that the poisonous wild cherry laurel berries that killed Gregory grew all over the Marron estate. Which was an interesting wrinkle. The police thought so, too, because, according to

Margo's write-up, they'd searched the Marron mansion for any cookware that might have been used to boil and concentrate the cherries into a deadly brew. A forensics team had tested every available pot and pan, only to come up empty. They'd also combed every room and even the grounds for a syringe that could have been used to inject the juice through the cork and into Gregory's wine. They did find a stash of medicinal syringes on the property, but those legitimately belonged to Gig, a diabetic. And he swore that all were accounted for.

What intrigued Carly most about that aspect of the report was not the surprise that they'd found no incriminating evidence on the Marron estate. After all, what sort of idiot boils up poison in his or her own kitchen then leaves the murder weapon lying around? What intrigued Carly was the fact that, contrary to Katie's assertion that Jack was trying to pin the crime on Mike, the Oakdale P.D. clearly was investigating Gregory's own family.

Margo and her team had done an amazingly thorough search. They didn't just analyze the cookware, they tested the cutlery and even the glassware. They'd inventoried every bottle of wine in the Marrons' cellar and checked it against their credit card statements, looking to see if maybe a recently purchased bottle of Château Petrus might have gone unaccounted for. They fingerprinted the staff, as well as Gig, Aurora, and Monica. These were not the actions of a police department that believed there was an open-and-shut case against Mike Kasnoff.

Carly took that as a positive sign. If Jack wasn't trying to pin the crime on Mike—or anyone else for that matter—that probably meant he had nothing to hide. It meant that he was doing his job honestly, without any ulterior motive.

Carly was almost ready to breathe a sigh of relief and begin the slow, torturous process of convincing herself she'd overreacted, when she saw the handwritten note Jack had paper-clipped onto the back page of the official record.

According to Detective Snyder, Mike Kasnoff had possessed ample opportunity to learn about cherry laurel berries' deadly qualities while working on the Marron estate fifteen years earlier. He could have easily slipped onto the property, picked the berries, and prepared them at an outside location before poisoning Gregory's wine. It was Detective Snyder's opinion that the use of cherry laurel berries was a deliberate attempt to implicate a family member for the crime, and thus pointed even more strongly in the direction of an outsider familiar with the grounds.

So maybe Katie Peretti was delusional.

Or maybe Jack really was trying to frame Carly's former lover for murder.

Carly needed some answers, and there was only one place to get them.

She hid the file back under the sink and headed for the police station.

Carly asked Margo for permission to visit Mike Kasnoff.

Margo wanted to know why Carly hadn't asked Jack. She also wanted to know why Carly had deliberately waited until she knew Jack was out of the precinct before making her request.

Carly told Margo the truth — almost. "Mike is my friend," she said. "At one time, he was much more. I want to help him if I can. Jack is the officer on his case. When you want to talk to Hal, do you ask Tom to set up the meeting?"

Margo Hughes's husband, District Attorney Tom Hughes, was not the father of her older son, Adam. Her former partner, Detective Hal Munson, was.

Margo looked at Carly for a long moment. And then she said, "I'll get Mike for you."

When Carly walked into the visiting area, Mike was sitting behind a metallic table, drumming his fingers on it impatiently. He paid no attention to Carly. He didn't say a word, express surprise, or even look up until, in an attempt to jumpstart their conversation, Carly sat in the chair across from him and said, "Who knew we had so much in common?"

Her non sequitur at least got him to stop drumming. He looked up. "Say what?"

"Gregory Marron Jr. You're not the only one who's got a past with him."

"Oh, yeah? He sent you to prison, too?"

"In a matter of speaking."

She finally had his attention. "What are you talking about, Carly?"

She told him the whole story. Just as she'd told it to Jack. And just like Jack, Mike didn't seem particularly surprised to hear about her social-climbing past. Carly supposed she should be offended. But she had more important issues on her mind.

She said, "My case isn't exactly the same as yours. Gregory just threw me over. Not very ceremoniously—I believe he said something about my boring him; the words *cheap* and *trash* may also have come up once or twice—but it's still not the same as being locked up in prison."

"Yeah, he wasn't a very nice guy, I think we can all agree on that."

"That's why I'm here," Carly said.

"You want equal time to rebut all the nice things that are going to be said about him at his funeral? Maybe the minister can just reuse the tribute Katie wrote about him for the gala."

"I'm here to say that out of everybody in this town, I understand why you would want to kill Gregory Marron. And I don't blame you. In fact, I want to help you."

Mike looked down at his palms. He pursed his lips. "You believe I killed Gregory Marron?"

"Did you?" That was the question of the day, wasn't it? The one on which Jack's future, which meant also Carly's and Parker's and Sage's, hung.

Mike smirked. Or maybe it was just a reflexive twitch—as if he'd been hit. "Your husband slapped the cuffs on me yesterday."

"He did have evidence."

"Yeah . . . he did. Just doing his job. Jack's real good at his job."

"Are you saying you didn't do it?"

"If I didn't do it, how did my prints get on the wine bottle?"

"Mike!" Carly's last nerve snapped. "What the hell is the matter with you? Why are you acting like this? You are the most straightforward, honest guy I know. Why are you playing games? Why can't you just come out and say what you mean? What the hell is going on here?"

"What did you really come here for, Carly?" Mike refused to match her strident tone. If anything, his voice grew even quieter in response to her outburst.

Carly tried to rein in her temper. But it wasn't easy. Her heart was beating so quickly she felt like it had lodged in her throat, making even the simplest of lies a challenge. "I . . . I told you. I understand why a person could be driven to kill Gregory, so I want to help you by maybe—"

"What? Maybe what? Come on, Carly, what can you really do for me?"

"I . . . I don't know."

"This visit isn't about me. We both know that. It's about Jack."

"Jack?" Carly was taken aback. Did Mike know? Had he figured out that Jack was the one framing him? And had Carly's telling him about her past with Gregory finally supplied Mike with the last missing piece of the puzzle—Jack's motive for doing such a thing? Had her attempt to protect her husband actually given Mike the necessary ammunition to destroy him?

"Everything you do, Carly, is about Jack."

"That's not true."

"It is," Mike said, indicating he wasn't about to argue the point, so she might as well concede it. Not that there was anything to argue. "Tell me the truth: Did Jack put you up to this?"

"Of course not!"

"Jack didn't send you in here to talk to me, figuring I'd open up to you because of our past together? Because, you know, even if I confess to Gregory's murder on the spot, even if I tell you how and why I did it every bit is still inadmissible evidence. You can't use it to convict me. It would all be hearsay. Your word against mine, you've got no proof."

"Mike . . ."

"I know how this game is played, Carly, okay? Been there, done that, got the record. When the Marron family wants you in jail, the Marron family sees that you end up in jail. Little things like evidence don't stop them. Still, this isn't like Jack, using you—"

"He isn't using me, I swear."

"Fine. Have it your way." Mike leaned back in his chair and proceeded to stare straight at a spot above Carly's head.

"I came here on my own, Mike. Go ahead, ask Margo. I waited till I knew Jack was out in the field and I came in to see you specifically so Jack wouldn't know."

"Because you want to help me?"

"Yes. I know you, Mike. I loved you once, remember?"

"That was a long time ago."

"Not so long that I've forgotten the kind of man you are." Carly had been talking nonstop since she came in. Suddenly she actually found herself listening to the words she was saying. "You're not a bitter man, you're not a malicious man, and you're most certainly not a vindictive man. When you found out that Sage wasn't yours, you had every right to hate me. You had every right to hate, or at least to resent, Jack. Instead, you came to our wedding. You said a blessing for us— and for Sage. It takes a big man to do that."

"That was different."

"No, it wasn't. You just don't hold grudges, Mike. You're a forgiving man. For God's sake, Henry Coleman faked a back injury and planted himself on your living room couch so Katie wouldn't divorce him for you, and you risked your life to save him just a few months later."

"Being mad at Henry is like being mad at a kid. He always screws up and then he's always sorry and then he always promises never to do it again and then he does."

"Your old girlfriend cheated on you with her former stepfather, got pregnant, and you married her anyway."

"And you know how long that lasted. We were over within months."

"Katie chose Simon over you. Three times. And each time, when she asked, you took her back."

"I love Katie."

"My point is, Mike, you're a forgiving guy, okay? On paper it may look like you spent years seething with resentment over what Gregory did to you, but that isn't the case, is it? You're not the sort of person who holds grudges, then intricately plans his revenge a decade later."

"You mean you think I'm too disorganized to have killed him?" Mike asked, but, for the first time since she'd come in, Carly saw the trace of a genuine smile tugging at his lips.

"Yes," Carly said. "That's exactly what I mean, Mike."

The smile faded as quickly as it dawned. "Katie thinks I did it."

"Did she say so?"

"She didn't have to. The look on her face when Jack put the cuffs on me . . . She's never looked at me like that before. Like she didn't recognize me."

"She was probably just in shock. I know how I would feel," Carly confessed. "If I were in her shoes right now."

"I never lied to Katie, you know. She knew I'd done time, it wasn't a secret. But, I guess knowing about it and seeing it. . . ."

"You two just need to talk it out. Katie knows the kind of person you are. If you just give her a chance to think it through—"

"Like you did right now?"

"Was I that obvious?"

"Kinda. You came in here saying you wanted to help me beat a murder rap, then, a couple minutes later, you're telling me why I couldn't have done it. Almost gave me whiplash there for a minute."

"But at least you know I mean it when I say that no one who really, really knows you could ever believe you are a cold-blooded killer. Give Katie the same chance I got. Let her remember the terrific guy she landed. I promise you, once she does, there won't be any more doubts."

Mike nodded. "It's a great plan, but kind of tough to enact while I'm a guest of the state. Katie tore out of here as soon as I told her I didn't want a lawyer. Hasn't been back to see me since."

"So you go to her."

"Again. Carly. Guest of the state. This isn't a hotel you can just check out of anytime you feel like it."

Carly asked, "Have they charged you formally yet?"

"No. Not yet."

"And it's been twenty-four hours since Jack went to the house and arrested you, right?"

"Yeah. He was a real early bird."

Carly stood purposefully. "The cops can't hold you for more than twenty-four hours without charging you. I know because Jack complains about this all the time. I'm going to call Margo in here right now. We're getting you out of jail, Mike. Leave it to me."

10

Katie realized she'd been robbed. What other explanation could there be? She had probably left the house in such a tizzy this morning, stressing over her appointment with Gig and Nancy, that she forgot to lock the door and a thief had come in and cleaned her out.

Katie's first concern, when she heard the ominous footsteps in the kitchen, was her bunny, Snickers, and his little companion, Snickers II, vulnerable and defenseless in their hutches upstairs. She had to protect her furry little guys from the intruder. It was her solemn duty as a pet owner.

Katie looked around for a brass candlestick, a wooden bat, or a sturdy golf club. Unfortunately, she didn't own any of those items so she made do with a large volume of her childhood encyclopedia.

Clutching it in both hands, she inched toward the

kitchen, when the noise of feet hurrying down from the second floor prompted Katie to jump and spin around.

"Mike!" Katie shrieked.

"Katie," he easily caught the book before she had the chance to do any damage. He smiled down at her. "Nice to see you, too."

"What—what are you—"

"They let me out. They didn't have enough evidence to charge me with Gregory's murder."

"They did? I . . . but that's great! That's terrific! The misunderstanding with the fingerprints has been cleared up? You're a free man? It's all over? Oh, my gosh, Mike, that's awesome—we should celebrate!"

Katie threw herself at him, thinking about one of those world-famous hair-curling kisses she knew Mike must have been dying to give her after his two days in the slammer, but all he did was gently take the encyclopedia from her hands and set it down on an end table. He shook his head. "Not exactly, Katie."

"What do you mean not exactly? You said they let you go!"

"Because they didn't have enough evidence to arrest me, not because they think I'm innocent."

"But who cares what they think? Unarrested is unarrested. We can worry about your reputation later."

"I care about what the people in this town think of me. And so do you. Besides, Katie, have you noticed how the living room looks?"

She had. And then she'd just as quickly forgotten it in her excitement over seeing Mike. "You mean the robbery—"

"It's not a robbery. It's the result of a search warrant. Same time as the police let me out, they informed me they'd be coming home with me to search the place. They're looking for evidence that I brewed the poison that killed Gregory. That's why they're taking all our pots and pans. For analysis."

"Well, good luck to them. The only thing that might be stuck to the bottom of those pans is old macaroni and cheese. They're not going to find a thing, and *then* will you be home free?"

"Not exactly." Katie turned around toward the voice from the kitchen. Margo walked out of it, looking at Mike. From behind her back, she produced a bottle of wine Katie had never seen before. Margo held the bottle forward so Mike could take a closer look at it. She asked, "Care to explain this?"

Mike didn't budge, but Katie leaned over to read the label. "Château Petrus . . . Mike, isn't that the brand—"

"That Gregory Marron drank," Margo confirmed. "Mike, any reason why you'd have a bottle of five-hundred-dollar wine hidden under a tarp in your garage?"

"I was saving it for a surprise," he said. "For Katie."

"Katie," Margo asked, "was Mike often in the habit of purchasing bottles of wine that cost more than your monthly mortgage?"

"I . . ." Katie began, unsure of what to say. "He said it was for a surprise."

"Well, surprise!" Margo pulled a folded plastic evidence bag out of her pocket, shook it open, and slipped the bottle inside. "I'll be taking this down to the station."

"Knock yourself out," Mike said.

Margo hesitated. She turned toward the kitchen and called for a pair of uniforms to bag the cookware, as well. And then she addressed Mike, telling him, "You know, you are not helping yourself with this attitude. I want to help you. Truth be told, every single cop down at the station would like to help you. You're just making it impossible."

"Sorry. Been a while since I read my *How to Be a Perfect Prisoner Handbook.*"

"Don't do this, Mike," Margo pleaded. "Don't do this to Katie."

"I'm fine, Margo," Katie said. Even though she'd been thinking the exact same thing, she wasn't about to let her older sister play the role of her protector. Whatever issues Katie and Mike had, they'd work them out for themselves. "Don't worry about me."

"We'll be in touch," Margo told Mike as she and the policemen walked out the door, carrying half of Katie's household possessions.

"Are you okay?" Katie asked Mike. "They didn't hurt you or anything down at the jail, did they?"

"I'm all right. I could use a shower, clothes I haven't slept in, but I'm okay. No rubber hoses. No bamboo under the fingernails." How could he be joking? Katie wondered. If she'd just been held for two days on suspicion of murder, she certainly wouldn't have been joking.

She decided to jump right into the heart of the matter, pleading, "Mike, tell me what's going on here, please. Why didn't you want Jessica, or anybody else, to defend you? Why was that bottle of wine hidden in our garage? Why are your fingerprints on the bottle Gregory drank from?"

"There's a reason, Katie," Mike said. "But I can't tell you right now. You need to trust me."

"Why can't you tell me? I would never betray you, you know that."

"I know. But things are . . . complicated. I'm trying to protect you. Believe me, you don't need to be involved."

"I am involved. Mike, I love you—that means that I'm involved in whatever you're involved in."

"Not this time, Katie. It's for your own good."

She knew it was the absolute wrong thing to utter under the circumstances, but she couldn't help herself. "That's what Simon used to say. That he lied to me to protect me. For my own good."

Mike recoiled. Katie could actually see him withdrawing from her.

"I. Am. Not. Simon." He enunciated every word.

"Then why are you acting like him?"

"Have it your way," Mike said. He moved toward the door, reaching for his coat and pulling car keys out of his pocket.

"Where are you going?"

"I'll find someplace else to stay."

"No! You don't have to leave."

"Actually, I think I do." He paused before walking out. "Ever since we got together, you've been waiting for me to disappoint you. Just like Simon. Looks like you've finally gotten your wish. Are you happy now, Katie?"

Katie was most definitely not happy. She was crushed. For the first two hours after Mike left, Katie could do nothing more productive than sit in her ravaged living room, hugging a couch pillow and periodically whimpering. These were, admittedly, not the actions of a resilient, independent woman of the twenty-first century. They were not even the actions of Katie on a good day.

But this had not been a good day.

Was Mike right? Had Katie just been waiting for him to screw up? She didn't feel as if she had been. But then why had her first thought, upon seeing Gregory's dead body hit the pavement, been that Mike had committed the crime? Surely, a woman who wasn't lying in wait for her man to prove himself a fraud or worse, wouldn't have automatically leaped to such a conclusion.

Katie needed to do something. Something productive. Or risk going crazy from the anxiety she was experiencing.

She wished she still had a job to go to, though she figured Gregory's death pretty much put the kibosh on her doing any more work with the Marron family. Katie's only professional option these days was her stake in the health club. The detective agency—despite her earlier boast to Margo—was pretty moribund these days. She hadn't been to the gym since Friday, when Mike had dropped her off then peeled away in a huff. Usually Katie liked to pop in at least once a week to see how things were going. She preferred to do this on the weekend, which was the club's busiest time. It was a lot more heartening to see the place half full rather than empty, as it was most weekdays. This weekend, though, she'd been kind of busy.

Well, she wasn't busy now. She might as well head on over.

With any luck, the club might prove to be the one thing she didn't screw up today.

                    *   *   *

No such luck.

When Katie got to the Butt Buster, all the lights were off. Just what she needed. Another blown fuse. Or Henry had forgotten to pay the electricity bill. Either way, this was not the way to attract new clients, or to keep old ones. Katie parked her car behind the health club, and unlocked the back door rather than walking all the way around to the front. Whereupon she discovered that the place was silent as well as dark. This really wasn't good. Where the heck was their daytime manager? Where the heck was Henry, come to think of it? Inside the club which smelled a little damp and sweaty, and very flowery, thanks to the air freshener they used, Katie almost immediately bumped, chest-first, into the handlebars of a stationary bicycle.

She grimaced in pain but at least the collision helped her orient herself to where she was. She took three more steps forward, and promptly bumped her shins on a rowing machine. Oh, she was really making progress now. If her calculations were correct, six steps to the side meant she could swing her arm and hit—ow!—the weight stacks.

Okay, now she knew where she was and how to get to the fuse box.

Arms stretched out in front of her, Katie was proceeding in the direction of the fuse box, when, halfway across the room, she heard the dragging sound of footsteps.

Katie stopped moving.

But she could still hear the other footsteps.

She wasn't alone.

Katie's first instinct was to call out. But that would be letting her intruder know that she was on to him or her. And while that could be a good thing, it could also prove very, very bad.

Gathering her wits, Katie figured her safest, best bet was to move faster, reach the fuse box, and blind the intruder with the light.

So Katie broke into a run, tripping over a medicine ball on the way, but still managing to hit the wall with the fuse box at full speed, sending her head spinning. She reached up above her to pull on the metallic door, when she felt another body slam into the wall, just a few inches from her.

"Leave me alone!" Katie screamed, her arms and legs flailing like windmills in the direction of the intruder. She raised her knee and blindly rammed it into soft flesh, hoping to make contact with a particularly vital organ.

Katie heard a thump, followed by a very distinctive "Ooooof."

Katie flicked on the lights.

"Henry!" she shrieked. She sank to the floor where he appeared to be curled up in pain. "What are you doing here?"

"Yelping in pain," he managed to gasp out between clenched teeth. "And how are you, Bubbles?"

"Why didn't you say you were you?"

"Why didn't you say *you* were *you*?"

"I was afraid you were someone who'd broken in."

"Ditto."

"Are you okay?"

He sat up gingerly and winced. "I've always wanted to perform with the Vienna Boys' Choir."

"I'm sorry," Katie said. "But you shouldn't have grabbed me like that."

"What are you doing here on a Monday? Monday is my day to work."

"I just needed to get out of the house. Why were the lights off? Why was the club closed?"

"I got a call from the morning guy saying the lights were out and to come down here to fix it. I told him to wait until I arrived, so naturally he left as soon as he hung up the phone. I came in through the front door, started feeling my way toward the fuse box when I heard footsteps. I thought someone had seen the lights out and decided to break in and rob the place—of course, the joke's on them, considering how much we've got in the register. When I got close enough, I tackled. You've got a mean knee there, Bubbles. You ought to consider getting it bronzed."

"I said I was sorry. Oh, God, this just hasn't been my day!"

"Yeah . . . about that. Margo wouldn't tell me, but is Mike a suspect—"

"They arrested him Sunday morning."

"Oh my God! He's in jail?"

"Well, he's out now."

"Really? Fantastic news. The getting out part, not the arrest," Henry clarified.

"That's what I said, too. Fantastic news! But, apparently, I was wrong. There's still the minor detail of Mike's prints being on the bottle."

"Mike's what on the where now?"

"Oh, yeah. That's Jack Snyder's big evidence for bringing him in. They found Mike's fingerprints on the bottle of wine that poisoned Gregory Marron. And you want to know the kicker? Mike won't tell me, or more importantly, the cops how they might have gotten there."

"He won't? Really? Why?"

"He says it's complicated. He says he's protecting me for my own good. He says I should trust him and everything will work out. Now who does that sound like to you?"

"Katie. Don't. Mike Kasnoff is no Simon Frasier. Believe me, the man stole my wife from me, and I can still say he's a jolly good fellow."

"Then why won't he level with me? I can keep a secret. Heck, maybe there's even something I can do to help. I can help, you know."

"Men are weird, Katie. They like solving their problems on their own. It's a very common condition called testosterone poisoning. It keeps you from thinking straight."

"That's what I should do." Katie sat up on her knees. "I should help him. Whether he likes it or not, I should keep going until I figure out who really killed Gregory."

"Bubbles."

"What?"

"You're in over your head."

"I am not. I've figured out things before. I know how to investigate. Like here's a good question, Henry: Since the wine bottle was in your car all day, can you think of how Mike's prints might have gotten on it?"

"Absolutely not. Margo asked me the same thing. Well, not exactly the same thing. She didn't tell me about the prints—confidential police business or some other nonsense. But she did ask me if Mike had access to the wine bottle that day."

"And did he?" Katie asked hopefully.

"No, Bubbles, he didn't. I wish I'd known what was going on before I told Margo that, though. I could have made up some harmless reason for his touching it and cleared this whole mess right up for both of you. But I didn't, and if I change my story now . . ."

"No, Henry. I don't want you to lie. That would only make things harder for everybody. What I need to do now is follow the clues—the real clues, the ones Jack Snyder is too stubborn to pursue—and they should lead me straight to the real killer."

"And then what?"

"What do you mean, and then what? And then Mike will be off the hook, and he'll see that he was wrong, I don't always think the worst of him. I'm on his side and he can trust me."

Henry rose to his knees. He faced Katie and took her hands in his. "What I meant was, what if those clues you follow lead you straight back to Mike?"

"That's impossible." She stood up, using Henry's shoulder to balance herself. "Mike did not kill Gregory. I would know if Mike were capable of killing Gregory."

"Katie, listen to me. If Mike is innocent like you think, then he doesn't need your help. Jack and the Gang in Blue will get to the bottom of things eventually and Mike'll be cleared, no harm, no foul. But, if he is hiding something—or somebody else is, somebody willing to go as far as they have to, to cover their tracks, you could be in a lot of danger. Bubbles, if you insist on sticking your nose in places it doesn't belong, you could get hurt. Really, really hurt. As in permanently."

11

~

Maddie thought fast as she looked at the angry expression on Lisa Grimaldi's face and then at Monica Marron who was now gazing at her suspiciously.

Monica Marron had been about to spill who she thought poisoned her stepfather and why. But Lisa Grimaldi was demanding to know what Maddie thought she was doing playing salesgirl in her boutique. Unless Maddie came up with a kick-ass answer for the latter, the odds were she would never get to hear the former. So Maddie thought fast. Extra fast.

"Mrs. Grimaldi," she said, "I'm sorry, I know you said I was too young to work here. But I thought if you saw what a great job I could do in your boutique, you might change your mind."

"You don't really work here?" Monica asked.

"She most certainly does not!" Lisa placed her hands on her hips. "Now, Madeline, while I may admire your initiative—and I do, a young lady with moxie always has a place in my heart; I used to have quite the bit of moxie myself back in the day. Nevertheless, this sort of fraud is not acceptable. I cannot have you lying to my loyal customers. Miss Marron, I apologize. I assure you, this will never happen again."

"But, Mrs. Grimaldi, please, I really need the job," Maddie pleaded.

Monica interrupted, "Excuse me, Mrs. Grimaldi, are you going to hire Maddie?"

"Well, no," Lisa said. "It's—Madeline is simply too young to work in the hotel, maybe in a few years. . . ."

"Great." Monica turned to Maddie. "Then how would you like to work for me?"

"What did you say?" Maddie's head spun. And it wasn't just from her attempt at fast thinking.

"You'd be perfect. You're exactly what I'm looking for."

"To do what?"

"Well, as Mrs. Grimaldi can tell you, I'm a major shopaholic. I'm in here, what? A couple of times a week?"

"Oh, yes," Lisa said. "Miss Marron is one of our best customers. She's constantly stopping by, looking at the new styles, updating her always very chic look."

"The problem is, for people like me, the non-supermodel-size ones, there aren't many clothing choices out there. Everything is either cut for much taller women, or it's for little kids. I don't want to wear an outfit that hangs down my arms and legs, and I don't want to look like I'm still in high school. No offense, Maddie."

"Oh, hey, none taken. High school is pretty much the pits."

"For the last year or so, I've had this radical idea: Why not open a clothing store that caters to petite women? But petite women with a sense of style and adventure. I mean, they've got those big and husky, or whatever they're called, stores for men. How about some equal time for the tiny and cute?"

"That's a totally awesome idea!" Maddie chimed in. Partially because she really thought so, and partially because she suspected she knew where this was going.

"Yes, Miss Marron." Lisa did not seem to be nearly as keen on the idea. "It does seem like a workable concept—on paper. But surely you realize that opening a brand-new boutique involves a great deal of work, on both the retail and the administrative ends. It's a complicated endeavor."

"Exactly why I need a personal assistant to help me get started. Would you be interested?" Monica asked Maddie. "You could work part-time after school—and maybe a few weekends here and there?"

"Interested? Oh, yeah!"

"We'd have to work out of my house, unfortunately. I don't have an office yet. Would it be too much trouble for you to travel out to the boonies every day? I'd pay for the cabs."

"No trouble," Maddie swore. "No trouble at all."

"Terrific!" Monica turned to Lisa, "I happen to like moxie, too. And I've got no age limit for rewarding it. Have a nice day, Mrs. Grimaldi."

*   *   *

Monica offered to drive Maddie home, and Maddie jumped at the offer. How often did she get the chance to investigate a murder—while riding in a cherry-red Lexus?

Monica was saying, "You have a good eye for color and style, plus your salesmanship is awesome. You had me ready to whip out my credit card and buy every one of those T-shirts, and you weren't even on commission!"

"Thanks." Maddie fought the urge to giggle with glee. "So were you thinking of opening this new boutique right away, or do we still need to do a lot of research?"

"Both. I mean, I've already done some basic research. I've got my eye on a few potential locations for the store, plus some terrific designers. I'd have been ready to get started months ago, actually, but, well, my stepfather, he's the Mr. Moneybags—he kept me on an allowance, can you believe it? Like I'm some high-school kid. No offense."

"None taken."

"Gregory thought the boutique was a lousy idea. Honestly, he thought any notion I had was a lousy idea. He said, 'How many high-fashion pygmies do you think are out there to make this vanity-project of yours financially feasible?' He wouldn't give me the money. I even went to my mother to see if she'd like to invest. I figured Aurora loves clothes, she gets fashion, she knows there's a market out there for this. But I guess I must have had an attack of temporary amnesia—or maybe it was insanity—if I thought she would take my side against his. Gregory had her on an allowance, too, so it's not like she'd ever do anything to upset or anger him. You know, Aurora told me once that she married him to ensure our financial security. Some security, having to grovel for every penny."

"But now that your stepfather is dead . . ." Maddie tried to hide her excitement. There was nothing like a clear motive to kick a murder investigation into high gear.

"Free at last, free at last, thank God Almighty, we are free at last. No offense, Reverend King."

"None taken," Maddie answered automatically.

"We're finally free. Me, my mother, even my grandfather. You should've heard how Gregory spoke to his own father. To his face, he called him a crazy, senile old man for giving all our money away. At least Granddad's cash went to worthy causes. With Gregory, it was all about me, me, me."

Maddie said, "Actually, speaking of your dad . . ."

"Stepdad. He always made that part perfectly clear. He liked to remind me that just because Aurora bullied him into adopting me and giving me the Marron name, there weren't any blood ties between us. That was his favorite idea of a joke: Blood is thicker than water, and you, Monica, you are not even a trickle to me."

"Yeah, well, so speaking of blood ties, here's the thing. . . . You know Henry Coleman?"

"Who?"

"Henry Coleman, he drives for your family?"

"Oh! Henry! Henry Coleman. Right, the tall guy? Sandy-haired? Thinks he's really smooth with the ladies?"

"That's the one."

"Poor guy. The look on his face when Gregory went splat right in front of him. . . . I hope the police don't think Henry is to blame. He's so sweet and awkward and—"

"He's my brother," Maddie said.

"He is?"

"Yeah. I guess I should have mentioned it before."

"I don't see why . . ."

Really? Because Maddie could most definitely see why. "Well, because, maybe your family might not like me—Henry's sister—hanging around your house. It might remind them—"

"Oh, please. Henry wasn't to blame for what happened. Granddad has the police investigating every possibility, and there simply isn't any evidence connecting Henry to Gregory's murder. I mean, there's a good reason why his fingerprints were on the bottle. It's that other man, Mike Kasnoff, the one who robbed us years ago—I was just a little kid, like seven or something, but I remember how furious Gregory was about his precious car being stolen. I remember Mike a little, too. I thought he was very handsome."

"If you like that whole tall, dark, and muscular look, then, yeah, I guess . . ."

"At seven, I thought he looked like Prince Charming in all the Disney movies. But, anyway, he's probably the one that killed Gregory, don't you think?"

"I . . . I guess so."

"The police are coming to Gregory's funeral tomorrow. Detective Jack Snyder, I think that's his name—he's really good looking, too—will be there. He probably wants to observe the crowd and check out potential suspects. That's what the cops always do in the movies, right? I don't know why he's bothering. It's not like Mike Kasnoff is going to come pay his respects."

"So you think Jack Snyder believes your dad's—I mean Gregory's killer—might be at the funeral?" Maddie asked. "Where is it being held?"

"St. Stephen Cemetery in Oakdale, and then there will be a reception afterward, and there is absolutely no reason on Earth for you to be there," Henry said firmly.

Maddie had arrived home to find her brother in the kitchen. Henry was making his specialty, a martini wrap. The recipe called for a slice of whole-wheat bread folded around an olive recently dipped in gin and vermouth. Henry then drank up the remaining martini to wash down his sandwich. A compact—and vegetarian—meal.

He added, "It's bad enough I have to go to the funeral. But I figured if the cops are looking to pin this murder on me, then I can't give them any ammo. No suspicious behavior. None of that hiding my face in shame or guilt. I am going to be right out in the open, front-row center, next to the bereaved, offering them a hankie." He hesitated. "On the other hand, isn't returning to the scene of the crime considered a dead giveaway, too? What if Snyder thinks I'm returning to the scene of the crime? Do you think I should put out a press release or something beforehand? Clarifying my position?"

"That's why I should go with you. No one would think you're returning to the scene of the crime if you've got your little sister in tow. How sick would that be?"

"Why all this interest in Gregory Marron's funeral?"

"Because, I believe loyal family employees should show their respect."

"Uh-huh . . . Loyal family employee. That would be me . . ."

"And me!" Maddie announced excitedly. "I just got a job working for Monica Marron! Isn't that cool?"

"Monica Marron?"

"Gregory's daugh— his stepdaughter."

"I know who Monica is. I've driven her a million times. She's a sweet girl. God only knows how that family managed to produce someone like her. You're working for Monica Marron now? When did this happen?"

"Right now. I ran into her at Fashions—"

"Fashions? What were you doing at the Lakeview?"

"I was trying to get a job, but Lisa Grimaldi said I was too young, so—"

"Since when did you want to get a job?"

"Didn't you read my press release?"

"Ha-ha, that was almost funny enough to distract me. Now, what's this about your needing a job? You don't need a job. I told you, I've got everything under control."

"But, you shouldn't have to. Henry, I showed up on your doorstep, announced I was staying, and enrolled myself in private school. It was unfair of me to ask you to pay for all that. I mean, look what happened—you had to go into debt!"

"That's all taken care of now."

"Because the guy you borrowed money from just happened to end up dead? I don't think we can count on being so lucky the next time you borrow money."

"Even if Gregory hadn't met with . . . unfortunate circumstances . . . it would have been fine. Your big brother always has a plan, you remember that."

"Well, then, if you can have a plan, why can't I? Monica Marron hired me to be her personal assistant for a fashion business she wants to start up. Why shouldn't I jump at the opportunity to learn a whole lot, plus make some money in the bargain?"

"So you'd be working for Monica?" he clarified. "Just Monica? Not Aurora and definitely not Gig?"

"Just Monica."

"But this is out at the house? So you would probably bump into the others every once in a while?"

"Maybe. I don't see why they'd take any interest in me."

"They'd take an interest."

"Henry, you're acting weird again." Maddie demanded, "Is there some reason in particular that you don't want me working for Monica?"

"Monica Marron is fine. Monica Marron isn't the problem. It's the rest of them. Maddie, when you drive people, you hear things. . . . They're a weird bunch out there. Gregory may have been the worst of the lot, but he definitely didn't hold exclusive rights."

"To what? What's wrong with them?"

"Just hang around Monica, okay? Hang around Monica, and you'll be fine."

"So I can take the job?"

"Yeah. Sure. I guess. I mean, it would be kind of nice to have some extra money coming in. Not have to work two full-time jobs. Today was a real pain in the posterior, I don't mind telling you. I had to break the speed limit racing over to the health club for a few blown fuses. Of course, I wasn't counting on Katie going ninja on me—"

"You saw Katie today? How is she? Crushed and devastated to find out Mike is a killer? Did you comfort her?"

"Madeline!"

"What? Is it a crime to be interested in your brother's well-being?"

"Try to comprehend this, Madeline: I will not be using the misfortunes of my friend Mike as an opportunity to make moves on my ex-wife Katie."

"Who you're still in love with."

"Maddie!"

"What?"

"The funeral tomorrow. Wear black. I don't want us sticking out from the crowd. We are going to look like normal, respectful people who have absolutely nothing to hide. You got that?"

12

Carly wore black to Gregory Marron's funeral. She would have preferred mauve or teal or maybe a lovely chartreuse. She chose black because today was not the day to dance on Gregory's grave. She would have to settle for a private celebration in her heart.

Today was about Jack, and his insistence on going to Gregory's funeral. He said it would give him a chance to observe the mourners and look for potential suspects. Carly wondered if it would also give him a chance to return to the scene of his crime.

After all, who more than an officer of the law would have ample opportunity to sneak onto the Marron property? If anyone noticed his car parked by the side of the back road, they would hardly call him on it. And who better than a police officer to brew the deadly poison, then hide the evi-

dence where it would never be found—especially if the field
officers were told not to look there. Jack would have had
plenty of time to do it, too. Carly still had no idea where
he'd gone the afternoon before the benefit, or what "private
matter" he'd supposedly been taking care of. The only detail
Carly hadn't quite figured out yet was how Jack might have
managed to get Mike's prints on the killer bottle. But, then
again, who else but a cop could seamlessly tamper with a
forensic report?

Jack may have been going to Gregory's funeral to watch
for potential suspects. But Carly was going to watch Jack.

They took separate cars, since Jack was driving his official ve-
hicle, and Carly would be leaving from home. She'd hit a bit
of a snag when Jack asked her why she felt she needed to
come. "I thought you hated the guy."

"I do. I want to make sure he's really dead."

Jack smiled mirthlessly. "Suit yourself."

Carly intended to.

At the funeral, she stood off to the side, directly across
the grave from Jack, both of them somewhat behind the as-
sembled mourners. She noted him taking stock of who'd
come. The family, of course, a visibly shaken Gig, Aurora
the widow, and Monica. Plus, their lawyer, one of those over-
tanned, reptilian types who only went by initials—O.K.?
F.M.? B.S.?—and always seemed to be counting up billable
hours in his head. Several doctors from Memorial, including
Ben Harris and Bob Hughes. A dozen other assorted busi-

ness associates. Servants. Plus Carly recognized various faces from the country club, and even one or two from their New York days.

She also observed that Gig seemed to have surgically attached himself to Nancy Hughes's side, much to Aurora's displeasure. Because Aurora was working very hard at playing the grieving daughter-in-law. First, there was the outfit—widow's veil and black suit. Then there was the dramatic way she kept dabbing tears with a white handkerchief. Carly was willing to bet money that beneath her veil, the widow's eyes were dry. There was also Aurora's last-minute embrace of the coffin, which Gig didn't appear to notice because he had turned away, whispering something to Nancy.

Aurora was not pleased at being ignored.

However Carly could see that Monica, for one, noticed her mother's histrionics. The girl all but rolled her eyes as she looked in Maddie Coleman's direction.

Maddie and Henry stood next to Katie and, catching sight of the group, Carly felt a twinge of kinship with the young woman. It almost pierced through her overall dislike of Katie Peretti. Carly understood Katie's reasons for being here. Her reasons were exactly the same as Carly's. Katie was here to try and save the man she loved. Of course, if Katie's mission to clear Mike in any way interfered with Carly's objective to protect Jack, Carly fully intended to squash her like an insignificant, perky blond bug.

But first, she had to get through Gregory's funeral—complete with its fawning eulogy and warm reminiscences by friends and family—without laughing.

To begin the ceremony, a minister read off a long list of the Marron family's charitable deductions—sorry, donations. Next, Monica read her stepfather's eulogy from Oakdale's favorite tabloid, *The Intruder*. Leave it to publisher Emily Stewart, Carly thought, to write an ode to a man so hated he was actually poisoned on the way to his own tribute. Of course, Gregory had been mega-rich, which meant the family he left behind might be grateful enough for Emily's face-saving fibs to help *The Intruder* out in the future.

Aurora read Gregory's other obituary, the one published by their more respectable paper, *The City Times*. There, publisher Lucinda Walsh had taken the easy way out and simply written up a history of the Marrons in Oakdale. Just facts, no editorializing. Lucinda was rich enough in her own right; she didn't need to tell a fellow millionaire lies about his murdered son.

Finally, a handful of men Carly assumed to be Gregory's golfing, gambling, and vintage-car-collecting buddies said a few words, the gist of which was, "He cheated at golf only sometimes," "He paid his debts eventually," and "Boy, did he love those cars."

At that, Carly sneaked a look at Katie. Gregory Marron's cars were a pretty loaded topic these days. The allusion made Mike's girlfriend look down at the ground. Henry wrapped a sympathetic arm around her shoulder. She smiled at him gratefully.

Carly waited until the coffin was lowered into the ground and the black-clad crowd was invited to drive to the Marron estate for a reception, before heading for her own car. She and Jack briefly crossed paths in the parking lot. He waved to her as he was climbing into his front seat, but Carly could see that Jack's mind was clearly someplace else.

Watching him drive away, Carly decided to stop into the ladies' room in the church before hitting the road herself.

When she came out of the stall, she bumped straight into Aurora.

Gregory's widow had taken off her veil and was standing in front of the mirror, dabbing powder on every inch of her face. She'd already spread a thick layer of concealer under her eyes and outlined her lips in pink pencil before filling them in with a rosewood gloss.

Aurora glimpsed Carly coming out behind her and, without turning around, smirked, to indicate she knew exactly who Carly was. Carly didn't doubt it. Back in New York, Gregory had gotten a perverse thrill out of bringing Carly to social events that Aurora was also expected to attend, then manipulating them into close quarters and disappearing.

Speaking carefully, so as not to smudge her lipstick, Aurora enunciated, "Whore."

Carly stepped up to the mirror, removed a hairbrush from her purse, and smoothed down her bangs. If Aurora had meant to rattle her, she'd chosen the wrong plan of attack. As long as her kids weren't around, Carly was not the kind of woman to fall apart when foul words were lobbed in her direction. There were very few she hadn't heard before.

"And here," she drawled, "I'd been about to offer my condolences for your loss. After all, I, more than anyone, knew exactly how much Gregory meant to you."

Aurora actually almost smiled at her sarcasm. She took

out a tube of mascara, shook it, and proceeded to lift it to her—as Carly had suspected all along—utterly tear-free eyes. "That's terribly kind of you to say, Miss Tenney."

"Actually, it's Mrs. Snyder. Mrs. Jack Snyder."

"Please offer Mr. Jack Snyder *my* condolences."

"You know," Carly figured as long as they were chatting like old pals . . . "I always thought, if Gregory were ever murdered, you'd be the one to do it."

"Once again, that's terribly kind of you to say. And as classy as always, Carly."

"Mrs. Snyder," Carly corrected and continued blithely, as if uninterrupted by the attempt to put her in her place. "I mean, your marriage was hardly—"

"Any of your business?"

"Gregory told me how the two of you got together. It was a business deal, pure and simple."

"My business. And Gregory's. Definitely not yours."

"And Gig's?" Carly knew it wasn't ladylike of her, but she enjoyed how her question almost made Aurora drop the mascara. "I said that Gregory told me everything. I know he agreed to marry you in exchange for a nice big check from Gig."

"At least my husband got something of value from marrying me. What did Mr. Snyder get from you, except a second-hand tramp?"

"My husband got a loving home," Carly said. "A family, a daughter—"

"Gregory and I have a daughter."

"Born several years before you met. Not quite the same thing."

Mascara application completed, Aurora returned for a second coat of lipstick. "Monica is Gregory's only legal child. And I'm his legal spouse. No matter how hard you schemed to alter that fact."

"So," Carly asked casually, "did you kill Gregory?"

Aurora laughed out loud. "Women with high-priced tastes don't kill men who pay all of their expenses. Which is something you'd have known if any man had ever offered more than a crumpled twenty from the backseat for you."

Again, Aurora had better try a lot harder if she expected Carly to get the vapors and pass out cold. "Women with high-priced tastes also quite often outgrow even the most generous of stipends, and start pining away for the true golden goose."

"Which means precisely what, Carly?"

"Which means I saw your little theatrical performance at the funeral. You were going out of your way to demonstrate your terribly sincere and heartfelt grief, all for Gig's benefit. What, do you figure with Gregory gone, you finally have a shot at the real wheeler-dealer in the family? You think you have a shot at Gig?"

"Don't be absurd."

"Gregory's estate is probably worth a couple of million, sure. But that's nothing compared to the kind of money Gig has at his disposal."

"For now, yes. But Gig Marron is a doddering old man who is fading fast. His son's death might just be the final push that drives him over the edge. He'd have barely managed the family finances these past couple of years if Gregory hadn't stepped in and cleaned up Gig's messes. We have documented proof of how far his father's mental capacity had deteriorated, and Gregory was going to use it to have Gig declared incompetent."

In the blink of an eye, all of Carly's painstakingly constructed theories and fears about potential motives for Gregory's murder flew out the window. *Gregory was going to have his father declared incompetent?* "Did Gig know that?"

"Of course not. Do you think Gregory was an idiot?" Aurora, visibly unhappy with the results of her careful makeup application, pulled down her veil and turned toward the exit. "If Gig found out what Gregory was up to before the final papers were signed, Gig would've killed him."

It was too easy.

Carly had to remind herself of that as she followed Aurora out of the restroom and into the parking lot. It would be way, way too easy a solution if the truth proved to be that Gig had poisoned his own son to keep Gregory from wresting control of the family fortune away from him. And it would be way, way too convenient for Carly's sense of justice if Aurora had been his accomplice.

And yet, both of those possibilities made Carly very happy.

She got into her car, starting the engine and pulling out of the lot to drive to the Marrons' house where she intended to search for clues to support her new theory. But when Carly flicked on her right-turn signal, she noticed that Aurora, in the car directly in front of Carly's, had signaled a left.

It could have been a simple error. Was it possible that Aurora felt so shaken over having revealed more than she'd meant to, to Carly, that she was mistakenly driving in the opposite direction of the estate? It was definitely possible. Or was Aurora purposely driving someplace else? Under the circumstances, there was also only one thing Carly could do.

Follow her.

Carly followed Aurora at a safe distance, letting at least two, sometimes more cars get between them. Luckily, Oakdale was such a busy metropolis that Carly was able to drive almost twenty blocks without even so much as losing Aurora around a corner, or getting stuck at an inconvenient traffic light.

Aurora parked in front of a two-story home in a neighborhood that hadn't yet been completely gentrified. Carly continued to hang back, making sure that she wasn't spotted as Aurora locked her car, clutched her purse tighter, and high-heeled it up the stairs leading to the second-level home.

From the shadows of her front seat, Carly watched as Aurora rang the doorbell and looked around. The door was opened by a man in a purple polo shirt and chinos.

Aurora threw her arms around the man and allowed him to lead her inside.

This, Carly thought, was an exciting development.

So exciting that Carly wanted to know more. And there was only one way to do that—she had to find out who the guy was and why seeing him immediately after her husband's funeral was so important that Aurora would risk being late for the reception.

Leaving her own car parked at the far corner, Carly

sneaked up the same stairs Aurora had taken just a moment earlier. What she would do if the door suddenly opened and the Widow Marron chose that moment to step out, Carly didn't know. But, the way she figured it, Aurora already hated her, and she already knew that Carly suspected her of being involved in—if not outright masterminding—the plot to poison Gregory, so what harm was there in Aurora knowing that Carly was snooping around?

There was no name printed on either the mailbox or the doorplate of Aurora's mysterious host. There wasn't even a handy piece of mail lying around that she could sneak a peek at to make a quick I.D. Not that a mere name would have told Carly all that much, but it would be a solid place to start.

Instead, she was forced to go with an even more potentially hazardous plan and risk a quick peek into the side window.

Whereupon the first thing Carly spied was a hand. Holding a needle and syringe pointed in her direction. It took Carly a good beat before she was able to stop staring in horror at the potential weapon long enough to recognize that the syringe was being maneuvered by Aurora's gentleman friend. And that he was aiming it, not at Carly but actually right at Aurora. Right at Aurora's face, as a matter of fact.

Aurora was sitting, it looked like to Carly, in a makeshift dentist's chair, her hands in her lap. The veil had been removed and her hair was pulled back in a headband. The man was injecting something to the side of each of her eyes and around the nose. Then he moved up to her forehead. In her pursuit of Gregory's real killer, Carly had, instead, managed to uncover Aurora Marron's top-secret, and vitally important Botox injections. She felt like a big idiot.

She'd heard about places like this; doctors who catered to a clientele so desperate to keep their cosmetic enhancement a secret that they would only receive the injection at odd hours in out-of-the-way places—and pay dearly for the privilege.

Considering how unhappy Aurora had appeared with the face that stared back at her from the church bathroom mirror, she'd probably decided that a little Botox touch-up was mandatory prior to making her grand entrance at the reception.

And now Carly, who only a few moments earlier felt certain she had this case cracked, was back where she'd started from: in possession of a lot of wild speculation, some random facts, a few Marron family insights, and no way to make them fit together to produce the outcome Carly demanded.

Except for one thing.

Prior to slinking away from the window, Carly did notice that the doctor kept his box of sharp, shiny Botox needles right out in the open.

And utterly accessible should a resourceful client need to borrow a handful, for her own purposes, while his back was turned.

13

Katie had come to Gregory's funeral with Henry and Maddie, but when Nancy asked if she wanted a ride out to the estate with her and Gig, Katie jumped at the opportunity—just as Nancy must have known she would. The woman was really a marvel.

Gig didn't say much during the ride. He simply sat in the backseat of the limo, staring out the window and periodically pulling out a pocket handkerchief to wipe his balding head, though, thanks to the air-conditioning blowing full blast, it was impossible for anyone to work up even the semblance of a sweat.

Twenty or so minutes into the ride, Gig turned to Katie. "I hear your Mike has been let go for now."

"That's right. The police didn't have enough evidence to charge him, so—"

"What about the fingerprints? He say yet how his finger-prints got on that bottle?"

"Not exactly."

"Aren't you curious?"

"I am," Katie admitted.

"I understand why he did it," Gig said. He leaned forward to tell Katie, "Gregory shouldn't have been so hard on him. That jail sentence was utterly unreasonable under the cir-cumstances. Can't blame the boy for being furious, carrying a grudge. Look how it ends. Gregory brought it on himself. He was the one with the choice, not Mike. Understand what I'm saying?"

"Um, yes, sir, I do, I guess," Katie hedged. Then she couldn't help adding, "You told me this before. At the Lake-view Hotel? When I ran into you and Mrs. Hughes having lunch. A couple of days ago."

"Oh, yes, right, I remember," Gig said. And he turned back to the window. He didn't utter another word for the re-mainder of the trip.

Katie had visited the Marron estate several times while she was working on the benefit. This time, though, knowing that the cherry laurel berries that had killed Gregory and made Mike's life a nightmare might have grown and been picked right on this same property, made the entire compound feel sinister. Every tree swaying in the wind seemed to be snicker-ing in Katie's direction, even the innocent elms and firs. The white stone drive up to the entrance was no longer a graceful curve, but a mocking question mark demanding to know what Katie thought she was doing here. And the cavernous foyer, the one with a ceiling so soaring it once made Katie feel like a princess when she stepped over the threshold now seemed a cruel, English-class metaphor for her high aspirations and inevitable, crushing descent.

At least the buffet was good.

Katie had to give Aurora credit. While she'd mocked Katie's—all of Oakdale's, really—idea of haute cuisine, her spread was a study in high-class fare . . . for the calorie conscious. A uniformed waiter helpfully informed Katie that her dining choices included guava-chipotle–glazed scallops in mango-fennel salsa with watercress-basil broth; citrus-poached asparagus and gazpacho gelée ("Jelly?" she asked. "Gelée," her waiter corrected); maple-smoked tenderloin of pork with glazed golden beets; and flame-roasted Fuji apples with Irish oat pudding. What he couldn't tell Katie, however, was where Mrs. Marron was so that Katie could pay her respects.

She looked around, figuring Aurora was probably mingling, thanking people for coming, urging them to take a Tupperware of gazpacho gelée home for a snack later—the usual hostess things. But, surveying the various groups of mourners amassed, apparently by income level, Katie couldn't spot Aurora with any one of them.

As a result, Katie found herself migrating back to Gig and Nancy, figuring that even repeated information was better than no information and, heck, maybe hearing it all again would help Katie finally untangle this mess.

She caught up with the couple back at the buffet table where Gig was telling Mrs. Hughes, "Look at this! Just look

at it. Have I been talking to myself all these years? Do you
have any idea how many hungry people could have been fed
with the money Aurora wasted on impressing her friends?
What is half of this stuff, anyway?"

"Guava-chipotle–glazed scallops in mango-fennel salsa
with watercress-basil—" the always solicitous waiter began,
but Gig cut him off.

"Fruity shrimp and salad. Is that what I'm hearing? Fruity
shrimp and salad?"

Unlike Katie, the waiter, a seasoned professional, obviously grasped when the questions lobbed in his direction
were rhetorical. He merely continued smiling politely and
serving, as if Gig hadn't ranted a word.

Of course, a second later, Gig was acting as if he hadn't
ranted a word, either. He turned to Katie and asked, "The little girl you were standing with at the funeral, the one over
there talking to Monica now. Who is she?"

Katie turned her head to make sure she and Gig were discussing the same person before answering, "That's Maddie
Coleman."

"Coleman? Any relation to Henry Coleman?"

"She's his sister."

"There's something fishy about that fellow. You see it? All
twitchy and weasely when you talk to him. And he's taller
than he looks, you know. That's suspicious."

Katie felt like she'd lost the conversational thread.
"What is?"

"Being taller."

"Taller than what?"

"Than you are." Gig turned to Nancy to help explain his

meaning, but when she appeared as mystified as Katie, he sighed in annoyance and explained, "Look at that boy. He's got to be six feet if he's an inch, probably more. But look at the way he's standing hunched over, shoulders up like he's trying to swallow his neck. I ask you, what's he trying to hide? I hate folks who are always trying to hide something. Don't trust them. And he was the last person to see Gregory alive. Got him that cursed bottle of wine, too. Sure hope the police are taking a good long look at him. Because, mark my words, that young fellow is standing there, deceiving the lot of us. Mark my words."

Katie, who knew that Henry had a tendency to lie instinctively when asked such tough questions as "How are you?" and "Do you have the time?" had to give Gig credit. Because, point of fact, Henry had been acting very peculiar lately.

Their run-in at the club had been just bizarre. It was one thing for Katie, the small and defenseless, to keep quiet when she thought an intruder was in the dark with her. But Henry was a guy. A big, strapping guy surrounded by weights/weapons, who could easily have hollered out to try and scare away whoever it was he thought had broken in. And yet he hadn't. Instead, he'd stalked Katie and attacked her. Which wasn't at all like Henry.

It was also unlike Henry to stake out a position so far from the free food. But that's exactly what he'd done. He, Maddie, and Monica were ensconced in a corner, three heads bent together and deep in conversation. They didn't even look up when Aurora finally came through the door—almost an hour late and not even vaguely apologetic. In fact, she didn't seem to be much of anything at all. Her face was a total, frozen blank. Katie wondered if she was in some sort of shock.

"Mrs. Marron?" Katie asked hesitantly. "Hi. Remember me? Katie Peretti?" She considered mentioning that bonding moment a few weeks back when Aurora had mocked her culinary choices, but decided to let it go for now.

"Yes?" Aurora sounded as if it were physically difficult for her to speak.

"I—I just wanted to say how sorry I am for your loss."

"Thank you." The "you" part of her perfunctory reply was already floating in the air as Aurora turned her attention toward a more important guest.

Prompting Katie to pack the rest of her carefully prepared statement into a hectic burst. "But, the thing is, I wanted you to know that Mike Kasnoff, my boyfriend, the one the police are calling 'a person of interest' in relation to the crime, he didn't do it. I'm certain that he didn't do it, which is why I'd like to talk to you about who you think might have killed your husband so I can get to the bottom of this, which I'm sure will be a great load off both your mind and mine. It would be great if we could work together to solve this case, don't you think?"

With her back already to Katie, Aurora paused in place. She cleared her throat. And then, without even acknowledging that Katie had said anything beyond expressing her condolences, Aurora moved on to dutifully embrace another guest.

*   *   *

Was that strike one, Katie wondered? Or had she, in the course of her clumsy investigation, already struck out several other times, but just failed to notice?

With Aurora making it clear that she had no interest in speaking to Katie, and Monica taking on her mother's role of hostess and greeting Carly Snyder after Aurora had just walked by Jack's wife without so much as an insincere "Thank you for coming," Katie found herself gravitating back toward Gig. However, as he once again sang the praises of superphilanthropist Andrew Carnegie, Katie decided that this was definitely one well she'd already pumped dry.

With a whispered aside to Nancy to keep Gig occupied and a wink back from Mrs. Hughes confirming she intended to do just that, Katie asked the young woman circulating through the crowd with a silver tray filled with assorted juices and sparkling waters (serving wine, under the circumstances, would obviously have been in poor taste), where the powder room was.

She was directed to a discreetly hidden door just off the kitchen. Katie dutifully headed in that direction. Then she made a sudden right turn and scampered up the freshly polished walnut stairs instead.

She made it to the second floor without getting caught or stopped, and she found herself facing a carpeted hallway, with three closed doors on either side, and a stained-glass window featuring the Marron coat of arms: yellow and black stripes with a prancing dog atop a knight's helmet to signify the Marron family's 1066 contribution to Duke William of Normandy at the Battle of Hastings (never let it be said that Katie Peretti failed to do her homework!), along with this particular Marron family's motto, in Latin: *In necessariis unitas, in dubiis libertas, in omnibus caritas* (in certain things unity; in doubtful things liberty; in all things charity).

From having come up here before with Gig to snap a digital picture of their crest to scan onto the benefit's napkins, Katie knew that this was Gregory and Aurora's wing of the house. He had the three rooms on the right, she the three on the left. Katie tried the first door on the right, Gregory's study, and found it unlocked. The police had obviously searched the room, as evidenced by the identically bound books stacked not on the shelves but the floor, and a couple of the desk drawers still ajar after being yanked open. Katie recognized Oakdale P.D.'s decorator style from her own tossed home.

Otherwise, Katie presumed the study remained exactly as Gregory had wanted it. Who but the owner of a string of vintage cars that he never actually drove, would adorn his rooms with what appeared to be the white elephants of the world? There on his desk was a Cartier Temple Gate clock, featuring lapis Egyptian friezes on mother-of-pearl, which he'd bought at auction for over a million dollars. Katie had stumbled over that scintillating fact on the Internet while researching the Marrons. And yet it still ticked two minutes behind the plastic Wonder Woman watch Mike got Katie as a gag gift for her last birthday. She recalled he'd told her that was how he saw her, as his Wonder Woman; but Katie didn't dare think about that right now, or she might cry.

There was also a solid-brass umbrella stand which held Gregory's collection of walking sticks. And naturally there was the assorted overstuffed furniture, overweight drapes, and overpriced art.

Katie sat in the chair behind Gregory's desk and began opening drawers. Even the inside of Gregory's desk was swollen with the ornate and unnecessary. In the shallow center drawer she found a pile of gold, silver, even jewel-encrusted fountain pens, as well as Arturo paper he'd apparently used for scratch. In one of the deeper side drawers, shoved indiscriminately in among bank statements that testified to the strict allowances Gregory kept his wife and daughter on was a wrinkled photograph of tiny Monica, dressed in a T-shirt with the Marron crest on it and blowing out a pair of birthday candles, "To Daddy—From Monica" scribbled on the back in distinctively adult handwriting. At least in the beginning, Aurora had clearly done her best to coerce her new husband into falling in love with her child. And, last but not least, a handmade felt hat had been tossed in the very bottom drawer.

The only thing the desk—the entire room, really—didn't have, was a clue to who might have killed its owner.

Which, in the end, was really all that Katie cared about.

Katie was about to exit the study and head for the next room down the line, when a noise from the hallway and the click of a doorknob turning prompted her to give up that plan in exchange for a quick dive behind the overweight drapes.

Katie held her breath as she heard footsteps—they were light, so it was probably a woman—enter the room. She wondered what Aurora would do if she found Katie hiding in her late husband's private sanctuary. She wondered if Gig would be angry or whether he would claim to understand her reasons for doing it. She wondered what Nancy would think of Katie's lousy sleuthing and if she'd ever agree to help her again.

And then she wondered why Aurora, in the middle of Gregory's wake, would feel the need to come upstairs to his desk, and begin rifling through it.

Katie poked her head out from behind the curtain.

"Carly?" she asked, shocked.

Katie had never actually seen another human being jump up in surprise until she saw Carly do exactly that.

Carly whipped around and half-whispered, half-screamed, "What the hell are you doing here, Katie?"

Katie pointed to the myriad of drawered items Carly had spread out atop the desk and begun rifling through. "Same thing as you, I'd guess."

"I . . . I'm not . . ."

"Did Jack put you up to this?"

"Absolutely not. I'm here on my own. I swear."

"Why?" Katie asked.

"Because."

"That really clears things up."

"Because . . . I . . . I . . . I want to get to the bottom of this as much as you do. Mike is my friend. He's a very good friend. I don't want to see him go to jail again."

"You're here for Mike," Katie said in a tone that conveyed her disbelief.

"Yes."

"I don't think so," Katie said. "I mean, you love Mike and

all. But you love Jack more. And you would never, ever screw up an investigation of his. Not even for Mike."

"Maybe you don't know me as well as you assume you do."

"And maybe you knew Gregory Marron Jr. a heck of a whole lot better than the rest of us . . ."

"What's that supposed to mean?"

"How did you know where his study is located?"

"I took a guess."

"The way Aurora looked at you downstairs . . ."

"So what?"

"Carly, were you having an affair with Gregory? Is that what all this sneaking around is about? Did you leave some clue behind and you're afraid that Jack—"

"Just leave Jack out of this, all right?"

"Carly," Katie asked as diplomatically as she could while trying to keep her own excitement under control. "Do you know something about Gregory's death that you're not telling the police?"

"No," Carly snapped and angrily slammed a drawer shut. "That's the problem. I only wish I knew something that they didn't so I could figure this mess out and get Jack as far away from this case as possible."

"Jack," she repeated. And then understanding dawned. "This is about Jack. Oh my God, Carly, are you afraid that Jack found out about your affair and killed Gregory?"

Carly stared at Katie for what felt like an eternity. Finally, she looked away and, with great effort, allowed herself to admit, "Something like that."

"Then you know that Mike didn't do it!"

"I don't know that Jack did it either," Carly quickly replied.

"But he's heading the investigation. He shouldn't be allowed to—"

"I swear to God, Katie, if you breathe a word of this to anyone, if you get Jack into trouble with his superiors, or cast doubt on his integrity in any way, I will rip you to shreds and serve the pieces up for dinner. Is that clear?"

"You really must think that Jack is guilty."

"If he is, then it's all my fault, you get that? If Jack does or did anything wrong, it's because of me. I'm responsible. Which is why I have to get him out of this."

"By framing Mike."

"I had nothing to do with what happened to Mike! I even went down to see him at the jail, I asked him to explain his fingerprints on the bottle—"

"Did he?" Katie asked eagerly.

"No. He wouldn't say a word. Which isn't exactly the reaction of an innocent man, now is it?"

"Mike didn't do it."

"Neither did Jack."

"Okay. So how do we prove it?"

"Well, obviously by proving that someone else did." Carly indicated where they were standing. "Isn't that why we're both here?"

"You know," Katie suggested, "I bet if we worked together and pooled our resources, we'd get a lot further than we did apart."

"You just want to keep an eye on me and make sure I don't do anything to hurt Mike's case."

Katie shrugged and didn't deny it. "Keep your friends close and your enemies closer. Isn't that how it goes?"

"So which ones are we?"

"I guess this is our chance to find out." Katie held out her hand. "Deal?"

"Deal." Carly extended her hand, only to find that there was no time to shake.

Because the doorknob was turning again.

Carly and Katie both ran to hide behind the drapes.

Neither one made it.

The newest arrival wasn't Aurora or Gig or even Monica.

Maddie Coleman stood in the doorway, looking from Katie to Carly, a puzzled expression on her face.

"Hey, hey," Carly drawled. "The gang's all here."

14

Katie decided not to bother with either explanations or de-nials. They were standing in a room they shouldn't be in, and that standing time should probably be cut to a mini-mum, so she cut to the chase. "You're here because you're afraid that Henry killed Gregory."

"No!"

"Don't be shy. Carly is here because she's afraid it was Jack."

"Katie! I warned you . . ."

"You said I couldn't say a word to the police. If Maddie were interested in talking to the police she'd be there, in-stead of here. With us."

Maddie said, "I don't think Henry did it. Not really. I just think he might, well, I'm afraid he might know something about someone who did. He's been acting so weird lately. I mean, weirder than usual."

"Don't worry, Maddie," Katie reassured her. "Carly and I will get to the bottom of all this. We've got a plan. We'll work together and we'll—"

"Oh, me, too, me, too," Maddie said. "Please. I want to be a part of this. Please, let me help you."

"Absolutely not," Carly said. "This is an R-rated operation. No one under eighteen admitted without an adult."

"But I can be a huge help. I'm working for Monica Marron now, did you know that? Right here, in this house. There's no telling what kind of dirt I could dig up with access like that."

"She has a point," Katie told Carly.

"Fine," Carly snapped. "Whatever. You want to put Mike's future in the hands of a child, you go right ahead. In the meantime, it's not doing any one of us any good to be searching the same place at the same time, especially since none of us has any idea what we're looking for. We should split up. Oh, and Maddie, if you really want to play Three Musketeers, then here are some ground rules: We share all our information. No secrets. You got that, too, Katie?"

Katie said, "Absolutely. Share and share alike. No secrets."

"Just as long as we're clear."

"So how about you go first, Carly? Tell us something about this case that Maddie and I don't know."

"Yeah, that would be really great," Maddie agreed. "But shouldn't we first be getting the heck out of here? If anyone caught us, don't you think it would look kind of suspicious?"

"The kid has a point," Carly said.

"I am not a kid."

"Yeah, okay, in a minute." Katie nodded without meaning it. "First, though, Carly, you're on."

"What?" Carly was halfway to the door before realizing that Katie was still fishing for proof of her commitment. "Oh, okay, fine. How's this? Aurora? She's a Botox addict."

"And this is relevant how? Gregory wasn't killed by a botulism toxin."

"It's relevant because her doctor happens to be very free with his needles." At the blank looks on Katie's and Maddie's faces, Carly added, "Hello? Needles? How did the poison get into Gregory's wine? Someone injected it. How easy would it have been for Aurora to steal a syringe from her doc, use it to kill Gregory, then wash the thing out and drop it right back into the pile on her next visit?"

"Wasn't she afraid the next patient might get poisoned too and the police would trace the needle to the doctor, then back to her?" Maddie asked. And Carly had to admit to herself that the kid was quick. She had never thought of that.

"Fine, so she didn't return it. She just chucked it in a Dumpster outside his house. I bet the guy constantly has medical waste. No one would give it a second thought."

"Okay," Katie asked. "So how do we prove that?"

"Hey, I did my part. I supplied a nice piece of information. One for all and all for one. Now you guys come up with the next step. In the meantime, like the kid said, let's get out of here."

"We three shouldn't go back down together," Katie said. "It will look peculiar. Maddie, you go first. Then Carly, then me."

"Why do you get to stay up here alone?" Carly demanded as soon as Maddie left.

"What's the matter? Afraid I'm going to find some incriminating evidence to use against Jack?"

"More like destroy something that points the finger at Mike."

"Just go downstairs, okay, Carly, I'll be right behind you."

"I'm watching you, Katie."

"That's very comforting."

Katie shut the door behind Carly and then, using both Gregory's fancy clock and her Wonder Woman watch just to be extra careful, waited a solid four minutes before she opened the door for herself.

And came face to face with Aurora.

"What the hell are you doing in my husband's room?"

Katie didn't say anything. Technically, *gulp* was not a word.

"Were you trying to steal something, is that it? Was that what all this twaddle about the benefit was about? Were you just coming here to scope the place out?"

"No!" Now that Aurora was asking specific questions, Katie felt much more comfortable flinging about self-righteous denials. "No, no, of course not! I was just— I just . . . this is such a beautiful house, I wanted a chance to look around—"

"Then you were snooping! Even better. What was that nonsense you spouted downstairs? Something about us working together—oh, don't make me laugh—to get to the bottom of Gregory's murder."

"That would still be very helpful, Mrs. Marron."

"Come on, Kathryn. We both know who killed Gregory. And it's just a matter of time before the police have enough evidence to make the charges stick."

"Mike didn't kill your husband."

"Actually, for your sake, you better hope that he did. And that this case is closed sooner rather than later. Because digging around in Marron family business can be very, very dangerous. Like war, it isn't healthy for children. And other living things."

"Where have you been?" Carly asked when a shaken Katie finally made her way back downstairs.

"Getting threatened by Aurora Marron."

Carly's eyes widened for a moment, but then she shrugged. "Been there, done that, got the claw-and-burn marks to prove it. Just another day in the life."

"She said that digging into Marron family business could prove very unhealthy."

Carly shook her head. "Forget about Aurora and her threats. We have more important things to talk about. I didn't want to say anything while the kid was around, because, well, if she's anything like her brother, I'm not certain that she's trustworthy."

"And you and I are?"

"Honor among thieves. Assured mutual destruction, whatever. The fact is, I know how your devious, self-centered mind works—"

"It takes one to know one?"

"Which is why I can trust you . . . to a point. I don't know

Maddie Coleman, and I have no particular desire to expand my social circle to the high-school set. Anyway, the thing I wanted to tell you was, Aurora said something very interesting to me this afternoon—I don't think she meant to, it just slipped out—I bring out the best in her. After I accused her of playing up to Gig in order to snare him for herself and grab an even bigger piece of the Marron pie—"

"Ew, that's disgusting. He's her father-in-law—that's gross."

"She told me that Gig may be the one who controls the money now, but that Gregory was in the process of trying to have him declared incompetent so that Gregory could take over managing the family fortune."

"Good-bye Andrew Carnegie, hello bad, expensive clocks?"

"What?"

"Never mind," Katie said, then agreed. "This is a big deal."

"Not to mention a hell of a motive for murder."

"You think Gig poisoned his own son?"

"Gig. Or Gig and Aurora."

"Okay." Katie hated to nag, but . . . "So how do we prove that?"

It was almost time to leave. The caterer was packing up, and the girl with the silver tray was carrying around more dirty glasses now than filled ones. Plus, Aurora was standing by the open door, saying good-bye to her guests—so Katie decided to take one more pass at Gig.

Based on the number of times he'd tried to tell her the

same story that afternoon alone, Katie had no trouble believing the patriarch of the Marron family might be drifting a bit out of touch with reality. The question was, had he drifted far enough away to be declared legally incompetent. Or far enough to commit murder?

"Mr. Marron?" Katie took his hand and shook it enthusiastically. "I just wanted to say good-bye and, again, how sorry I am for the loss of your son."

"Thank you, Katie, thank you very much. Always a pleasure to chat with such a lovely young lady."

"Also, I was wondering if now, with your son gone, you might be in the market for a personal assistant? I kind of need the work, and I thought how it will probably be difficult for you, having to assume all of Gregory's responsibilities, so—"

"Gregory had no responsibilities."

"Excuse me?"

"The Marron Foundation is mine. My son had nothing to do with running either the investment or the endowment areas. That was all me."

"Oh, I'm sorry, Mr. Marron. I thought I'd heard that Gregory had been taking on more and more responsibilities because you were planning to retire soon."

"Retire" did sound so much nicer than "being forced out by your own flesh and blood," though Katie knew that, quite often, it meant the same thing.

"Balderdash."

"I see . . ." She didn't.

"I have no intention of retiring. Not when there's so much more good work to be done yet. I bet I can guess where you heard this rumor, Katie. Was it from my daughter-in-law? My board of directors? Hospital busybodies? Seems like I've been hearing the R word a lot lately. Everyone telling me to take a breath, sit back, enjoy my accomplishments. Don't think that I didn't figure out that's what this benefit was about. Isn't that right, Nancy?" He playfully nudged Mrs. Hughes with his elbow. She smiled politely in reply, neither agreeing nor disagreeing. "Nobody said it out loud, but when they decide to honor you for fifty years of work, it usually means somebody thinks fifty years is plenty. Hate to disappoint the buzzards, but this old goat isn't going anywhere. Long as I'm still breathing, I'm still in charge."

After Katie and Nancy had said their good-byes to Gig and Aurora and were walking down the front path toward the cabs waiting to take guests without cars to their respective homes, Nancy asked, "How did you know?" Nancy had her arm linked through Katie's as she navigated the twisting path, and she leaned her head in to whisper conspirationally, "How did you know Gregory was planning to have Gig deemed incompetent? That is what your little chat back there was all about it, wasn't it?"

"So it's true?" Katie cried out in surprise, then guiltily lowered her voice, not wanting to appear ill-mannered at a funeral, or holler secrets at the top of her lungs.

"Yes, it's true. Bob told me Gregory was working with several neurologists at the hospital to get the paperwork ready for presentation to a judge. Ben Harris was the only one in the department who refused to go along, I hear. Everybody else was too blinded by Gregory's promise of more research funding in exchange for their help with his very 'delicate' problem."

Katie stopped short. "Ben was the one who declared Gregory dead."

"Yes," Nancy agreed. "What of it?"

"I don't know." She resumed walking, but slower now, thinking out loud. "It just seems kind of coincidental, I guess. That Ben was the only one on Gig's side, and then he ends up being the one who decides that Gig's son doesn't need to be resuscitated."

"My goodness, Katie, surely you don't seriously believe someone as principled as Ben Harris could be involved in a conspiracy to kill Gregory Marron, do you?"

"I don't know," Katie repeated. That seemed to be the only answer she was sure of these days. "I'm just looking at all the possibilities. The fact is, Ben's not stupid. Unlike everybody else who was dazzled by Gregory's big promises of more funding, what if Ben actually realized that the first thing Gregory would do when he got control of the family fortune was put an end to their charitable endeavors? What if Ben took it upon himself to stop him? I mean, think about it, Nancy. Why was Ben the only one going against the other neurologists' medical opinion? Maybe Gig really did need to be removed, but he and Ben struck a deal to—"

Nancy said, "Gig Marron may ramble a bit, but he's far from incompetent."

"Does Gig know what Gregory was trying to do to him?"

"It's possible. Any one of the doctors helping Gregory could have mentioned it to a hospital board member, who might have wanted to either warn Gig, or taunt him about it.

Gig Marron inspires all sorts of emotions in people. You never do know some people's agendas."

"So do you think Gig might have tried to do something to stop Gregory?"

"Like perhaps slip some homegrown poison into his son's favorite beverage, then lure a doctor on board to make sure Gregory never came back to life?"

"I know, it sounds so horrible . . ."

"Gig Marron is a complicated man, Katie. And very unpredictable. To be honest, I very often haven't the slightest idea how he might react in a given situation. Especially when it's a perceived threat."

"You mean you really believe Gig Marron is capable of killing his own son?"

Nancy hesitated, then said, "Katie, I'm a mother. You probably don't know this but, almost exactly fifty years ago, my daughter, Susan, drowned. She was just a young girl at the time."

"Oh, Mrs. Hughes, I didn't—I'm so sorry . . ."

"I know what it feels like to lose a child. So when you ask me whether I think any parent is capable of deliberately . . ."

"I understand, I shouldn't have brought it up, forget I said anything."

"In my heart, I know that if I really believed Gig was capable of killing Gregory, I wouldn't be able to stay in the same room with him, much less keep a civil tongue in my head, or even go through the motions of a friendly acquaintance. So, in answer to your question, no, Katie, I can't believe Gig had anything to do with Gregory's death."

"Thank you, Mrs. Hughes. That helps a lot."

"But, my gut instinct is hardly evidence," she added softly.

They were standing in front of the gates now, waiting in line for their taxis. Nancy said, "Oh, poor Katie, you look so glum. I know these last few days have been horrible for you. Would you care to come home with me? I can't promise a particularly exciting distraction from your woes, but I'm happy to offer a sympathetic ear."

"That's really sweet of you, Mrs. Hughes, and you know how I love to blather on about my problems. But I'm afraid I have to get home. Snickers the Second has an appointment at the vet's. Ever since the cops spooked him by turning the cottage upside down, he's been acting a little strange." She opened her taxi's back door and added, "Kind of like everybody else in this town."

Back home, Katie changed out of her black mourning outfit and sensible shoes into a pair of jeans, a gray sweatshirt, and comfortable sneakers. When Mike was around, Katie liked to dress up a bit more. Tight, tailored slacks, short skirts, clingy tops in ice-cream colors, and definitely shoes with heels (at five foot one, Katie needed all the statuesque-help she could get). Katie sincerely believed that a man coming home from a hard day's work deserved to be greeted by a woman looking her best—this included makeup and jewelry. Otherwise, what was his incentive to come home? With Mike out of the house and possibly out of her life for good, though, Katie could barely motivate herself to don the gray sweatshirt without the mustard stain instead of the lime one with a big, drying squirt right on the sleeve. She was not at her best and, at the moment, Katie didn't care who knew it.

Once she walked through the door of the veterinary clinic with Snickers II, though, Katie found herself wishing she'd put at least a minimum token effort into her appearance before coming over.

Because standing right in front of her, was someone with a very familiar face.

As the reception was ending, Carly looked for Jack.

They hadn't talked at all since arriving at the Marron house. Carly had been too busy going into the sleuthing business, while Jack had proceeded to melt discreetly into the background, watching and waiting. He never once, as far as she could see, directly approached any member of the Marron family, or questioned a single one of their friends. And yet, wherever a Marron — any Marron at all — was, Jack would materialize on the sidelines, seemingly everywhere and nowhere, at once.

Carly had known that her husband was a talented detective, the best on the force. But actually seeing him in action, Carly's heart ran as if she were encountering Jack for the first time. Watching him move so confidently from room to room, group to group, without once losing his cool or drawing unnecessary attention to himself flooded Carly with an erotic pride of possession. This was her man. Hers and no one else's. She'd gone through a great deal to make that fact an unalterable truth.

Of course, that unalterable truth didn't seem all that obvious to anyone observing them at Gregory Marron's wake. Not only did Jack and Carly never speak, he never so much as looked in her direction. Granted, he was working here, not socializing, but nonetheless, Carly wasn't accustomed to receiving the silent treatment from her husband.

That's why she sought out Jack at the end of the wake.

He was getting back into his squad car when Carly stuck her head in through the open driver's side window.

"Hi, honey," she said.

"Hey, Carly."

"You know, I was thinking: What do you say we take the kids out tonight and do something really fun? Maybe a movie or miniature golf? You know how Parker loves it when you guys go golfing together, and we haven't been in such a long time."

"I'm working tonight, Carly." He started up the engine so that she had to strain to make out the last part of his sentence. "I'm going to keep working until I can safely put this whole sordid mess behind us."

Carly ended up driving around for over an hour after she and Jack said good-bye. Carly knew she should be heading home to the kids. Parker and Sage had been with Gwen all day, and though they loved her and she was great with them, Carly knew that it was time for her to take over.

Except for the fact that just thinking about walking into her house, all warm and cozy and bustling—without Jack, filled Carly's throat with a bitter bile that no amount of diligent swallowing could suppress. Jack should have been home. Jack would have been home. If it weren't for her.

Because even if Jack hadn't killed Gregory, the fact was,

he wouldn't have been working so hard on solving the man's murder if he also wasn't trying to keep his promise to Carly about making sure that their kids never found out about her more-than-a-little checkered past. Taking that into account, how was Carly supposed to look Parker and Sage in the eye and answer their questions about "Where's Daddy?" with anything but a bottomless pool of guilt?

She couldn't do it. She couldn't spend another evening reassuring her kids that Daddy would be home soon. So Carly took the coward's way out. She kept driving around. For twenty minutes she simply circled the block of her house, until she saw the bedroom lights go off and knew Parker and Sage were in bed.

Only then did Carly dare to go back home, thank Gwen profusely for her help, and, once she was gone, settle down for yet another night of recrimination and guilt.

At around 9 P.M., Carly turned on the news, more for background noise to try to distract herself from the nonstop voices in her own head, than because she really cared what the local Oakdale broadcast had to say about anything.

Until she heard the top story.

And turned toward the screen to witness the murder of Katie Peretti.

15

Katie saw the murder, too.

She was inside the veterinary clinic, getting Snickers II's vitamin prescription from the nurse when she heard the screech of tires outside and the screams of passersby.

Grabbing Snickers's cage, Katie rushed onto the street, where she saw the beautiful, young blond woman, also holding a rabbit's cage in one now bloody hand, lying on the sidewalk, not moving, her head twisted at an angle so unnatural, she couldn't possibly be alive.

"It was a hit-and-run!" somebody screamed. "I saw the whole thing! Car came tearing out of nowhere, hit her from the back, and didn't so much as slow down. Bastard kept right on moving, full speed. He was practically all the way down the street while she was still flying through the air."

"Outrageous!" somebody else screamed.

"This used to be such a safe town . . ."

Sadie.

It was Sadie lying there. Dead.

Sadie, who everybody joked was Katie's double, her Separated-at-Birth identical twin. Because they looked so much alike. And they both had pet rabbits. Heck, Sadie had even gone out with Henry once.

Sadie, who had already been at the clinic when Katie came in, looking fresh and perky and making Katie wish she'd spruced up at least a little, because, in comparison to Sadie, she realized she looked really, really awful.

Sadie, who'd had the appointment just before Katie's, and so had ended up exiting the clinic, with bunny in tow, a few minutes earlier.

And gotten killed for it.

In the past, Katie had been accused of assuming that everything was about her, even when it possibly wasn't. When Margo had suffered from Hepatitis C and required a partial liver transplant and Katie volunteered to be the donor, some folks had accused Katie of making the crisis all about her and whether Simon would let her go through with the operation. Another time, when Mike's then-wife, Jennifer, went into premature labor with a baby that wasn't Mike's, a few know-nothing tongues wagged that Katie was, as usual, turning that emergency into a question of how soon she and Mike could get back together after he'd finished supporting Jennifer through her time of need.

But this time, Katie felt pretty certain that the hit-and-run had, in fact, been all about her.

She considered saying as much to Hal Munson, the detective who came to interview Katie and the other witnesses after poor Sadie's body was taken away by an ambulance. (Katie had been glad to see the medics gently transport the deceased rabbit, as well.)

"I really didn't see anything that could help you," Katie told Hal in a trembling voice. "But there was this other man. When I came out, I heard him say he saw the whole thing."

"Yes," Hal agreed. "Unfortunately, the more questions we asked him, the more obvious it became that he was, shall we say, embellishing just a bit to make himself look good. Turns out he was like everybody else and ran outdoors after the car struck the young woman. I'm not surprised. This corner is practically deserted after nightfall."

"So you have no clues, no idea who might have done this?"

"Not so far, no." Hal put a hand on her shoulder. "Are you alright, Katie? You look pretty shook up."

"Are the police treating this as just another accident? A typical hit-and-run?"

"What should we be treating it as?"

"How about murder? What if somebody ran Sadie down on purpose?"

"Why would you say that?"

Katie wanted to tell him. But, in the end, she couldn't. Because Hal had known her for a long time. And more likely than not, he would just accuse her of using another girl's tragedy to gain attention for herself. Katie had to face it. She'd cried wolf on too many occasions. This time around, she was totally on her own.

*   *   *

"You don't know that for a fact," Carly said. "Although, I admit, when I saw the news report about a blonde carrying a rabbit being killed—"

"You thought it was me, too, didn't you?"

"For a minute. Yes."

The two women were at Katie's house, Carly arriving first thing in the morning after the hit-and-run, in response to Katie's barely coherent telephone plea.

"It's Aurora, isn't it?" Katie was trying to finish cleaning up the mess the police had left behind after searching her house. "Aurora threatened me at the funeral, and a couple of hours later . . ."

"Sadie could have had enemies, too."

"You don't believe that."

"No," Carly admitted. "But it seemed like the polite thing to say. You're right, of course, Katie, you are much more the type of person that people would want to kill."

"Thanks." Katie dragged the coffee table back to its place in front of the couch. "What am I going to do, Carly?"

"Well, I suppose if we can figure out who's after you, it would lead us right to whoever killed Gregory."

"So what are you suggesting?" Katie asked. "That I go stand in the middle of the road and see who comes gunning for me next?"

"Don't be ridiculous."

"Thanks."

"Nobody would be stupid enough to pull the same stunt twice."

The phone rang. Which was a good thing, because Katie and Carly were about a barb and a half away from committing their own homicide, rather than investigating one.

"Hello?"

"Katie! Hi! It's Maddie. I've got great news!"

"It's the kid," Katie told Carly. Then, "Hey, Maddie, what's up?"

"So check this out: So Monica goes to me how she'd really like to find a place soon where she could have her boutique—that's what I'm helping her with, setting up a boutique that sells cool clothes to short girls like her. And I said, you know, my friend, Katie, she's got a gym that's in a neighborhood that's full of great stores and it would be a totally awesome location for your boutique, we should go and check it out and we should ask you to come along because you could give us advice about, you know, what's the foot traffic like and what kind of people shop there. Isn't that great? While we're all doing that, you and me, we can pump Monica for details about her dad and who killed him." Maddie was finally forced to take a breath.

"Kid," Katie said, grinning broadly at Carly, "you're okay."

Monica Marron, driving the cherry-red Lexus, pulled up in front of Katie's cottage at four o'clock the following afternoon and tapped the horn playfully. Maddie was riding shotgun in the front seat and she waved madly as soon as Katie stepped outside.

"Thanks so much for agreeing to do this with us, Katie,"

Monica said. "Maddie tells me you really know the retail area."

"Maddie's a smart kid," Katie agreed.

They drove on in silence for a few minutes, though the third time that Maddie pulled down the passenger side sun-visor, ostensibly to apply another coat of lip-gloss, but really so that she could make faces in the mirror that urged Katie to start questioning Monica, Katie got the message. "So, Monica, I guess things are still pretty rough around your place. How are your mother and grandfather holding up?"

"Oh, they're fine. It takes a lot to knock that pair off their bearings. Though they did both lose their cool right after Gregory's funeral. Granddad wanted Mother to observe a proper mourning period—whatever that is—but basically meaning that everybody should stay locked up in the house or else how would it look? But Mother insisted on going out. I'm not usually on her side about anything, but this time around I was glad. If Mother got to go out the night of the funeral, then I can go out with you two today without Granddad lecturing me on suitable behavior for"—she affected a laughable British accent—"young ladies of my station."

"Your mother went out the night of the funeral?" Katie asked, thinking of poor Sadie.

"Uh-huh." Monica pulled off the woodsy two-lane road that ran by Katie's cottage and turned onto a busier street leading downtown. "I suppose it's no secret that she and Gregory didn't have one of those lovebird marriages. She's not exactly broken up over his death."

"Yeah," Katie said. "I kind of got that feeling at the funeral."

"You mean you didn't buy her performance? Mother will be crushed! She really wanted to come across as the grieving widow."

"But who was she trying to impress?" Katie asked, remembering what Carly had said about Aurora and Gig. "It's not like your grandfather was paying much attention—"

"Oh, Granddad always pays attention. Even when you think he isn't looking, he's really taking it all in."

"So then your mother was doing it for his benefit?"

"My mother does everything for his benefit. She married Gregory because Granddad wanted her to. Aurora Marron is not stupid. She knows what side her croissants are buttered on," Monica said. And then she pointed: "This is the area I had in mind."

They spent the next half hour driving back and forth across Oakdale's key shopping district, checking out available storefronts for rent and debating potential locations for Monica's boutique-to-be. Later, they got out of the car to view the possibilities up close. For almost an hour they walked through town, sometimes together, sometimes splitting up and keeping in touch by cell phone, debating the pros and cons of each available property, brainstorming names, color schemes, and interior decor.

The whole enterprise proved to be so much fun that all three were reluctant to quit and go home, even after the sun began to set and dusk brought with it a persistent drizzle. Even though they insisted to each other, "It'll clear up soon," the sprinkles turned to substantial drops, and they agreed to call it a day. Driving back along the two-lane road toward Katie's cottage, the three were still wondering whether "Monica's Miniatures" made the boutique sound like it sold precious enamel figurines when Monica squinted into the rearview mirror and asked, "See that car? The one right behind us? Has it been following us since we turned onto this road?"

Katie and Maddie swiveled around to look.

"I didn't notice it before," Maddie said.

"I'm probably just imagining things." Monica shrugged. "It's spooky out here. I don't know how you do it, Katie, living alone so far out in the middle of nowhere."

Katie decided not to point out that Monica also lived in the middle of nowhere, albeit in a house surrounded by cast-iron gates and security guards to provide that warm and cozy feeling. She also decided not to point out that she wouldn't currently be living alone if it weren't for Monica's family. Instead, she merely replied, "It's not so bad."

"Well, I admire you, nonetheless," Monica said.

A few minutes later, though, Monica observed, "The car is speeding up. Look."

They did. Monica was right. The car, which had once been a few lengths behind them, now seemed to be practically on their bumper.

"Maybe it wants to pass," Katie suggested.

"Then pass," Monica rolled down her window, stuck out her hand, and motioned for the driver to go around them.

The car stubbornly stuck behind them. And the driver turned on his high beams, practically blinding them in the process.

Katie winced, unbuckled her seat belt in order to sit up on

her knees for a better view, and held up one hand to shield her eyes. Because of the rain, the steamed-up back window, and the high beams, she could barely make out what was going on. All she knew for sure was that, instead of heeding Monica's signal to go around if he was in that much of a hurry, the driver of the car chose to accelerate and nudge his bumper, hard, into theirs.

"What's this nut's problem?" Monica demanded, proceeding to speed up herself.

"I think he wants us to pull over," Maddie said, sounding alarmed. "He's waving his arm like he wants us to pull over."

"Oh, right, that's exactly what I'm going to do," Monica snapped. "Three girls in a car on a dark road, and some guy is telling us to pull over."

"Let's get out of here," Maddie suggested. "Get back on the main road."

"Good idea." Monica looked around, stepped on the accelerator, and whipped the steering wheel sharply to the left.

Katie felt herself being flung against the far door, her head hitting the window, as the tires of the Lexus screeched in protest and the puddle Monica accidentally plowed them into spun the car until, instead of making a 180-degree turn, she ended up whirling them almost three-quarters of the way around. They were now stopped defenseless across two lanes, with the other car bearing straight down on them.

"Get out of the way!" Maddie shrieked as Monica managed to jerk the car to the left before they were smashed in half.

Unfortunately, her last-minute escape plunged their car

off the road and into the woods, where wet leaves made gaining any kind of traction even harder.

"Maybe he'll leave us alone now," Maddie suggested. "Maybe it was just some stupid kid playing chicken."

"He's coming back!" Monica wailed and practically ground her accelerator into powder attempting to bump back onto the road and away.

"Let's just get out of here," Katie said, rubbing her bruised head.

"I'm trying, I'm trying, but he's gaining on us." Monica did her best to speed down the road.

"There's a side road." Katie pointed. "Take it. It leads to the main road."

"Where? I can't see—"

"You missed it!"

"Turn around," Maddie suggested.

"No. He's getting closer."

"Just keep going straight," Katie instructed.

"Maybe I can cut through the woods here and double back."

"No, that won't work. That's not a road, that's—"

The rest of Katie's words were lost in Monica's scream as she realized they were headed straight for a thick cluster of trees, with nowhere to turn in either direction. She panicked and let go of the wheel.

"Here, let me—" Katie threw herself over the front seat, arms stretched out as she attempted to grab the wheel and steer them into a clearing.

But the last thing she saw was the dashboard hurling itself straight at her head. And then a lot of pretty colors.

16

"My name is Henry Coleman, I got a call about my sister being brought into the emergency room." He drummed both hands on the counter of Meg Snyder's nurse's station, trying to prod her into action. "Madeline Coleman. Maddie. Where is she? Is she all right? I need to go see her."

Meg, Jack Snyder's cousin, smiled reassuringly and looked through her stack of charts. "Maddie Coleman. Car accident, right?"

"I don't know. They didn't tell me anything over the phone except to get down here. And bring an up-to-date insurance card—they were real clear about that last part. How the hell could Maddie have been in a car accident? She doesn't own a car. Was she hit by a car? I need to speak to a doctor. No, make it a specialist. No, make it Bob Hughes. He knows what's going on around here. He doesn't need a chart to—"

"Henry!" A voice from behind him called. "I'm over here, I'm okay. Chill."

"Maddie!" He whipped around, trying to simultaneously hug his sister and hold her at arm's length to get a better look at her. "You're okay! What happened? Whose car were you in? What's going on here? Are you hurt? Do you feel faint? Should we sit? I feel faint. Let's sit."

Which was how Maddie, with a bump over her left eye and her right arm bandaged and throbbing from six stitches where the passenger-side window had sliced her as it shattered, ended up supporting her woozy brother into a blue plastic hospital chair a few steps away from the nurse's station. "It's okay, Henry," she said, sitting down beside him. "Just take a deep breath. Everything will be okay."

He groaned and bent over to put his head between his knees. "What the hell happened, Madeline?"

"Well . . . see, Monica wanted—"

"Monica Marron?"

"Yeah. I started working for her yesterday, I told you that. Monica wanted to drive around downtown Oakdale and look for a retail space for her boutique."

"Monica was driving? Monica was in the accident, too?"

"She's fine."

"You're sure?"

"Yes. Geez, Henry, why do you care so much?"

"Because the last thing our bank account needs is for another Marron to meet their doom in a car with a Coleman. You following my drift, kiddo?"

"Monica is fine. She had her seat belt on, too, and she

was behind the wheel. If Katie hadn't leaned over she'd have been—"

"Katie was in the car? What the hell were the three of you doing together? Since when are Monica Marron and Katie shopping buddies?"

"They're not. And we weren't shopping—try and pay attention Henry, okay? Monica was looking for a place for her boutique, and since she was looking in the same area where you and Katie have the gym, I thought Katie could give her some good advice."

"Wonderful. Brilliant. Fantastic. Just what I needed." He sat up and put on the most fake smile Maddie had ever seen. "I'm sorry, go on, you were saying?"

"Are you okay?"

"Never better. Please continue."

Maddie had no idea why her brother was behaving so strangely. So she stuck to the facts and waited for him to elaborate. "We checked out the stores for a couple of hours, and then we were driving home and this car came up behind us and tried to force us off the road—"

"Why? Who was driving the car?"

"I don't know. Monica tried to lose him, she even turned around to drive the other way, but then we got stuck in a ditch or something and we ended up off the road and Monica didn't know where to go—it was dark—so Katie tried to help but she was in the backseat and she tried to reach the wheel, so when we crashed into the trees she flew forward and she was unconscious, but the guy in the ambulance said—"

"Katie is unconscious? Oh my God, oh my God, oh my God."

"I'm sure she'll be okay. The guy in the ambulance said it was probably just a concussion and they'd check her out and—"

"Okay, this is it. This is getting out of hand. First, Sadie, now some guy trying to drive Katie off the road—"

"Sadie?"

"She was killed in a hit-and-run accident the night before last. Coming from the same vet's place Katie was at, with a rabbit in her hands."

"Oh my God," Maddie repeated. "Oh my God, oh my god, oh my God."

"Good," Henry said grimly. "Now you're with me. How many times have I told you, Madeline, with all due respect to Mr. Rudyard Kipling: If you can keep your head while those about you are losing theirs, chances are you haven't fully grasped the situation."

"You think the person who drove us off the road was trying to kill Katie?"

"Was it the 'oh,' the 'my,' or the 'God' that you found unclear, sweetheart?"

"The same person who killed Gregory?'

"That would be a reasonable guess." Henry stood up, heading determinedly off in no particular direction. "We have to tell somebody. We have to tell them everything, not leave anything out this time. We've got to go to the police, and we have to lay our cards on the table. Katie's life is at stake now."

"Tell them what?" Maddie had to run double-time to catch up with his strides.

"Yes, Henry, tell them what?" Monica Marron stepped out of Examination Room 3. There was a scratch on her chin from where it had scraped the steering wheel, and she was moving stiffly, wincing from a presumed assortment of bruises.

"Hi, Monica," Henry said.

"Hi, Henry. Maddie," she rubbed the other girl's shoulder with her hand. "I'm so glad you're okay. I was worried."

"Thanks," Maddie said. "I'm okay. It's just Katie . . . She hasn't woken up yet."

"She will. I'm sure of it." Monica turned her attention to Henry. "I'm so sorry about what I've gotten your sister into. If I'd had any idea—"

"It's not your fault," Maddie blurted out. "Henry thinks whoever ran us off the road was after Katie."

"Katie? Why would someone try to hurt Katie?"

"Henry thinks it's because of what happened to your dad—I mean, stepdad."

"I didn't say that," he interjected and glared at Maddie. "I'm sure there is no connection between Gregory's death and Katie's accident. What connection could there be?"

"Then what was it that you wanted to tell somebody?" Monica asked. "I heard you. You said you had to tell the police everything?"

"About the accident," Henry said. "I was telling Maddie she had to tell the police everything that she remembers about your accident, so they can get this guy."

"Oh, of course. In fact, I just called the precinct again to demand they send an officer down to take our statements as soon as possible. It would probably be useful for Maddie and me to get our stories straight. That way, we won't send the police off in a dozen different directions. They're already working overtime looking for Gregory's killer. They certainly don't want us to waste their time. Isn't that right?" She looked from Maddie to Henry for confirmation.

"Absolutely, Miss Marron," Henry said.

"The sergeant I spoke to said they'd have someone here soon. Why don't the three of us just sit down and wait for them together?"

"Okay," Henry said, sitting back down.

Maddie had never seen this side of her brother before. This wasn't Henry her brother, Henry the dreamer, Henry the wannabe bon vivant, or even Henry the periodic conniver. This was Henry Coleman, servant. And whatever Miss Monica Marron said, obviously went.

To Maddie's discomfiture, he'd visibly deflated the moment Monica had stepped into his path. As a result, Maddie had no idea of how to act, so she merely followed her brother's pathetic lead and did as Monica commanded. She was, after all, a Marron employee now, too. And she wanted to remain one for at least a little while longer.

She sat down between Henry and Monica and dutifully went through every detail of what she remembered about their accident, until Jack Snyder arrived and asked her and Monica to go over it again.

"I'm responsible," Monica confessed to Jack. "If I had just stayed calm and been more careful and not lost control of the car . . . Let me know as soon as you have any leads about who might have done this, Detective Snyder."

"Actually," Jack said, and he was looking pointedly at Henry as he said the words, "we have a pretty good idea of who is responsible for this."

Katie was dreaming.

Or, at least, she sincerely hoped that she was dreaming. Because if any of this was happening in real life, she was seriously screwed.

She was walking on the Marron property. The cherry trees were thicker than she remembered, the branches not merely brushing Katie's head, but actually scraping along her arms, slithering inside her shirt and along her stomach and up her back.

Katie kept moving. She heard gunfire somewhere behind her, but she refused to turn her head to look. She started running.

She ran through the woods, being pelted by branches and cherries, her ankles tangling in weeds, her nostrils dilating as she gagged from the smell of rotten, toxic fruit. She kept running until the woods suddenly cleared and, in the distance, Katie saw a barnlike structure. With a huge Marron crest over the front door.

She stepped inside.

And came face to face with Mike, who was wearing blue jeans, a denim workshirt, and a welcoming smile.

At first, Katie was so shocked to encounter a Mike who

wasn't mad or accusing her of waiting for him to fail, that it took her a moment to realize he was welcoming her into the Marrons' vintage-car garage.

Mike reached under the front seat of a golden convertible parked in the corner and pulled out a bottle of wine. When he put it lovingly into Katie's hands, she could see every one of his fingerprints gleaming from the glass as if painstakingly scratched in silver. She was about to ask Mike what he expected her to do with it, when he bent over and brushed her mouth with his. First gently, then more forcefully, not taking no for an answer.

The bottle slipped through her fingers. It didn't shatter when it hit the ground. It simply disappeared. As did the entire floor because, in the next instant, Katie was lying in the backseat of the car, Mike looming on top of her, smiling and reaching to pull off her sweater. She let him, raising both arms to make it easier and savoring the way his hands felt on her bare skin as he slid his palms down her back, arousing every nerve ending in her body. She felt him brush past her neck, flicking her hair, and Katie languidly closed her eyes, letting the sweater slip over her face before opening them again. She looked up. And saw Simon perched where Mike had been.

They weren't in Gregory Marron's garage anymore. And they weren't inside one of his cars.

Katie and Simon were back at Burt's Garage, back in Nancy Hughes's convertible. And now Simon was holding the bottle of wine, smearing Mike's fingerprints with his own until Katie could no longer tell which was which.

It was starting all over again. The lies, the fears, the horrible surprises. And there was nothing Katie could do to stop it.

Except scream.

"Katie!" Margo was standing over her bed, holding Katie by
the shoulders to keep her from flailing about and knocking
over the IV that led from the back of her throbbing palm into
a tube of clear liquid on a pole. "Katie, it's okay! It's me. It's
just Margo. You're all right. Thank goodness you're all right."

Katie looked up, her vision coming in and out of focus,
her stomach coming in and out of her throat, and saw Margo
hovering over her.

A nightmare, she told herself. The Marrons, Mike,
Simon. It was just a dream.

"Could I have some water, please?" Katie managed to
croak out. Margo poured her a cup. Katie waited to see if it
would stay down. After several false alarms, it finally did.
Katie ventured another attempt at speech. "Where . . ."

"You're at Oakdale Memorial."

"Wh-what happened?" Her head pounded. "I don't remember . . ."

"You were in an accident this evening."

"Car?"

"Yes."

"But, I wasn't driving, right? I was . . ."

"You were in the backseat. Monica Marron was driving."

"Monica Marron?"

"Maddie said the three of you were out looking for stores
to rent? Is that right? You and Maddie and Monica—"

"Are they all right?" The events of that evening came bearing down on Katie as powerfully as had the car crashing into the trees. "Maddie and Monica were in the car, too. Are they okay?"

"They're fine. Just some scratches. I think Maddie needed a few stitches. But you're the one we're worried about."

"Am I okay?"

"Looks that way. You've got a hard head, Katie, Mama always said so. Nice to know it can come in handy once in a while."

"Margo?" Katie asked. "Were you crying?"

"Seasonal allergies."

"Oh. Right. Sorry."

"Damn it, Katie, don't you ever scare me like that again!"

"I'm sorry. I don't know what happened. We were just driving home, when all of a sudden, this car, it came out of nowhere and started following us."

"Did you recognize the car?" Margo asked, slipping into police mode.

Katie tried to recall. The whole afternoon was so fragmented now. She could barely remember whether she, Monica, and Maddie were jabbering blithely on their cell phones before the accident or after.

"It was dark," she finally said. "It was raining. Monica was driving so fast . . ."

"What about the driver of the other car? Anything familiar about the car or driver?"

Katie tried to shake her head, but that hurt too much, so she settled for, "It was a man. At least, I think it was a man."

"Why do you think that?"

"Well . . . Maddie—I guess it was Maddie—said something about a guy motioning for us to pull over."

"It was a guy. You and Maddie were right about that."

"You mean you know who did it?"

"We think so. He didn't try to run after the accident. In fact, he was the one who called the police and the ambulance."

"So he didn't mean to run us off the road?"

"I don't know, Katie."

"Then why was he following us? And why did he bump our car and continue chasing us when we tried to lose him?"

"He says that after you spun around he only came back to see if you were okay."

"And before that? Why was he trying to force us off the road?"

"He says it was because of you, Katie."

"Me? The driver knows me?"

Margo nodded.

"The driver"—she took a deep breath—"the one who drove you off the road, was Mike."

17

Katie spent the next forty-eight hours at the hospital pushing the on-call button and requesting pain pills. It wasn't that she was in so much pain. The worst of the headache went away after the first day, and once they took the IV out, her sore hand felt fine. What Katie found comforting about the pain pills was that they stopped her from thinking. The last thing she wanted to do right now, was think.

After Margo told her that Mike was the one driving the car that had almost killed her, she began thinking comforting thoughts such as, "Mike would never deliberately hurt me, so there must be a logical explanation for all this," and disturbing thoughts such as, "Mike was trying to kill me, so he must know I'm looking into Gregory's death and he's determined to stop me by any means possible."

Margo told Katie they had Mike in custody, that Jack had already interviewed him once and intended to do so again.

"Did Mike say why he was in the car following us?"

"He said it was to protect you, Katie."

Simon, Katie recalled, was also always claiming to do things to protect her. There was even one instance, after Simon came back from the dead, that he and Mike worked together to "protect" Katie. Simon was living his life on the run and Katie was determined to go with him. But Mike and Simon got together and decided that Katie would be better off staying in Oakdale. They also lied to her about when and where she and Simon would supposedly be departing for their new life. Which meant that Katie showed up at the docks, ready to throw all caution and comfort to the wind in the interest of supporting her man, only to watch from behind a wire fence her man swiftly departing as he shouted that he and Mike were only doing this to protect her.

"What did Mike say he was protecting me from?" Katie asked.

"He didn't say," Margo admitted.

Katie wondered what it was about her nightmare that had made her wake up screaming. Was it the sense that everything rotten that had already happened to her was about to happen again? Yeah. That was it.

How many times was Katie supposed to go through this torture, anyway? Was this somebody's idea of a joke? Was this a test? Was she a fool to have given Mike a second chance?

Maddie certainly seemed to think so. The first thing out of her mouth the day she visited Katie in the hospital was, "I told you Mike Kasnoff was no good. Henry, on the other hand, is a good guy. Henry wouldn't keep secrets from you. And he certainly wouldn't try to kill you. Ever."

"There is no way in heaven or hell Mike would ever do anything to hurt you. To hurt any woman," Carly insisted when she dropped by after Maddie had left. "There is more going on here than meets the eye. You said Aurora threatened you at the wake. And Monica said her mother was out of the house the night Sadie was killed. So maybe she was driving that first car that was aiming for you, but hit Sadie. And maybe she was also behind the car that hit you."

"You think Aurora wanted me dead so badly, she'd risk her own daughter's life?"

"Monica is fine. You're the only one who was seriously hurt."

"But she couldn't have controlled that."

"Who knows? Maybe she knew exactly what needed to be done to just get you and not Monica."

"And what about Mike? How does Mike fit in?"

"I don't know," Carly admitted. "But we'll find out."

Later that day, Katie got the chance to ask another visitor, Mrs. Hughes, a disturbing question that she just could not get out of her mind. "When you said that Gig Marron was unpredictable and you didn't know how he might react in a situation, especially if it was a perceived threat—did you mean you thought he might do something like . . . this?"

Nancy hesitated. "I don't believe that Gig Marron would ever do his own dirty work."

"So you're not saying that he wouldn't run me over, you're just saying you think he'd hire someone to get the actual job done."

"Yes, I suppose that is what I am saying. But please, Katie, we are speaking in theoreticals."

"Someone who owed him a favor, maybe? Or someone who he promised to help in the future? Help with something important. Like, say, getting a murder charge dismissed? Or even just making some really key evidence disappear?"

"Katie, I don't think this is good for—"

"Someone who has as much to lose as Gig does if a particular piece of information got out?"

"Now you truly are speculating, my dear."

"Someone like Mike?" Katie asked innocently.

"Katie."

"Mike."

She was finally sitting up in her hospital bed, eating pudding from a white plastic bowl. Her hair was pulled back off her face but she hadn't yet had a chance to wash out the dried blood left by the cut on her scalp. Mike stood in the doorway, looking as if he feared Katie would call security.

It was not their most romantic moment ever.

Still, Katie managed to keep from bursting into sobs of frustration over everything that had transpired in the last forty-eight—no, seventy-something—hours. "Hi," she said.

He hesitated. "Can I come in?"

"Sure."

He came in. He stood several feet from the bed and nodded, though there was nothing to agree on. "Glad to see you're doing okay."

"Thanks."

"Going home soon?"

"Maybe this afternoon. They just have to do a couple more X rays, make sure nothing's more broken than it looks."

"I swear I didn't try to hurt you, Katie. I've never wanted to hurt you."

"Well, you did." Katie could feel the tears coming. "How could you move out like that? I don't even know where you're living now. How can you treat me like this? Just walk away, give up, act like you don't even want to try and fix—"

"I had to do it, Katie. You didn't believe me—"

"There was nothing to believe! In order to believe someone, they have to give you an answer one way or the other! You just clammed up."

"I asked you to trust me."

"And I asked you to trust me."

"It's not that simple, Katie."

The tears had made their way from the clog in her throat all the way to the base of Katie's lashes, threatening to spill at any moment. But she had too many questions still left to risk that. So Katie dredged up the one strategy she had to keep from crying. She went on the offensive.

"Margo said you called the police after we crashed the other night."

"I did."

"Did you come to see if we were okay?"

"I tried. But when Monica and Maddie saw me coming, they freaked out, started screaming, warning me to stay back. I tried to yell and tell them who I was, but I think I was too far away—they couldn't see me in the rain. I didn't want to make things worse, scare them further, so I stepped back, called the police and waited for them to come."

"And then you turned yourself in?"

"I didn't have to turn myself in, Katie, I just told them what happened."

"So what happened, Mike? Why were you on the road, following us? Or are you going to say it was just a coincidence, that you were heading home, looking to apologize so we can start putting this relationship back together?" Katie uttered the stinging words with as much sarcasm as possible for a woman who desperately wanted them to be true.

"I was at work," Mike said. "I'm adding another room to Lucinda Walsh's guest house. She says so many people ask to crash there, she might as well turn it into an orgy-friendly commune."

"That sounds like Lucinda. Except for the words *crash*. And *orgy-friendly*."

"I'm paraphrasing." He smiled. She saw dimples.

"I'm listening." He expected her to melt at the sight of the dimples. And Katie did. But she was damned if she was going to let him see that.

Mike waited for Katie to react. When she didn't, he cleared his throat and went on. "Anyway, I was at Lucinda's, finishing up for the day, cleaning up, when I got this call on my cell, with the number blocked. It was a woman, she was screaming, "They've got Katie! They've got Katie! She's in danger. They're driving south on Old Mill Road in a red Lexus. If you hurry you can catch them!"

"And you didn't ask who it was? You didn't ask for any details?"

"Look, Katie, I know how stupid this sounds. I know how stupid this makes *me* sound. Big, dumb, Neanderthal man, going off half-cocked over what, in all likelihood, was some kid's idea of a practical joke. But, that's who I am. I'm the kind of guy who, if he thinks there's even a chance that the woman he loves is in trouble, he goes off after her. Without stopping to think. Katie, I saw what happened to Sadie. I couldn't not take the phone call seriously if it meant saving you from what happened to her!"

"So you also think whoever got Sadie was really after me?"

"I don't know. Katie, I was just trying to protect you."

"But why were you trying to force us off the road?"

"I wasn't. When I saw exactly what the woman warned me about—a red Lexus with you in the backseat, I had to make sure you were okay. Yes, I followed you, yes, I turned my lights on to get your attention, and yes, I even bumped the car a couple of times to try and get you to look over and notice me signalling for you to pull over. I just needed to see for myself that you weren't in any danger. I certainly didn't expect Monica to panic like that . . ."

"It was pretty scary out there, Mike."

"It was a stupid thing for me to do, I don't deny it, and if Monica wants to press charges, that's her right—I won't fight her. But I need to hear that you don't think I was actually out there trying to hurt you on purpose. Katie, I love you. I want you to believe and to trust that."

"Then help me. Make me believe."

He stepped up to her bed. He leaned over so that his knuckles were resting on her blanket and his face was level with hers. "Look at me, Katie," he ordered. "Look at my eyes.

Anything you need to know about how I feel about you, anything you need to know about who I am or who I might turn
out to be, it's all in there. You just have to see it for yourself."

She looked into Mike's eyes. She looked deeper and
harder than she'd ever looked for anything before. She tried
to hack past what she thought she knew, to reach for what
she definitely felt. What she definitely believed. The problem was she didn't feel she knew enough yet to make any decision one way or the other.

She said, "I'm sorry, Mike, but . . ."

He stormed out of the room, slamming the door behind him.

It turned out it wasn't X rays the hospital wanted to take
before releasing Katie, it was an MRI of her brain. She wasn't
sure what they were looking for, but she went along with the
procedure nevertheless. She was especially pleased that Ben
Harris would be doing it.

Even since Mike's plea for faith, followed by her failure to
supply it, followed by his door-slamming exit, Katie had
been thinking a lot about just who she presumed Mike was.

When they first met, she'd thought he was her hero. The
man who would do anything for her. The man who would
put her needs before his own, who would be always truthful,
always noble, always gallant, and always there.

A pretty tall order for anyone. Even a natural Boy Scout
like Mike.

No man could live up to those heights of expectation;
it was all bound to collapse under the weight of day-to-day
realism.

But did it have to, in this case, collapse so dramatically?

In the space of one night, Katie's champion became Katie's thief/murderer/liar.

So what did that say about her?

It said that she was the kind of woman who was eager, willing, and able to believe each and every horrible rumor she heard about a man she professed to love. It said that she was shallow, that she was self-absorbed. And that she needed more facts before she made a decision about Mike.

Which is where Ben Harris came in.

Ben and Mike grew up next door to each other in Milltown, Oakdale's working-class neighborhood. They'd been friends in high school. If anybody could offer Katie insight into Mike's character, it was Ben.

Which was why, as he was helping slide Katie into the sterile white tube of the MRI machine, she looked up and asked Ben, "Do you have a minute to talk to me about Mike?"

"Um, I'm a little busy right now."

"What I meant was, what are you doing after this MRI?"

Ben chuckled. "You really are something else, Katie, you know that?"

"Is that a yes?"

He eased her head all the way into the tube. "That's a yes."

Having found nothing to worry about in the results of Katie's MRI, Ben invited her to go ahead and get dressed, check out, sign the obligatory stacks of paperwork, then stop by his office afterward.

She did just that, easing into the fresh clothes Margo had

brought her from home and telling the nurse's aide she could burn the ones she had arrived in. Even if they weren't torn and bloodstained, Katie knew she'd never want to look at them again.

In his office, Ben urged Katie to take the chair across from him. Sitting down, Katie felt tiny compared to his six-foot-plus frame. It was as if they were the ultimate opposites—she, short, perky, and ultra-whitebread, and he, tall, broad-shouldered, serious, and black. Ben put away the file he'd been reading, folded his hands, and gave Katie his full attention. "So what was this about Mike?"

"You and he were friends when you were kids?"

"I like to think we're still friends now, but, yes, I understand what you mean, we were closer in high school. Which was a bit unusual, I must say. Where and when Mike and I went to school, the white kids hung out with white kids, the black kids hung with black kids, and rarely did the twain meet."

"Did you see much of Mike after he dropped out?"

Ben hesitated. It wasn't a difficult question and yet, all of sudden, Ben was acting like it was. He scratched his beard thoughtfully and looked away for a moment. "A bit," he finally admitted.

"But not that much?"

"Look, Katie, shocking as it may seem—considering that I grew up to be a neurosurgeon with one failed marriage and several broken engagements behind me—I was quite a nerd in high school. AP classes, Junior Achievement, National Honor Society, Science Club. . . . Under normal circumstances, guys like Mike should have been stuffing me into lockers for sport. We didn't really have a lot in common on the surface, and especially not after he dropped out of school."

"Is that the kind of guy Mike really was? Someone who stuffed nerds into lockers for sport?"

"Come on, Katie, what do you think?"

"That's just it," she admitted. "I don't know what to think. I used to think I knew Mike. That I knew everything about him, knew how he'd react in a given situation. But now, I . . . Gig Marron told me he didn't blame Mike for stealing their car all those years ago, or for killing his son now, because Mike was just like a million other guys he knew. Poor, angry kids who got so frustrated with everyone having more than they did that they couldn't help but lash out into violence and crime. It was inevitable."

Ben seemed amused by Gig's description. "This is Mike Kasnoff we're talking about?"

"I know. It made no sense to me, either. But Gig seemed so sure of it."

"Gig Marron has some very strong opinions. But that's all they are. Opinions, not gospel."

"Any other day of the week, I'd agree with you. But the way Mike's been acting recently . . . I said I thought I knew how he'd react in a given situation? I never dreamed that he could be accused of something like murder, and then just shrug his shoulders and refuse to defend himself. Or that he wouldn't tell me the whole truth about stealing a car when he was a kid. Or that he'd almost get me killed."

"That last one, from what I understand, was an accident."

"Yeah. It's what Mike wants me to believe. But how can I when every time I look at his face, I see a stranger?"

Or, rather, she didn't dare add, someone all too familiar.

"So that's why you're here. Okay, I get it now. You want me to tell you which Mike is the real deal—the one you thought you knew, or the one Marron described."

"That would be great, yeah."

He chuckled again. Katie truly was pleased that she could bring a decent guy like Ben so much joy in the space of one afternoon. What a shame that every time he got that bemused expression on his face, Katie felt her own hopes growing dimmer and dimmer.

"All right, Katie, here is what I can tell you. Having known Mike for over twenty years, I'm pretty confident that Gig Marron is barking up the wrong tree. Yeah, Mike didn't have a lot growing up—none of us did. But I'm not out there holding up liquor stores or dealing drugs, and neither is he. So, from my perspective, that destiny might not be quite as inevitable as Marron believes. As for hurting you, running you off the road on purpose? No way, no how, not ever. I'd stake my life on it. Mike is crazy about you and, even if he wasn't, there is no way that man would deliberately hurt any woman. He just doesn't have it in him."

Katie considered leaping over Ben's desk and kissing him.

But then he added, "As for his other alleged crimes, like poisoning Gregory . . . all I can say is that Mike would need a hell of a good reason to do something so drastic. And when it comes to Marron, I just can't imagine what that could be."

"Gig thinks Mike was still holding a grudge over Gregory's sending him to jail."

"Why would Mike hold a grudge about that? He was guilty."

Katie was so shocked she couldn't speak for a moment. "He was? Are you sure? I mean, he said that he pled guilty, but this is Mike we're talking about. Isn't it possible that Gregory railroaded him into prison to cover up some shady dealings on his own part? I was thinking, what if Gregory had the car stolen himself, for the insurance money, and Mike was just an easy scapegoat and—"

"Katie, hold up." Ben raised both his hands. "Hold on a second. Let's not turn the boy into a saint, here. Mike did steal Gregory Marron's car."

"But how can you be so sure?"

"Because," Ben said, "I helped him do it."

18

"You, Ben?" Katie almost shrieked.

Learning Mike had a record was one thing. Despite his general all-around nice-guy vibe, he did have a bit of the sexy, unshaved rebel about him. But finding out Ben had committed a crime worse than jaywalking was like discovering Mother Teresa ran a bordello on the side.

"I took an afternoon or two off from Science Club," he admitted.

"You and Mike . . ."

"Stole Gregory Marron's car. Mike disabled the alarm and did the driving. I was the lookout man. I was also the guy who hid the car. Which is why the police didn't find it after they picked Mike up. They searched all the logical places he might have hidden it. They didn't know about me. They never found out it was me, either."

"What did you do with the car? Sell it eventually?"

"Nah. I was too scared. Figured the cops were on the lookout, could trace it back to me. I finally just got a tire-iron, beat that gorgeous frame practically to bits so nobody would recognize it, then took it to a junkyard. Stayed there till I personally saw it get crushed and melted down into nothing, to make sure we were home free."

"And Mike never said a word."

"No. Nothing. Not even when the D.A. offered him a shorter sentence if he told them who his accomplice was. Not being able to find the car convinced the cops that Mike was in on it with somebody else. And cops hate conspiracies. Makes them look stupid. That's why they offered Mike the deal. Plus, with two punks to string up instead of one, Gregory Marron might have gone easier on Mike. Wouldn't have lobbied so hard for a maximum sentence. Mike could've saved himself a lot of grief if he'd just mentioned my name."

"Or you could have turned yourself in," Katie pointed out.

"That would have been the right thing to do, wouldn't it?" Ben said, lowering his gaze to his desk. "All those AP courses I took in rhetoric helped me convince myself that, while turning myself in might theoretically be the right thing, it wouldn't help Mike. After all, the reduced-sentence deal was on the table only in case he snitched, not if I voluntarily surrendered. Better for me to stay on track. Scholarship to college, medical school. On track, I could serve all of humanity, not just one man."

"You must have aced your rhetoric final," Katie observed.

"Actually, I got a B minus. Teacher found my logic far-fetched and self-serving. I ended up not making valedictorian because of that grade."

"I'm sure that made Mike feel a whole heck of a lot better."

Ben didn't try to make excuses. "I owe Mike a lot," he said. "I realize that. I also realize that there's nothing I can do now to make up for my cowardice back then."

Except for . . .

Katie recalled an earlier conversation she'd had with Nancy Hughes. And she said, "Ben, you were the one who declared Gregory dead, right?"

"Yeah." He nodded.

"You're the one who decided not to give him CPR or whatever."

"It wouldn't have done any good. He was dead by the time I got to him."

"Right," Katie agreed. "That's what you said."

Ben immediately grasped what she was intimating. "Wait a minute. I don't believe this! Are you seriously sitting there thinking that I let Gregory die in order to avenge Mike?"

"And maybe clear your guilty conscience in the process, yeah." There were also her earlier suspicions about Ben and Gig being in on it together, but Katie decided not to mention them now.

"Oh, come on, that's ridiculous. Yeah, I feel bad about turning my back on Mike, but, believe me, there's plenty of blame to go around on that account. My cowardice and

Gregory's vindictiveness were not the things that hurt Mike most from that incident. It was actually his family's reaction to the arrest that really broke his spirit."

"You mean his brother and sister?"

"Sarah, Mark, his mom, too. When the police came to question Mike, they all acted like . . . like they'd been expecting it. Like they always knew Mike was a bad seed and it was just a matter of time before he screwed up. Can you imagine what that must have felt like for him, not only to be arrested, but to turn around and realize that the most important people in his life just automatically assumed he was guilty?"

Katie didn't reply.

She tracked Mike down at Lucinda Walsh's estate, by the guest house out back, behind a workbench, sawing on a piece of wood, his shirtsleeves rolled up, his forearms covered with sawdust.

"Mike," she said.

"Katie." He set down the saw.

"I wanted to say—"

He picked up the freshly sawed board and proceeded to carry it inside the half-completed addition to the guest house. Katie followed and found herself standing in a room that was a mere skeleton of its ultimate shape. Katie knew the feeling. Since getting out of the hospital, she'd felt pretty raw and unsteady herself.

Katie said, "I talked to Ben Harris."

"How is Ben?" Mike turned his back on Katie to settle what she presumed would be a windowsill.

"Still feeling guilty about not coming forward fifteen years ago."

Mike paused for only a second. His back stiffened and the board wavered. But, as she noted, only for a second. He went back to work almost instantly. He didn't say a word in response to her statement.

"Why didn't you ever tell the police Ben helped you steal the car?"

His back still to her, Mike snapped, "I don't rat out my friends, Katie. Not even to save my own hide."

"Is that why you didn't want to talk about what you did back then? Because you were protecting Ben?"

Katie took a tentative step forward and attempted to rest her hand on his shoulder, but Mike shrugged it away and strode to a farther corner of the room.

"Believe what you want to believe, Katie." He stepped back outside and headed for his car. "People like you always do."

Three days after the accident, Maddie was back at work. It wasn't that Monica insisted, it was more that Maddie was itching to get back into the Marron house to continue snooping.

Monica didn't require much cajoling for the company. "Gig is out of town donating something to somebody in Gregory's name," she said. "And Aurora is off on another of her top-secret appointments, what else is new? There are servants, and security up the whazoo, but I have to admit I feel better having a friend to talk to. It's so creepy being here all alone and thinking about Mike Kasnoff still lurking out there, probably dreaming of other ways to get at us."

Maddie was sitting at the computer in Monica's room, Googling for a complete list of exclusively petite designer labels, while Monica was gazing out at the grounds from her window seat. "I don't know what the police are thinking, letting Mike Kasnoff out again, especially after he tried to run my car off the road. All of us could have been killed."

Maddie said, "Mike claims driving us off the road was an accident. He says he got a phone call from a woman who—"

"Oh, I know, I know. He phoned me personally to apologize and explain himself. I swear to God, I thought I would have a heart attack right then and there when I picked up the phone and heard his voice."

"You don't believe him?"

"A mysterious woman screaming that Katie is being kidnapped? Can you think of anything more preposterous? I guess it's like Gig always says, most criminals don't get caught because the cops are so smart, but because they're so stupid."

Maddie continued typing. She paused and pointed at the screen. "This designer here, Khait Couture, they technically don't make petite sizes, but their small size looks really, really small. We should consider stocking them, as well. Take a look."

Maddie pivoted the monitor and Monica got up from the window seat for a closer inspection. "Khait Couture . . . You know, I think my mother has a few of their items. Not the

small size obviously, she's almost twice my height. But, yeah,
I think that's the brand. If it's twenty years too young for her
to wear, she's got it somewhere in her wardrobe. For an actual young person . . . they're not bad."

"Want me to go to her room and pull a couple of samples
out?" Maddie asked as nonchalantly as possible, trying to
hide her thrill over a chance to look around Aurora's room.
"It's so hard to judge stuff like texture and material from a
digital photo."

"Okay," Monica agreed. "You know which room is hers?"

I have the entire floor-plan of this place memorized, Maddie thought.

"Remind me, again?" she said.

Unlike her late husband's study, Aurora Marron's bedroom
was not overstuffed with the excesses of many lands. Her
excesses were limited to the European continent, including
an intricately carved wooden bed complete with matching silk sheets, pillows, and duvet, three mirrors—one full
length, one waist-up, and one magnifying—each with its
own overhead lamp, an ivory inlaid armoire, a hand-painted
English tea cart, a gold-leaf-engraved writing table, and
a jade, somewhat-Vietnamese-influenced-though-French-if-
you-went-by-the-artist's-signature-on-the-side, chest. All of
the items were gorgeous, priceless . . . and locked.

The latter she knew for sure, because Maddie had given
a firm tug to everything that seemed like it could harbor a
potentially useful scoop.

Well, wasn't this just great?

It looked like Maddie was destined to exit this potential treasure trove of crucial information without even those items that she'd been sent to fetch because Aurora's closet was locked, too. Which totally wasn't fair.

About the only thing left for Maddie to go through was the woven elephant-hair trash can by the writing desk.

Maddie wasn't proud. She went for the trash can.

On TV, the police always put on rubber gloves before Dumpster diving. Maddie had no such luxury. She simply stuck both hands into the refuse, hoping extremely hard not to encounter anything squishy.

What she found after dumping its contents on the floor, was a seemingly infinite collection of crumpled tissues with different shades of lipstick on them—as if Aurora had gone through a dozen tubes testing and rejecting each color in turn, plus a pot spilling a recently deceased plant, a stack of unopened condolence cards, two pairs of ripped and crumpled pantyhose . . . and a *Vogue* magazine subscription card, the kind that falls out while you're turning the pages.

With Mike Kasnoff's name and cell phone number scribbled on the back.

"Aurora did it," Maddie triumphantly announced at the meeting she'd called over at Katie's house. "Just look at this number. This proves it. I can't think of any other reason for Aurora to call Mike, unless it was to freak him out about Katie's being kidnapped by a red Lexus, can you?"

Actually, Katie could. It was the same reason that she could think of for Gig to call Mike. They were in it together and Mike was doing Aurora a favor, getting rid of a snooping Katie before she identified Gregory's killer to the police, in exchange for having his own role in the death covered up. Not to mention the more banal reason that Aurora could simply have been calling Mike because she wanted some construction work done on her house. Or because he happened to be very good looking and she happened to be newly available.

"This card means that Jack, Henry, and Mike are innocent," Maddie concluded.

Katie hated to be the downer, but . . . "This is hardly the kind of conclusive proof that's going to make the police lock Aurora up and throw away the key."

"But it's a start," Maddie insisted.

"What we need," Carly pointed out, "is to prove that Aurora had access to the wine bottle at some point during the day Gregory died, so she could poison it. Once we prove that, everything else, like Sadie's death and Katie's accident and probably even Mike's prints, will fall right into place."

"If Aurora set Mike up to kill me," Katie said.

"And me," Maddie hated to be left out.

"She must think I'm close to proving that she killed Gregory. She must think that I spotted something incriminating in his study the day she caught me up there. I just wish I knew what it was Aurora thinks I know!"

"What *did* you find up there?" Carly asked. "You were there longer than me."

"I have no idea! But I guess I must have overlooked a significant clue."

"This phone number proves it," Maddie insisted. "Aurora called Mike to get him to scare us into crashing. We all could have been killed."

"That's the problem." Carly shook her head. "I have no trouble picturing Aurora Marron cooking up a plan to get rid of her husband. They had a horrible marriage. And I have no trouble imagining her framing Mike or Henry or any other person for the crime to cover her tracks, or accidentally running down Sadie while she was gunning for Katie. But the more I think about it—and I know what I said to you at the hospital, Katie, but I wasn't thinking straight then—I can't picture Aurora having her own daughter killed because Monica had the misfortune of riding in a car with you."

"Monica and her mom don't get along all that well, either," Maddie offered.

"And weren't you, Carly, the one who suggested that Aurora may have knocked off Gregory in order to get closer to Gig, who controls the real money? Maybe, if that's what Aurora was really interested in, she saw Monica as just another heir in the way."

"I can't . . ." Carly threw her arms up in the air. "I'm sorry, I can't see a mother deliberately harming her own child."

"You know," Katie pointed out, "just because Maddie found Mike's number in Aurora's trash can doesn't necessarily mean Aurora was the one who used it. What if someone was trying to frame Aurora and make it look like she was the one who called Mike, by using her phone and then leaving the evidence in her trash?"

"Someone like who?" Carly asked. "The only other woman in the house, except for the servants, is Monica."

"And Monica hardly called Mike to tell him to come kill her," Maddie agreed. "Besides, she was with us all afternoon. She couldn't have made the call at the time that Mike says that he got it, which was what? Like ten minutes before he caught up with us?"

"It could have been Gig," Katie said. "Gregory planned to have his dad declared incompetent so he'd stop giving the family fortune away to charity. It's likely that Gig found out about Gregory's scheme, Nancy Hughes told me. Gig might have killed Gregory to stop him. And he might be the one who thinks I'm on to something. That's why Sadie died. That's why Mike was sent after me."

"Except that Mike said he was called by a woman," Maddie reminded her.

"Nancy also said she didn't believe Gig would ever do his own dirty work. How simple would it have been for him to have one of the female servants make a call at a pre-arranged time—he didn't even have to be anywhere in the house; he didn't even have to be in Oakdale—from Aurora's phone, then drop the card with the number on it in the trash-can. The card with the number written on it doesn't even have to be a setup. It could just be his accomplice being sloppy."

"Aurora is still the one that makes the most sense," Maddie insisted, unwilling to let go of her triumph, or the bragging rights that would come with being the one to break the case. "She's got means, motive, and opportunity."

"Now all we need is a shred of physical evidence," Carly said.

At midnight, while Jack and the kids were upstairs asleep, Carly was still sitting at the kitchen table, poring over her illicit copy of Gregory Marron's case file for what felt like the umpteenth time. Carly sorted the interviews from the forensic reports from the other evidence collected at the Marron estate. If Aurora was on the warpath because she believed Katie had noticed something in Gregory's study that pointed to his wife as his killer, then Carly wanted to make sure she knew about every single item that the police had found in his study.

As she looked at the black-and-white photographs of Gregory's study, all Carly could spy on the surface was an infinite hoard of junk. If a Cartier clock harbored the answer to Gregory's murder, Carly certainly wasn't seeing it. The same for the collection of walking sticks and pens. About the only thing of interest Carly did manage to find among the photos and papers in the file were photocopies of Aurora's credit card statements. According to a note in Jack's hand on the side, his men had gone through every purchase, looking for anything potentially incriminating, like poison, drugs, medical equipment, wine, etc. . . .

According to Jack's note, the Oakdale P.D. had found nothing of interest.

But the Oakdale P.D. were mostly men. (Sorry, Margo.) And they didn't know what Carly knew.

She didn't care that it was after midnight. Still looking at one credit card statement in particular, Carly grabbed the phone and called Katie, not even bothering to apologize for waking her up.

"Katie," she said excitedly. "I found the proof to nail Aurora!"

19

On Sunday morning, with Jack working his seventh straight day at the station and all of their regular sitters otherwise occupied, there was no way Carly could get away from Parker and Sage's commitments long enough to meet with Katie and Maddie. So they compromised. Carly would bring the credit card statement—and the kids—and meet the other two at the playground.

She deposited Parker onto the soccer field and reassured him that she'd be just on the other side of the wire fence, near the sandbox, watching Sage. She then plopped Sage into an unoccupied corner, admonishing her to "Play nice, no hitting with the shovel, you know the drill . . ." and sat down on a nearby bench, waiting for Katie and Maddie.

"What've you got?" They arrived together and sat down on either side of Carly, prepared to be dazzled.

"Check this out." She slipped the credit card statement

copy out of her purse, smoothed it out on her lap and leaned back so that both Katie and Maddie might take a good look. "See anything interesting?"

"Aurora is addicted to Botox?" Maddie guessed. "You told us that already."

Katie, however, asked, "If her credit card statement was in Gregory's room, does that mean Gregory paid all of her bills?"

"I would think so," Carly said. "Aurora doesn't have any money of her own. She loved calling me money-grubbing trash, but her own résumé didn't look so different."

"Why did Aurora call you money-grubbing trash?" Maddie wondered.

"Never mind."

Katie said, "This doesn't make any sense. Gig told me that he keeps—well, kept, I guess—all three of them, Gregory, Aurora, and Monica, on an allowance. But, if that's the case, why would Gregory be paying Aurora's bills? Wouldn't they all pay their own expenses from the money Gig doled out to them?"

"Monica told me it was Gregory who kept them on an allowance," Maddie said. "That's why she couldn't start her business until after he was dead."

"Then why was Gregory trying to have Gig declared incompetent, if he already had access to the family money?"

"Who cares?" Carly demanded. "Would you two look at the damn bill?"

Katie and Maddie scrutinized the bill.

"Do you see it?"

Maddie shook her head right away. Katie took another

moment to give the list of purchases one more glance, before doing the same.

"Look at this. Right here. It's a credit for Genrikh's in Chicago."

"Okay," Katie said.

"Genrikh's is a very high-end cookware shop. I used to live in Chicago. I'd pass by and peek into the windows at all the things I couldn't afford."

"Okay," Maddie said.

"You guys aren't getting this."

"That seems kind of obvious," Katie agreed.

"It's a credit for a high-end cookware store. Katie, have you ever bought a really fancy dress just to wear for the night, then returned it for store credit?"

"Never."

"That's a crock, but we won't go into it right now," Carly said. "I work in fashion. Women are constantly buying special occasion gowns, wearing and returning them. All sorts of people do it, too. Poor, rich . . . Aurora Marron has been both. What could be more natural for her than to buy a cooking pot, use it to cook up some poison, then ship it back the next day? The police will never find it. And there'll be no evidence to connect her to the crime."

"It sounds possible. I guess. But couldn't she have just bought a cooking pot for, you know, cooking?" Katie suggested.

"No. Aurora Marron does not cook. Aurora does not even dial for take-out."

"In that case," Katie mused, "I think we need to take a road trip."

*   *   *

Bright and early Monday morning, the trio was off to Chicago. Carly had hired an all-day sitter, Maddie had told both
Henry and Monica that she was going on a school trip, and
Katie, who was unfortunately on her own, didn't have to lie
to anyone.

Katie, who'd developed an aversion to backseats since
the accident, drove; Carly sat in the front seat beside her;
and Maddie perched on the very edge of the backseat, her
face planted squarely between the two headrests, lest she
miss a single word or an opportunity to offer her opinion.

For the first fifteen minutes of what would probably be a
two-hour trip, the conversation concerned which radio station to settle on. Katie liked soft-rock ballads, Maddie went
for jazz, and Carly, somewhat sheepishly, admitted to a fond-
ness for show tunes.

"It's Jack," she confessed. "Before I met him, I couldn't
stand that kind of music. But, Jack has a secret passion for
Smokey Joe's Cafe and *Bloomer Girl* and *Carousel* . . . He
sings them around the house all the time. He sings them to
the kids; for a while there, Sage could only fall asleep to 'Lul-
laby of Broadway,' and Parker would beg for Jack to do 'I
Won't Grow Up' from *Peter Pan*. Jack even sings them to me.
I couldn't help it. I developed a taste. I got to tell you, girls,
there is nothing like a man sincerely crooning, 'All I Ask of
You,' to make your knees absolutely melt."

Ah, yes, Katie was familiar with the knee-melting phe-
nomenon. In her case it was usually more a case of simmer-

ing to a languid, sensual boil. But the overall sentiment was one she could truly relate to.

"Mike does that for me just by smiling," she revealed. "I know, I know it's crazy. Everybody's got lips, everybody's got teeth, everybody smiles eventually . . . But there's something about the way Mike does it; like the smile is coming from inside of him, like it's something he's just been dying to share with you, and now you're here, and he's the happiest, luckiest guy in the world who's going to do anything he has to, to make you the happiest, luckiest woman." Katie shook her head. "I sound like an idiot, don't I? One minute I'm wondering if maybe Mike tried to kill me, and the next I'm writing greeting cards about his smile. I can't help it. It's like there are two Mikes out there. The guy I've been in love with for years. And this total stranger who keeps jumping out when I least expect it. I have to figure out which one he really is." She sighed. "Even when I'm furious with him, I can't help remembering all the stuff I love about him, too."

Carly looked at Katie sideways. "You mean you actually do love him?"

"Uhm . . . yeah, Carly. What did you think?"

"Frankly, I thought you were taking advantage of a genuinely nice guy after that jerk you're really in love with dumped you. Again." She shrugged apologetically.

"Speaking of taking advantage of a genuinely nice guy . . ." Katie turned the steering wheel a bit more sharply than was necessary. "All this talk of yours about being willing to do anything to protect Jack and preserve this flawless marriage of yours. You wouldn't even be here, suspecting your romantic, show-tune-singing husband of murder, if you hadn't cheated on him with a slime like Gregory!"

"You did?" Maddie exclaimed.

"I didn't!" Carly cried.

"Then why would Jack want to kill Gregory?"

Carly shook her head, and said nothing.

The hostile silence stretched on for a good five minutes, growing more and more uncomfortable until Maddie couldn't stand it any longer and, even though no one asked her, chimed in with, "Monica told me her parents had a rotten marriage. She doesn't think they ever loved each other. Or her."

"You know, I don't get that," Katie admitted, equally eager to break the tension, even if Carly continued to pout. "I see couples who were in love enough to make a baby, and then, a few years—heck, sometimes a few months—later, they can't even bear to be in the same room with each other. How does that happen? How do you go from love to total loathing?"

"That's the only way," Carly said out of the blue. "The more you loved someone, the more you hate them when it's over. It's only when you weren't really that invested, that you can remain friendly. Hal and I . . . I liked him when we got married. He was decent to me, and he's a great dad to Parker. That's why we're on good terms now. Because there was no major heartbreak there. Jack and I, though, every time we were apart, we wanted to rip each other to shreds."

"So you guys love each other that much, and you still cheated on him?" Maddie wanted to know.

"I said I didn't cheat on Jack!"

"You mean with Gregory?" Katie queried politely. "Or are we discussing Mike? Or Craig? Or Brad? Or Hal? Or—"

"Cut it out, Katie."

"Just wanted to know which story you were sticking to this week, that's all."

"I did not have an affair with Gregory. Not recently, anyway."

"So you did have one?" Maddie refused to be the only one not in the loop.

"A long time ago. Before I came to Oakdale. I had a six-month . . . thing with Gregory Marron."

"A thing?" Katie sought clarification.

"He bought me expensive items and I had sex with him."

"Ah. That kind of thing."

"I was young, I was stupid, and, God knows, I had no clue what love or a relationship really was."

"Carly, no offense here," Katie said, while Carly snorted at her disclaimer. "But, if Jack suddenly decided to start taking out every guy you'd ever slept with, he'd need to climb into a bell tower with a rifle. And bring lots of bullets. Why do you think Gregory Marron would drive him into more of a homicidal rage than Mike? Or Craig? Or—"

"Because. The day before he was killed, Gregory and Jack had . . . words."

"Words?"

"The kind of words that conclude with Jack slamming Gregory against the hood of our car."

"Ah. Those kind of words."

"I don't know what Gregory said to Jack. But I can make a

few guesses based on Jack's reaction. And then, afterward, at home, I just lost it. I went on and on to Jack about how terrified I was that Gregory would one day pop up out of nowhere to tell Parker and Sage the same rotten things about me that he'd spewed at Jack. I thought it would make my kids hate me. I thought I could lose them."

"Do you really think that's possible?" Katie asked gently.

"I don't know. All I know is, growing up, I hated my mother for being this awful, shallow, opportunistic social climber who cared more about money than she did about her husband and kid. I don't think I could stand it if Parker and Sage ever felt that way about me." A tear slipped from the corner of Carly's eye. She smacked it away, furious at herself for allowing such a vulnerable crack to show.

Neither Katie nor Maddie said a word.

Neither Katie nor Maddie knew what to say.

Embarrassed, Carly struggled to compose herself, explaining, "But Jack told me not to worry. That he would take care of the problem. And the next thing I knew, Jack was blowing off work for the afternoon to run some mysterious errand that nobody knew about. And volunteering that evening to oversee security at the Marron benefit. And then declaring Gregory Marron dead and having his body hustled away to his exclusive jurisdiction."

"Oh . . ." Katie said.

"Oh . . ." Maddie agreed.

This time, the silence in the car felt even more uncomfortable. Except that now Carly was the one desperate to end it.

"But that doesn't mean anything, right?" She looked

from one to the other. "Tell me that I'm overreacting again. Please. He wouldn't—Jack would never—"

"Well, the thing is, Jack does really love you a lot," Katie said. Carly wasn't sure how to interpret that. Was Katie trying to reassure her or was she suggesting that, because he loved her, Jack might be capable of . . .

"Jack's an officer of the law!" Carly reminded her.

"And he's broken the law before, Carly. For you."

"This is ridiculous," she insisted, though each of them, even Carly to some extent, realized the fervid assertion was more for her own peace of mind, than out of any genuine belief. If Carly really harbored no doubts about Jack's innocence, she wouldn't be protesting the possibility so vehemently. And she wouldn't be sitting in this car, heading for Genrikh's. "I'm sure that Jack didn't kill Gregory. Aurora did. That's why we're going to Chicago. To prove it."

"What if we can't?" Katie asked. "Are you going to let Mike go to jail if we can't come up with a better suspect?"

"Mike won't go to jail."

"He's got the entire Marron family, not to mention a detective on the Oakdale P.D., all highly motivated to see that he takes the fall. The last time that happened, Mike ended up in prison."

"The last time that happened, Mike was guilty. What makes you so sure this case is different?" Carly challenged.

"Because Mike wouldn't cold-bloodedly kill a man!"

"What about a woman? What about by 'accident'? What about you?" Carly pressed on.

Katie shook her head. "I know what I said. I know what I

feared. I've been so confused. But I believe in Mike's innocence. I owe him that much."

"That much and a lot more! The man has stood by you
through everything. And I'm not just talking about Simon,
here. I'm talking about that other crazy old flame of yours,
the computer geek who hired an actual hit man to kill Mike,
then tried to blow up the whole town because you didn't
want to play with his hard drive."

"That guy also had Henry locked up in a cellar," Maddie
reminded her.

"I know Mike didn't try to kill me. I've thought about it
and . . . and I just know." Katie tried to make them understand. "Mike Kasnoff saved my life. Not only literally, like
when he saved me from a bomb down in Australia, or from
Pilar and her knife, or when he saved me from that other
bomb, the one at the telethon here in Oakdale . . ."

"Boy, Katie," Maddie straddled the perfect balance between sarcastic and truly impressed. "You've sure had lots of
exciting things happen to you."

"It's her gift," Carly said, not even trying to hide the
sarcasm.

"The point is, Mike may have saved me from a bunch of
physical dangers, but he also saved me from losing my mind.
Simon had me convinced that I couldn't trust anybody. That
even the nicest-seeming guys had these dangerous secrets in
their closets and it was just a matter of time before they all
came shooting out—usually at me. Simon had me believing
that the only kind of man who would ever sincerely want to
be with me was a con artist looking for U.S. citizenship, or an
unhinged computer geek or—"

"Henry?" Maddie asked softly.

Katie bit her lip. "I loved Henry. I still love him. His friendship is one of the most important things in the world to me, and I will always, always be grateful for everything we've been through and all the jams he's pulled me out of. But Mike . . . Mike made me feel beautiful. He made me feel desirable and . . . worthwhile. Mike didn't only make me feel loved, he made me feel like I was worth loving. And I needed that. A lot."

Maddie said, "I'm jealous of you guys."

"Which one of us?" Carly asked. "The one who's afraid her husband killed her ex–sugar daddy, or the one who's afraid her boyfriend tried to run her down?"

"The ones who have somebody in their life that they love so much, they're willing to do anything to help them."

"Yeah, well, that and a nickel . . ."

"You have someone like that, too, Maddie," Katie reminded her. "You're in this car today because you're just as committed to protecting Henry as Carly and I are to helping Jack and Mike."

"Henry's my brother. It's not the same."

"Maddie, listen up," Katie said. "My brother, Craig, okay? He tried to blackmail me. Several times and on several different occasions. At the moment, I wouldn't drive across the street to help him out, much less to Chicago. And my brother actually is in jail."

"She's right, Maddie," Carly chimed in. "Katie's brother isn't worth one-eighth of yours."

"And Carly would know," Katie said under her breath. "She cheated on Jack with him, too."

Maddie said, "I just wish I had somebody in my life I was as crazy about as you two are."

"Believe me, Maddie," Carly said. "It ain't all it's cracked up to be."

"No," Katie couldn't help winking across the seat. "It's better."

As advertised, Genrikh's of Chicago proved to be an intimate store, crowded with more soup pots, stock pots, Crock Pots, saucepans, frying pans, sauté pans, and fondue sets than, well, had any right to exist on the planet.

"So all we need to do is figure out what exactly Aurora bought, and we're home free," Katie chirped. "That should be simple."

"Well, we know her store credit was for $347.96. The first thing we should do is find out what items sell for exactly that amount. It'll help narrow down the possibilities."

"Unless she bought more than one thing for that amount," Katie said.

"We'll worry about that later."

"Actually," Maddie interjected, "we should find out what items sell for exactly $312.99. We need to deduct the sales tax from the total. And the restocking fee."

"How the heck do you know what their restocking fee is?"

"I looked it up on their website. Thought the info might come in handy."

"You are a scary, scary, kid."

"Thank you, Carly."

The three of them spread out, each diligently turning over

every single sales tag in the place, until Katie finally got to whisper "Eureka!" and call them over with a stage whisper and frantic beckon.

"Behold! The Mauviel stainless-steel lined two-point-five-millimeter French Copper Saucepan. For the ultimate in cookware performance, you'll note. All yours for $312.99."

"You did it!" Maddie exclaimed. "Katie, you did it! This is the pan that can prove that Aurora killed Gregory!"

20

"Not exactly." If there was a balloon to burst, Carly always had a needle handy. "We can guess that this is *a* saucepan similar to the one Aurora bought, not *the* saucepan that she used to cook the cherry laurel poison. I doubt the store has only one model of every item available."

"This is the floor model," Katie insisted. "Isn't it likely they'd put a returned item out as the floor model?"

"Maybe. Maybe not. They've probably got another dozen in the back. Any one of them could be the saucepan Aurora returned. In fact, the saucepan Aurora returned could have already been resold."

"So there's only one solution," Katie shrugged. "We buy every Mauviel two-point-five-millimeter saucepan they have, take it to the police, and hope we get lucky."

"Katie! That could cost, like, five thousand dollars."

"We'll charge them. Well, you'll have to charge them, I'm a little over my limit at the moment. Long story, actually having to do with the Marron benefit, funny enough. But, obviously, this store takes returns."

"No," Carly said.

"Come on, just because it's my idea, doesn't make it stupid."

"The fact that it's stupid is what makes it stupid." Carly sighed. "Think about it, Katie. Even if we could afford to buy every saucepan in the place, our taking them to the police for analysis would just taint the chain of evidence. Even a marginally competent lawyer will be able to convince a judge that the three of us had plenty of opportunity to plant the poison before we gave the pans to the police. It would destroy the one physical piece of verification we potentially have."

Katie hated it when Carly had a point. But Carly had a point.

"Fine. So what do we do now?"

"We go back to Oakdale. We show Jack this receipt—"

"And tell him to deduct taxes and the restocking fee!"

Carly actually smiled at Maddie. "And tell him to deduct taxes and the restocking fee. We tell Jack what we've been up to, and then we let him use proper police procedure to figure out exactly which saucepan in this store is the one Aurora bought. We let Jack subpoena it, we let him bag it, and we let him test it."

Katie said, "Jack is going to want to know why you got involved in trying to solve Gregory's murder."

"Of course, he is."

"Are you ready to tell him everything?"

"No." She took a deep breath. "But I'm going to anyway."

Katie dropped Carly off in front of the police station. As she was pulling away, she rolled down the window and called, "Good luck."

"Thanks."

"No." After an afternoon of sniping back and forth, Katie understood why Carly might be hesitant to believe her. But she wasn't playing around now. "I mean it."

"Thanks," Carly repeated. But the sharp, sarcastic note had faded from her voice. "I'm going to need it."

Katie offered the one thing she knew she'd want to be reminded of prior to heading into the lion's den. "Jack loves you."

"Love has its limits."

"Not for you two. If it did, you two would have hit them a long, long, long, long—"

"Thank you, Katie."

"—Long time ago." Katie smiled.

"I'll let you know what he says."

"We'll be waiting."

"Oh, and Katie?"

"Yeah?"

"You and Mike make a cute couple. Don't know if I ever told you that."

"Thanks, Carly."

"Anytime."

*   *   *

"Carly?" Jack half rose from his chair in the detective's bull pen as soon as he saw her come in. "What's wrong? Did something happen to one of the kids? What are you doing here?"

"Everything's fine. The kids are fine. I'm fine."

He spread his arms. "Then what— I'm kind of busy here, honey. Can't this wait till I get home?"

"And when will that be?" Carly hadn't meant to go on the offensive, but his question reminded her of the long hours he'd been working lately.

"Soon. I promise. As soon as I can get this Marron business off my plate."

"But that's exactly what I want to talk to you about."

"Carly . . ." Jack said in a warning tone, looking around as if he expected a hidden microphone to materialize and record their conversation. "No. Not now. Not here."

"Then where? This can't wait."

He looked around again. No one in the precinct was paying attention to them. Hal was on the phone, scribbling notes and reassuring, "I'll get a uniform out there right away, just sit tight." Margo was busy at her computer. Jack and Carly, for all intents and purposes, were having a private conversation.

But it wasn't enough to satisfy Jack. He said, "Come on, if you really want to do this now, let's go talk."

They walked across the street to a park that consisted of a jungle gym and several trees to keep the worst of the car fumes from enveloping the playing children. At dusk, only the most dedicated of grade-school climbers were still hard at work, their mothers and sitters nearby.

Jack led her to a quiet corner of the park. "Carly, I told you, just let me handle this. I've got it under control—the Marrons won't be able to touch us."

"Under control?" Every fear she'd been doing her best to suppress over the past week came sweeping back like a wave looming so far over her head that Carly was left with no choice but to hold her breath and dive straight into the heart of it. "What does that mean? What are you saying?"

"It means that I'm keeping my promise. The Marrons won't harm our family. I've seen to that."

"Oh, Jack, I'm so sorry. If I could take back—"

"Well, you can't. What's done is done. We just have to figure out a way to live with it."

"I understand. And I want to help. I want to help you."

"The best way to help me right now is for you to just stay out of this whole thing. Don't go anywhere near this case. Let me handle it."

"You shouldn't have to do this alone."

"Alone is the only way I can do this. If you butt in, I won't be able to protect you. And if I can't protect you, you can't protect Parker and Sage."

"What do you mean, protect me—"

"I said let it go, Carly!"

"But I know something that could help solve this case!"

"Damn it!" Jack said. "Why can't you ever leave well enough alone?"

"Because. I think I know how you can prove that Aurora

Marron poisoned her husband. Well, at least that she was in on the plan."

"Aurora Marron?"

"Look, Jack." He appeared so shocked, Carly figured she'd better hurry up and show him her evidence, before the top of her husband's head blew off. "This is Aurora's credit card bill—"

"How the hell did you get that?"

"Katie Peretti." Carly did what Carly did best. She lied. Automatically and instinctively. Though unrehearsed, the reply tumbled so logically out of her mouth that Carly suspected some part of her must have anticipated Jack's question and was ready with a cover. "Katie has been looking into Gregory's death. You know, because of Mike's involvement. The afternoon of the funeral, she sneaked up to Gregory's study to look around and she found this bill. Aurora caught her. She must have known the bill incriminated her, and that's why she tried to have Katie killed."

"Say what?"

"I told you the night it happened, but you wouldn't listen! Sadie. The hit-and-run. It was meant for Katie, obviously. When that didn't work, Aurora sent Mike after all three girls . . . We have proof of that, too. Maddie found Mike's phone number in a trash basket in Aurora's bedroom."

"Maddie? Maddie Coleman? Katie Peretti? They've gotten themselves involved? Oh, God help us."

"It's all right. We've been working together."

"And that's supposed to make it okay?"

"Just listen to me, Jack, please. Yell at me all you like, later, but, right now, just listen to me. This credit card bill proves that Aurora ordered a saucepan from Genrikh's in Chicago, then returned it after a few days. You said the police tested all the cookware at the Marron estate, but they found no trace of poison, so you couldn't prove that it was made on the property. But if Aurora used the pan she bought and returned, she probably thinks the police will never find it. She thinks she's gotten away with it." Carly's voice rose with every revelation. "All you need to do is get the serial number from the store, track the pan down, test it, and you'll have evidence that Aurora was involved!"

Jack looked ready to take Carly up on her offer to yell at her all he liked. "You tampered with evidence?"

"No. No, I was really careful about that, I swear. Katie wanted to buy all the saucepans in stock, but I told her that would make it look like we had a chance to plant the poison and that you should be the one to get them, in your official capacity."

"I don't know if I can do that, Carly."

"But this could be a huge break in the case!"

"How am I going to explain where I got the credit card receipt? My wife and her friends did a little breaking and entering?"

"No!" Again, the lie came beautifully. "You searched Gregory's study legally. You must have a copy of this receipt. You just didn't realize what the credit meant."

Jack hesitated. "I suppose I could check the file . . ."

"I'm certain it's in there," Carly said.

"If I go track down this pot—"

"Saucepan."

"Whatever. If I do what you ask, do you promise me you'll drop this?"

"What do you mean?"

"I mean, no more sneaking into people's houses, no more stealing evidence, no more taking investigative day trips to Chicago . . . can I be any clearer, Carly?"

"I was just trying to help."

"Don't. You asked me to take care of your Gregory Marron problem. That's exactly what I've been trying to do ever since we ran into him. Let me do it my way. Trust me, Carly," Jack said sternly. "This is for all of us."

As always, Jack was a man of his word. Immediately after returning to the station, he went through the Marron file, confirmed that Carly was right about the store credit for a returned saucepan and, somewhat grudgingly but dutifully, filed the necessary paperwork to subpoena Genrikh's sales records.

After the correct saucepan was identified, requisitioned, tagged, and sent off to the lab, Jack told Carly that it would probably take at least three days for the forensic results to come in. Carly relayed the information to Katie and Katie gave the 411 to Maddie. And then the three of them settled down to wait.

In the time that it took the Oakdale P.D. to do its stuff, Carly cleaned her entire house from top to bottom. She went through all of Parker's and Sage's winter clothes to determine what still fit and what needed to be given away. She put away the snowsuits, snow boots, and sleds, and got out the blue jeans, baseball hats, and sand toys. Plus she darned a sock.

It was the very first sock Carly had ever darned.

Katie, meanwhile, did a lot of working out. She took an aerobics class, a spinning class, a step class, sports stretch, and African dance. All in one day. She told herself it was just to work off the tension of waiting for Jack to call with the forensic results. And had nothing to do with missing Mike at all.

As for Maddie, she went to school and she went to work at the Marrons'. The few times that her path crossed Aurora's, she observed the older woman closely, looking for clues that Mrs. Marron knew what was up.

"Oh, good morning, Madeline, are you here again today?" Aurora was standing at the top of the foyer stairs, dressed in a lavender suit with matching pumps, and looking down on Maddie, both literally and metaphorically.

"Um, yes, ma'am, I guess I am."

"Planning to do anything productive today, or is it to be more of the same?"

"Um . . ."

"Is my mother bothering you?" Monica appeared beside Maddie. When Aurora saw her daughter, she turned around and walked away without another word. Monica asked, "Did she say something nasty to you? Don't pay her any mind. She thinks that this project of mine is stupid, so obviously anyone associated with it is dumb by association."

"Oh, no, it's okay, she didn't—"

"That's good. She can't do anything to actually stop me

now. Thank goodness I don't have to stand around anymore, waiting for Gregory to write my allowance check while listening to him go on and on about how undeserving I am. It was like a little ritual with us. He'd sit at his desk and practically make me beg for it, while I had to keep my mouth shut and take it just in case he decided to slam the checkbook shut and go, 'Nope, sorry, not this week. I don't think you've earned it, my darling.' How's that for a father-daughter moment?"

"Gregory gave you your allowance?" Maddie asked, recalling the discrepancy Katie and Carly had brought up earlier. "Not your grandfather?"

"Granddad is only interested in his causes. Gregory dealt with Mother and me."

"That's interesting," Maddie said.

Jack said, "This is interesting."

"What?" Carly asked, so startled to see Jack coming home midmorning that she dropped the sock she'd been mangling.

"You were right, honey," Jack said. "We tracked down the exact saucepan that Aurora returned. And we found traces of cherry laurel on it."

"Oh my God!" Carly's shriek brought Parker, Sage, and the sitter running down the stairs, but Carly didn't care. This was good news. It had to be good news. Forget all the fears she'd articulated to Katie. Aurora killed Gregory. Jack didn't do it. This was good news. "Oh my God! That's it! Jack, you have her!"

"An officer is bringing her down to the station for questioning, as we speak."

"Are you the one who's going to question her?"

"I intend to be."

"Jack, please, you've got to let me hear this . . ."

21

Aurora arrived at the police station without a lawyer, wearing a light-green Chanel suit, carrying a dark-green Hermès bag, and declaring that this had better be brief, she had an important appointment very soon.

Jack asked her to please have a seat. Aurora replied that she would rather not. Jack suggested, rather strongly, that it would really be for the best if she accepted his offer.

"I'd like to speak to you about your husband's murder."

"I surmised as much."

Jack read Aurora her rights. She seemed unfazed and dismissed the opportunity he gave her to call her lawyer. He leaned back in his chair and gazed at her levelly. "Some new information has recently come up, suggesting that you may have been involved in the preparation of the poison that killed Gregory."

"That information would be in error. May I go now?"

"We found the cookware used to brew the potion."

"Fantastic. In Mr. Kasnoff's kitchen, I presume?"

"Actually, it wasn't in a kitchen at all."

"Really?" To the casual observer, even to Carly and Katie, who were watching the proceedings through a two-way mirror in the interrogation room (thanks to Carly's gentle yet persistent reminders to her husband regarding who'd brought him the evidence that delivered Aurora), the widow Marron appeared genuinely intrigued. "Then where? Buried in some Dumpster?"

"Genrikh's of Chicago," Jack said, and paused to gauge her reaction.

"I've heard of the store . . ." was all Aurora would admit.

"You more than heard of it, Mrs. Marron. You ordered a saucepan from it."

"Oh, don't be silly, my housekeeper is in charge of all that."

"You ordered a saucepan and used it to boil cherry laurel berries until you had enough cyanide to kill a small hippo, much less one man. Then you returned the saucepan to the store. We'd have never known about it, if it wasn't for the refund on your credit card statement."

"You would have never known about it, because it didn't happen. Honestly, Detective Snyder, is this your idea of a clever bluff? Because, I assure you, I never—"

He laid a copy of the credit card statement on the table in front of them. "Does this look familiar?"

Aurora angled her head so that she could review the document. Finally, she said, "It's mine. So what?"

"Note the credit from Genrikh's."

"It's a mistake. Not unexpected. Every single person who works there is perpetually making stupid mistakes."

"You sound like you know the store pretty well," Jack observed. "I thought you'd barely heard of it."

"Fine. I may have gone there once or twice for gifts. But I would certainly never shop there for myself. Mass-produced rubbish, all of it."

"You bought a saucepan there a little over a month ago." Jack didn't so much as blink. "The same saucepan that our forensics department reports tested positive for cherry laurels."

"No, Detective, I did not."

"Yes, Mrs. Marron, you did." Never taking his eyes off her, Jack reached into his file and placed a second photocopied sheet in front of Aurora. Katie and Carly couldn't see what she was looking at. But if they were to judge by the expression on Aurora's face, it was something pretty impressive.

"That is your signature, isn't it?" Jack inquired. "Right there on the receipt?"

"My signature," Aurora repeated.

"You bought that saucepan. And you used it to cook the poison that killed your husband."

Aurora nodded. It wasn't an actual, verbal confession, but still Aurora nodded. They all saw it.

"Is that what you did, Mrs. Marron?" Jack asked.

Aurora stopped nodding. She glanced up. She put her hands on the table and looked Jack straight in the eye. She said, "If I did kill him, I had a plethora of reasons to, didn't I?"

"I would assume so," Jack's voice, harsh and demanding only a minute before, had turned calm and cajoling. "For instance . . ."

"For instance my dear husband's womanizing—that's a good one to start with. The way he treated me . . . And not just me, his father, our daughter, too—like garbage, that's another gem."

"Yes, yes, I see."

"And of course there's always the classic motive—the money."

"The money?" Jack repeated, surprised. In his experience, this was the part right before the confession where the suspect tried to justify his actions, tried to appear sympathetic, righteous even, to persuade the police that the crime was inevitable and well deserved, to boot. Greed was hardly a sympathetic motive. But, then again, maybe in Aurora Marron's world, it was.

"What if I just got so tired of having my every little expense treated like I was asking for a handout? The man absolutely tortured us, forced me to beg for every tube of lipstick. The end of Gregory would mean the end of that little problem, wouldn't it? He'd be gone, and I'd be a wealthy widow."

"I guess 'divorcée' just didn't have the same ring to it?"

"Ring?" Aurora laughed. Definitely not the actions of a woman begging for mercy or understanding. If anything, she seemed furious. "As in cash register? As in precious jewels? As in finally being able to do what I want, when I want, with no one to answer to? As in finally being in control of my own destiny? No, Detective, 'divorcée' definitely had a different ring to it than 'widow.' "

Jack stood up. "Aurora Marron, you are under arrest for the murder of Gregory Marron Jr."

"I want my lawyer."

"We asked you earlier, and you refused—"

"I said I want my damn lawyer! Now!"

"We did it!" Katie grabbed Carly by the shoulders and shook her in lieu of an actual hug, which would have been too warm and too fuzzy too fast. "We did it! We solved the case!"

"Not exactly," Carly pointed out. "What Aurora just did— it wasn't exactly a confession. She didn't say she killed Gregory, she just spun out some scenarios of why she might have . . ."

"That's just a legal technicality. Did you see her face when Jack confronted her with the receipt? She knows she's busted. And if she's busted, that means Mike and Henry and Jack are cleared!"

Katie grabbed her cell phone, dialing Mike to tell him that it was all over, the case was solved, they could move on with their lives and pretend this little . . . stumble . . . never happened.

Of course, just at the moment of their greatest triumph, Mike's carrier reported that the customer she was trying to reach was unavailable.

So Katie went to Plan B and, as Carly stepped out of the room to speak to Jack, Katie went for the next person she knew would be thrilled to hear about how everything went down. She called Maddie.

Maddie was in class.

What was it with young people today? So responsible, so studious. So boring.

Katie left a message, but it still wasn't the same as actually telling somebody. And Katie really, really wanted to tell somebody. In person. So she could watch their reaction. And collect the appropriate accolades.

What good was cracking a major murder mystery if there were no accolades?

Fortunately, there was still one person she could think of who would love to hear the play-by-play. One who was also good at the accolades.

Katie went to the bakery, bought a dozen fresh mini-cannolis, and drove over to see Nancy Hughes.

"Tell me all about it!" As expected, Nancy was thrilled to see Katie and the cannolis, as well as to hear the latest scoop first-hand. "Was it something Gig said at lunch that day? Was it something you noticed at the funeral? Sit down, my dear. Sit down and tell me how in the world you put everything together."

Katie grinned. She took Nancy through the entire process step by step, making sure to emphasize the areas in which she proved particularly prescient—though remembering to periodically add that well, yeah, Carly and Maddie helped a bit, too—right through to the triumphant end, where Aurora confessed all and how it was obviously just a matter of time before Mike was officially off the hook.

"Aurora?" Nancy repeated. "Aurora confessed?"

"Well, according to Carly, not exactly in the legal sense. But it was so obvious from the way she was behaving. Aurora is the guilty party. Isn't it wonderful?"

"No, Katie, it's not."

"Oh, I know what you mean. It's a terrible tragedy and may Gregory rest in peace and hopefully Monica and Gig will be able to move on with their lives and—"

"That's not what I meant. Are you sure you know precisely what happened?"

"Well, not precisely-precisely. But I have a general idea. Aurora said it herself—in that roundabout way of hers—she did it for the money. Gregory had her on an allowance and she got tired of—"

Nancy held up one finger. When that finger went up, the world, and that included Katie, knew to be quiet.

"Not Gregory," Nancy said. "Gig. Gig had all of them on an allowance."

"Are you sure?"

"Positive. I've known Gig for a very long time, before Gregory and Aurora got married, and it's always been this way. The family trust is set up so that the children don't inherit until the father dies. Gig had to wait to take control of the fortune from his own father, and Gregory was champing at the bit to do the same. That's why he was attempting to discredit Gig. If Aurora said she killed Gregory in order to come into money—"

"She did. Sort of. She said she wanted to be a wealthy widow."

"Well, then, she's lying. Gregory had no money to leave her, even if he had been so inclined."

"So you're saying we've got the wrong motive?"

"Katie, I'm afraid Jack has arrested the wrong person."

Maddie's cell phone rang in the middle of sixth-period calculus class. Which was the absolutely wrong time for it to ring. Not only was she taking a test, chasing a recalcitrant X all over a triple-decker equation, but her teacher had, just the other day, finished a long lecture on the decline of polite society in general, and the rudeness of cell phones in particular. She informed her students that anyone who couldn't remember to put his or her phone on vibrate during class time deserved to have the item confiscated. And that she would be happy to do the honors.

Now, Maddie had just lived through a pretty exciting two weeks. What with the whole dead body, police dropping by, attempted vehicular homicide, cracking a murder case adventure. She'd had other matters on her mind besides turning her cell phone on vibrate.

Her teacher, however, did not.

She held out her hand and waited for Maddie to walk all the way from the third row to the front of the room to hand it over. Maddie did. But not before seeing that it was Katie calling.

"Please," she begged. "Can't I just go outside and take it for a minute? It might be really important."

"If you take that call, Madeline, you forfeit the midterm. It's your choice."

Maddie handed over the phone and went back to chasing her X.

She had to wait until the period was over to politely request the return of her phone, and then she had to listen to an addendum about the ill manners of young women, Madeline Coleman in particular, before her request was honored.

Once out though, she ran for a quiet corner and listened to Katie's entire message about Aurora Marron's confession, needing to squelch her squels of delight—and anger over not having been there to see it unfold live—by clamping a hand over her mouth.

A group of kids walking by, including Margo's son, Casey, mumbled something about Maddie being even weirder than they all first thought. Which was when she figured her vague fantasies of fitting in would have to wait to be fulfilled until she entered another school. Or maybe college.

But who cared if she would never be Maddie Coleman, homecoming queen. She was Maddie Coleman—Supersleuth! Take that, Casey Hughes!

Maddie looked at her watch. Two more hours of school and three more subjects—biology, gym, and history to go. Maddie figured she knew enough about the birds and the bees from reading D. H. Lawrence, had worked up an ample sweat being chased down by a speeding car, and had a chance to make some history of her own right here and now.

She blew off the rest of the day and caught the bus home.

*   *   *

Initially Maddie intended only to stop off at the apartment, dump her bookbag, change out of her itchy school clothes, and head over to Katie's. What she got, however, was a 3-D, live and in-person lesson in the birds and the bees from her brother—and Monica Marron.

22

They were about as close to naked as two still-clothed people could be.

Henry was lying on his back on the couch, pants off, every shirt button undone, yellow smiley face boxers on full display, while Monica was stretched out on top of him, her sweater pushed up beyond her bra strap, her skirt waving good-bye to her thighs.

Henry heard the front door open, raised his head, and froze. Well, actually, first he pushed Monica off of him, then he froze.

"Why aren't you at school?" Henry demanded.

"Why aren't you wearing pants?" Maddie shot back.

Henry looked down, realized she was quite right, and stiffly crossed his legs, as though that would either answer her question or rectify the situation.

"Hi, Maddie."

"Hi, Monica."

Her boss giggled. "Pretty awkward, huh?"

Maddie clicked her tongue against the roof of her mouth. "That's one word for it."

"We can explain—"

"There is nothing to explain," Henry said, putting on his pants. "I'm an adult, Monica's an adult, and you, Maddie, are a child. We don't owe you an explanation."

Monica said, "It's not that we wanted to lie to you, Maddie. In fact, the longer this went on, the more we both wanted to tell you everything."

"Uh-huh." Maddie dropped her bookbag on the floor and counted off on her fingers. "So you say this has been going on for a while? This must mean that you guys only pretended you barely knew each other back at her house after the funeral. And also at the hospital. That's really adult behavior."

"There was a very good reason for that," Henry said.

"Which is?"

"We didn't want you to know."

Monica, her tousled clothes now back in place, gently rested her palm on Maddie's elbow. "This is all my fault."

"Hey, hey, give me a little credit here." Henry, struggling to rebutton his shirt, jimmed his way into the conversation. "Poor girl couldn't resist that famous Coleman charm. Happens to everyone."

Monica said, "I was the one who asked Henry to keep our relationship a secret."

"And why might that be?"

"Because Gregory and Aurora would have pitched a fit if

they knew I was in love with the help. And not even full-time help, at that."

"Sleeping with a chauffeur sans dental plan," Henry explained. "That just isn't done in Monica's social circle."

"You know, Henry," Maddie said, "I've been meaning to mention this to you for a while now: You're not nearly as funny as you think you are."

"Hey, hey, hey. No reason to get snippy."

"Maddie," Monica held up both of her arms as if she were a referee. "Please try to understand. What happened between Henry and me was so out of the blue. . . . He literally swept me off my feet. It was like nothing I'd ever experienced before."

"That Coleman charm I mentioned earlier? It's really out of my control."

Monica continued, "At first, everything was so new, I wanted to keep it to myself. Just Henry and me in our own private world. I know it was selfish, but it added to the fun, our having this secret. It brought us closer together. Then, when I realized that this wasn't just a crush or a fling, that this could really be something meaningful, Henry and I decided it was finally time to go public with our relationship. We were going to tell my family after the hospital gala. But, then, Gregory . . ."

"You can see, Maddie, how that wasn't exactly the time for Monica to spring another shocker on the folks."

"I'm not Monica's folks," Maddie pointed out.

"Oh, I know that, Maddie, believe me, I know how you must feel. That's why when I ran into you at Fashions—"

"You knew who I was when you saw me at Fashions?"

"Henry had shown me your picture. He's so proud of you, you know. He told me everything, how you're a straight-A student, computer whiz. . . . I was dying to get to know you better. That's why, when we had that lucky run-in at Fashions, everything just fell into place. I thought if I offered you the job, we could become friends. Plus, I know how tight money has been for you two lately, and Henry refuses to take a loan from me—"

"No, no more loans from the Marron family, thank you," Henry said.

"I thought this could also be a way for me to help you guys out financially."

"You could have told me all this. I know how to keep my mouth shut."

"You're right," Monica said. "Now that I've gotten to know you, I know that you are absolutely right—we could and should have trusted you. Henry wanted to level with you from the beginning. I was the one who begged him not to. Because I was scared of whom you might tell. Henry only went along with my wishes because he's a gentleman. That's one of the main reasons I love him. They just don't make men like your brother anymore. He's this incredible throwback to a time when people still had manners and a sense of humor, not to mention style and class."

"Yeah," Maddie agreed. "He's something, all right."

"So if you're going to be mad at anyone, be mad at me." Monica smiled. "But, I hope you won't be mad for long. I've had so much fun working with you these last few days. I'd hate to think that was over."

Maddie looked away and crossed her arms.

"Henry"—Monica had to stand on her tiptoes to kiss him—"call me when you and Maddie have worked everything out. And Maddie"—she reached for her purse—"I hope I'll see you out at the house tomorrow. I've got a lot of cool stuff to show you." She smiled hopefully, said "Bye, guys," and closed the front door behind her.

Henry said, "Look, Maddie, I know this was a shock, but, the thing is, we really thought—"

"How convenient," Maddie observed.

"Say what now?"

"How convenient that Monica Marron discovered her great passion for you just before her dad gets mysteriously knocked off. In your car."

"Well, yeah, obviously the timing could have been better, but . . ." Henry trailed off as Maddie's implication finally hit him. "Oh, no, kiddo. No, no, no, no. Don't you even think what you're thinking, because you're wrong. Dead wrong."

"So it never crossed your mind?" she challenged. "Not even for a minute?"

"Never ever, not even for a minute."

"It's all just a coincidence, then? The boss's daughter, out of the blue, throws herself at you—"

"Coleman charm, baby. She was powerless to resist."

"You guys start up this hot and heavy affair and then her dad croaks in your car?"

"I know the facts, Maddie. Your repeating them over and over again isn't going to change the reality that Monica had nothing to do with Gregory's murder. The cops said his wine was poisoned, right? Well, Monica never had a minute alone to tamper with it, I was with her the whole time in the car—"

"You were what with her where?"

"Oh, God." Henry covered his face with his hands.

"Monica was with you in the car the day Gregory died?"

"You're making too big a deal out of this."

"I don't think so. Jack Snyder just arrested Aurora for Gregory's murder and it turns out Monica was in the car with you and the wine bottle before he died? You didn't think that little tidbit was worth sharing with Margo when she was over here?"

"Hold on, wait up, rewind. Aurora is under arrest? How do you know?"

"Katie told me."

"And how in the world did Katie know?"

The lies didn't come quite as easily for Maddie as they had for Carly, but there was still barely a pause before she managed to come up with, "Mike. Because of Mike. See, he was the primary suspect because of his fingerprints on the bottle, so Katie's been following the case very closely and I just happened to call Katie today, and she happened to, just coincidentally, have talked to Carly and—"

"Fast-forward," Henry urged. "Get to the part about Aurora being arrested."

"Oh, right. That. Somehow, I really have no idea how, Jack found these pans that Aurora bought and returned to the store that tested positive for the poison used to kill Gregory, so he confronted her and she all but confessed and now she's under arrest."

"But that's fantastic!" Henry exclaimed.

"Not really for her."

"It's fantastic for Mike. This will get him off the hook once and for all. Tell me, was Katie thrilled, was she over the moon? This is great, great news. I can't believe you didn't tell me this as soon as you walked through the door."

"You were kind of busy, remember?"

He remembered. "And Monica. This is great news for Monica."

"Oh, yeah, I know. If I heard my mom was in jail for poisoning my dad I'd be throwing a Mardi Gras."

"Well, not that part, obviously not that part. But she's been so nervous that if the cops found out she was with me in the car, they'd get all sorts of ideas—"

"Pretty reasonable ideas, if you ask me."

"Absolutely not. Maddie, baby, listen to me. This thing with Monica, she said it herself, what we've got, it's real. I haven't felt like this since Katie. This girl, she gets me. She gets my jokes, she gets my oh so painfully obscure cultural references, and she gets me."

"That's what I'm afraid of," Maddie said. "She gets what a nice guy you are, which means she gets how easy it is to make you see only the good in people."

"Thank you very much, Maddie. Thank you so, so much. Even my own sister thinks I can't get a girl to fall for me unless there's some ulterior motive."

He looked so crushed, Maddie was sincerely tempted to

walk out the door, all the way back to calculus class, and pretend this entire afternoon had never happened. But she couldn't do that. The best she could do was verbally backpedal, "Oh, Henry, I didn't mean it like that."

"Is there a nice way to say: Hey, dude, I think your gal pal played you for a fool and only cuddled up so she could knock off her stepdaddy and find a sucker to alibi her?"

"Did she?" In spite of loathing to hurt him again, Maddie couldn't help asking.

"Did she what?"

"Get you to give her an alibi, too?"

"No! Monica didn't need an alibi for when Gregory was killed, because she didn't do it."

"Then why didn't you tell Margo that Gregory's daughter had access to the wine bottle while it was with you in your car?"

"Because she didn't—why can't you get that? Monica and I were only together for about an hour. It was my lunch break. But man can't live by bread alone, you get my meaning?"

"Almost as if I saw it taking place right in front of me."

"Right. Well, anyway," Henry said, blushing crimson, "the bottle was in the bar in the back, which means I had my eyes on it the whole time we were there. It stayed in its place until it was time for me to serve it to Gregory."

"And you never left Monica alone for a second?"

"You heard the girl. I'm an old-fashioned gentleman. I don't multitask."

"Where were you guys that you could have sex in the back of a limo and nobody noticed?"

"Out behind Emma Snyder's farm. They have that lake everyone uses in the summer, then there's a deserted patch of wood. It's invisible from the highway. You have to know there's a dirt road. No signs or anything, so hardly anybody goes there, it's nice and private."

"Perfect place to ditch a murder weapon."

"Would you get off that, already! Didn't you say Aurora confessed? I'm a legal professional, Maddie. My private investigator license is still valid in several Illinois counties. I know what a confession means. It means: case closed!"

"And you don't think for a minute that they could be in this together? Mother-daughter bonding, not to mention they both hated him. A lot."

"Monica wouldn't help her mother kill time, much less Gregory. She is not that kind of person. She's decent and honest and—"

"Was Monica the person who called you right after Margo left? The one who you told not to worry, you didn't say a word about her?"

"You were eavesdropping?"

"Yes, I was, and you're the one who taught me how to do it."

"Drat, hoisted on my own petard."

"So was it Monica?"

"It was, yes."

"Which means your decent and honest girlfriend asked you to lie for her, Henry. On what planet is that considered decent? Or honest?"

"Hey, I didn't lie. If Margo had asked me: Say, Henry, was

Monica Marron by any chance in your car with you between the hours of one and two P.M. on—"

"You taught me that particular trick, too. We both know what a crock it is."

"Watch your language, young lady. There's a gentleman present."

"You have to tell the police about Monica."

"No, Maddie, I don't. They've got their woman in custody."

"And if Monica was involved . . ."

"She wasn't."

"What about Mike?"

"What about Mike? You said he was cleared."

"No. You said he was cleared. I only said they'd arrested Aurora. What if Jack Snyder tries to say they were working together, what then?"

"Maybe they were, how would I know?"

"So Mike Kasnoff, the guy you called your friend, beloved by your beloved, the guy you think is good enough to be with the woman you love—"

"Loved. Katie is in the past."

"You have no problem believing that guy might have had something to do with Gregory's murder?"

"I didn't say I knew. I said I didn't know."

"But Monica, who you've only been boinking for a few weeks—"

"Hey, I said watch your—"

"She's above suspicion?"

"Maddie, look, I gave Monica my word that I would keep

her out of this. She has a lot of very complicated feelings about her stepfather, and if she were forced to lay them out in front of Jack or, God forbid, a jury and, by extension, the media, I don't know if she could handle it. She likes to pretend she's tough, that nothing bothers her. But she is really very fragile. She needs someone to take care of her, someone to believe in her. God knows those rotten parents of hers never did. I promised to be that guy. I've sworn to be her champion. I can't let her down."

"Really?" Maddie asked. "Because, you know what? I can."

"Don't," Henry said. And it wasn't an order or even a request. It was a plea. "I am asking you, Maddie, not for Monica, but for me, please keep what I've just told you to yourself. I don't want to pull big-brother rank but, what the heck, it's the only card I've got. I have always looked out for you. I took you into my house and let you turn my life upside down and didn't say boo about any of it. Well, now, Maddie, I'm saying boo. I'm saying it's my turn to ask for a favor and your turn to go out of you way for me, for a change."

She knew that he was right. But that was only because he didn't realize that she'd already been doing that all along. "Henry, actually, the reason I—"

"I don't care what your reasons are, okay? I don't care if you're just mad at Monica and me for keeping secrets from you, or because you think you owe Katie and Mike some kind of consideration after all the stunts you pulled on them a while back—"

"They've both forgiven me for that. Well, Katie's kind of

forgiven me. I'm not sure about Mike. I think he just likes to pretend I never existed."

"It doesn't matter. Even if you don't believe a word Monica and I said this afternoon, I am asking you to keep my confidence. For no other reason than because I'm your big brother. And because I asked you to, Maddie."

23

"Have you heard from Maddie lately?" Carly asked Katie.

They sat side by side on wooden benches in the third row of the Oakdale courthouse, waiting for Aurora Marron's bail hearing to commence. Neither the judge, nor the lawyers, not even the suspect herself had arrived, but Carly and Katie wanted to make sure they had good seats for the proceedings.

"No. And it's weird, too. Because I left her a message yesterday saying Aurora had been arrested. I thought for sure she'd call back to get all the gory details."

"Maybe she didn't get the message?"

"She did. I called her again this morning. I wanted to tell her about the hearing, but she just blew me off. Said she had a big test to take and how I shouldn't call her again because the school didn't allow cell phones. It was strange. All the work she put in, and now it's like she's over it and on to something else."

"Well, she's a kid. You know how kids are. One day they're one hundred percent jazzed about this or that, the next week they couldn't care less."

Katie shrugged. "I suppose . . ."

"So tell me, how are things with you and Mike? Back on track?"

"No," Katie said. "I tried calling him yesterday, but he didn't pick up. I went to his worksite but one of his guys told me Mike was too busy to talk. So I barged in—"

"No one can accuse you of not being persistent, Katie, I'll give you that."

"Mike just looked at me. And then he asked, 'Katie, how did my fingerprints get on that wine bottle?' "

"He asked you that? What did you say?"

"What could I say? I said, 'I don't know, Mike.' And then he just looked away like I'd broken his heart all over again."

"You should have said, 'It doesn't matter.' "

"But it does matter! That's the problem. No matter how many times I try to tell myself that I know Mike, that he's a good person . . . it *does* matter. I can't live with all this . . . stuff . . . between us. I need him to trust me."

"And he needs you to trust him."

"How are things between you and Jack?" Katie asked.

Carly smiled wryly. "And most certainly no one can accuse you of being subtle."

Or willing to drop a subject of interest. Especially when it deflected attention from her own woes.

"Things any better with you two on the home front?" Katie wondered.

"Jack hasn't been home," Carly confessed.

"Oh, that can't be a good thing."

"You don't think so either, huh?"

The opening of the door silenced them. Carly and Katie turned their heads to observe Jack entering with D.A. Tom Hughes, followed by Aurora, dressed down for the occasion in a black suit and only a tasteful pair of pearl earrings. She was escorted by the overly tanned lawyer Carly first spotted at Gregory's funeral. What *was* his name? I.E.? A.I.? I.Q.?

"L.B." Aurora grabbed his elbow.

Ah! That's what it was! L.B.! Well, Carly had been close.

Aurora directed her lawyer's attention toward the two women. "What the hell are they doing here?"

"The courtroom isn't closed," Katie pointed out.

"I don't want them here," she said.

"I'll take care of it," L.B. promised, moving to address the judge who was coming in through a back entrance, and leaving Aurora with Carly and Katie.

"Are you happy?" she hissed at Carly.

"I'm not depressed, if that helps."

"This is all your fault. Don't think I don't know what you did."

"Now *that* makes me happy."

"Why couldn't you leave well-enough alone, you little tart?"

"I'm a lover of justice. Even the poetic kind."

"You don't know anything, Carly. You don't know anything about anything that really matters. And you—" Aurora turned to Katie. "Haven't you learned your lesson?"

Before Katie could reply, Carly butted in with, "What the hell does that mean?"

Aurora said, "Katie knows."

She might have been willing to say more. But, at that moment, the bailiff showed up to politely inquire if Mrs. Snyder and Ms. Peretti wouldn't be more comfortable in the hall? Carly and Katie assured him that they were fine where they were. He assured them that actually, they were not. And escorted the pair from the courtroom.

"She threatened me again, didn't she?" Katie demanded. "That was Mrs. Aurora Marron reprising one of her greatest hits, 'Let's Scare the Hell Out of Katie.' "

Once ejected, Katie and Carly didn't merely leave the courtroom. To avoid being chased away a second time—the bailiff may have mentioned something about a contempt-of-court charge—they walked down the hall and took the elevator to the main floor, exiting through the revolving glass doors to stand on the steps of the courthouse.

A crowd of reporters was concentrated on the sidewalk, jostling for an obviously nonexclusive shot of Aurora arriving. Just for the heck of it, Carly skipped down to tell them that Mrs. Marron was already inside—she must have used a back entrance.

The correspondents nearly ran Carly over, scrambling and elbowing to be the first inside. After them came the rubber-neckers, followed by folks who dared to have other business to take care of on the day of Aurora Marron's bail hearing. That left Carly and Katie alone on the steps. And prompted the younger woman to voice her fear about Aurora's obscure threats.

"It was nothing," Carly reassured. "Obviously she—or that lawyer of hers—understands that you're going to be called to testify about Sadie's murder and your and Mike's accident. She just wants to intimidate you."

"She's very good at it."

"She's behind bars."

"She's out," Aurora said.

In what must have taken barely fifteen minutes, the alleged husband-killer who'd publicly threatened Katie with, well, something indeterminately scary, was sweeping by her two accusers, again holding on to her lawyer's arm.

Only this time, she was also smiling triumphantly. "Have a lovely day, ladies."

"She's going to kill me," Katie said.

"No, she's not. She wouldn't be that stupid."

"Aurora Marron's I.Q. is all that's standing between me and certain death? I'd like roses at my funeral, please. And Henry should have custody of Snickers the First and Second."

"You're going to be fine."

"Sure, right, maybe I am. Maybe I'll get lucky and Nancy Hughes is right."

"What about Nancy Hughes?" Carly asked.

"Oh, didn't I tell you? Nancy thinks we've caught the wrong killer. She doesn't believe Aurora's motive and doesn't believe she did it."

"That's ridiculous. She practically confessed."

"Maybe there's another nut out there looking to kill me,"

Katie mused. "Or maybe, the nut who poisoned Gregory and the nut who killed Sadie are two different people. Maybe Sadie's murder had nothing to do with me. Of course, there's still the matter of Mike's running me off the road. He either did it himself or was prompted by Aurora. But why would Aurora do that if she didn't kill Gregory? And if Aurora didn't kill Gregory, why would she threaten me?"

"Calm down, Katie, you're babbling."

"I am not babbling. Babbling is what I do in the course of an average day. What I am doing right now is getting totally and completely paranoid. Which, of course, does not mean that they really aren't out to get me. Of course, I don't know who *they* are . . ."

Thankfully, Katie's cell phone rang.

It was Maddie on the other end.

She said there was something important she really needed to speak to Katie and Carly about, could they come see her right away?

Maddie told Katie and Carly everything.

They met her after school, arriving in separate cars and sitting down under a tree on campus to get the whole story. It took much longer than it should have. Maddie kept stopping, starting, apologizing for stopping and starting, changing her mind, explaining that she really did love and trust her brother and she only wanted what was best for him, and, at long last, bursting out with, "But, see, I owe you guys, too. You've been so nice to me. You've treated me like a grown-up. And, well, you two are like the first female friends I ever had." Then, while chewing on each fingernail twice over, she finally told Carly and Katie everything.

Carly summarized, "Monica had the opportunity to poison the wine bottle."

"And then toss the syringe into Snyder Woods," Katie added.

Maddie nodded her head, then shook it, disagreeing with herself before she even spoke. "Henry swears he was with her and would have seen if—"

"Henry is a man getting laid for the first time in—how long?" Carly asked Katie.

"A very long while."

"Then his judgment isn't admissible in court." In response to the doubtful looks: "No. Really. Check the statutes. Excessive horniness is a real condition and it makes for a completely useless witness."

Katie said, "I'm going to check it out."

"Please don't talk to Monica," Maddie begged. "She'll tell Henry and he'll be so mad at me if you don't find anything."

"I have no intention of talking to anyone. I'm going to Snyder Woods to see if I can find that missing syringe. Nancy Hughes doesn't think Aurora killed Gregory. Let's see if we can find evidence of who really did."

Neither Carly nor Maddie were thrilled about Katie's idea. But, as noted earlier, persistence was one thing Katie actually was pretty good at. She convinced Carly to drive Maddie home, while Katie went in her own car to the scene of the crime.

"You've heard of a needle in a haystack, Katie?" Carly recalled. "You do realize that, in this case, we're talking literally."

"I'm not going to search the entire woods. Henry said he parked at the end of the dirt road behind the pond. I know where that is. All I'm going to do is search the radius of where the average woman can throw. That's not that far."

"I hate to sound like a broken record," Carly said. "But chain of evidence, chain of evidence, chain of evidence—need I go on?"

"Hey, I love a chain of evidence as much as the next licensed private detective—"

"Actually, Katie," Maddie interjected, "Henry told me there was some problem with that."

"In any case, I understand what you're saying, Carly. But I also get that it was one thing to come to Jack with a credit card statement and convince him to investigate Genrikh's, and another to do this. Right now, we don't have any evidence chain to break. We only have Maddie's word—which is hearsay; see, I did read my detective handbook once or twice. The best Jack would be able to do with Maddie's information is go to Henry or Monica, who'll both deny the whole thing, and he won't have a legal leg to stand on. If he goes looking for the syringe based on Maddie's word, it could look like planted evidence. My way: I go to the woods and find the syringe. I bring it to Jack like any concerned citizen would do. We keep Jack's hands clean. Which is important, right, Carly? Do we want a defense attorney bringing up Detective Snyder's motive for being overly interested in Gregory Marron Jr.'s case?"

"You have a point," Carly said.

"Yes, I do. And I also know I'm doing this for all of us. I won't screw up. I promise."

Katie did her best to keep that promise.

It wasn't easy. For one thing, to get to the north side of Snyder Woods she had to drive on the same road where the car accident had happened. In broad daylight, with a dry pavement, the sun shining so hard she actually had to lower her visor, every potential pitfall brightly illuminated, it didn't look nearly as ominous. In fact, with the grazing deer and scurrying squirrels, the only thing missing was for Snow White to come skipping out from between the trees, stretch prettily, and get ready to greet a new day. There was absolutely nothing for Katie to be afraid of.

Except a suspicion she couldn't shake, that she was being followed.

The last time Katie thought she was being followed, it was back at the unnaturally dark gym, where the intruder was only Henry. Of course, now that Katie knew the latest about his peripheral role in Gregory's death, she couldn't help wondering: If Henry was in some sort of cahoots with Monica to kill her father, wouldn't he want Katie out of the way, too?

She decided not to go there.

Even if it *was* trivially easy to imagine Henry and Monica setting up Maddie to find them in flagrante delicto, then feed her the story about the tryst out in the woods knowing that she would run to Katie, and Katie would run straight to

a dark, secluded, out-of-the-way place where one good bru-
tal *wham, bam, shut up, ma'am*—and no one would ever
know what happened to her.

Just how deep was Snyder Pond, anyway? Certainly deep
enough to hide a dead body . . .

Katie firmly ordered her mind not to wander. If she kept
going down this creepy path, there was a danger it might decide not to come back.

And so she drove on, forcing herself to focus on the pretty
countryside and not on the less than pretty notions swirling
around her head like a blood-filled lava lamp.

If she couldn't think about who wanted her dead and the
many creative ways they might go about fulfilling that re-
quirement, then she would think about Mike. And not about
her hope that he wasn't the person who wanted her cre-
atively dead. Katie would think about Mike and what she
could do to make him believe she trusted him again. Even
though, if there was one thing she'd learned the last few days,
it was that, when you got right down to it—she didn't.

Katie didn't trust Mike. Not anymore, maybe not ever. If
she had, then why did she break up with him so many times?
Would a woman who truly trusted her man keep looking so
hard for more and more innovative excuses to stay away? Obviously, Katie's subconscious had understood her true feelings even before they were pushed to the surface by
Gregory's murder. Her subconscious knew that Katie didn't
trust Mike.

And yet, she still loved him. That was the crux of the problem. She loved him, and she wanted to be with him, and she

missed him. But she couldn't be with him. Katie wasn't even sure why anymore.

At one point, finding Gregory's real killer had been Katie's route for proving her loyalty. But then why couldn't she let the fingerprints-on-the-wine-bottle clue go?

It probably had nothing to do with anything.

A woman who truly loved her man would believe that.

Katie couldn't believe that.

If there was really nothing to the story, then Mike would have told her the story. But, he was hiding something. She didn't know what. And she couldn't live with that.

It was all Simon's fault.

But Katie was the one being forced to pay the price.

She saw her turn up ahead and skidded in between two hunched trees that masked a well-grooved dirt road leading straight to the outskirts of Snyder Woods. With oaks and maples blocking out the sun, what had just a minute ago been a lovely drive through the countryside began, disturbingly, to resemble the forest of Katie's concussion-induced nightmare.

When the woods got too dense, she parked her car, guestimating this was where Henry and Monica would have stopped, as well. The spot left her with three directions in which to search for the missing syringe. Katie tried to be logical about it. She imagined that, if Monica stepped out of the car to perform a furtive task, she would instinctively do it on the side closest to the woods, away from the road and from Henry's line of vision—which meant the right passenger side. She would also probably throw straight ahead in an attempt to hurl the syringe as far as possible, and aim for an already clogged spot. Which meant that, following this imaginary trajectory, Katie needed to begin her search right in the belly of the beast, around the most weed-covered tangle of bushes and overgrown stumps that she could find.

Katie took a deep breath. And got a nose and throat full of scratchy pollen that made her sneeze. She changed tactics and proceeded to inhale in quick, shallow puffs as she stepped toward her destination.

Her first step resulted in something crackling beneath her shoe, then hissing. Her second resulted in something squishing, then leaking. Katie didn't know which to prefer, so she simply kept moving.

About three feet in, right around where Katie thought a robustly tossed syringe might have landed, she found, to her disgust, inside a tangle of mushrooms and moldy leaves, a discard pile of another sort. She found condoms. Dozens upon dozens of multicolored, used-and-thrown-away condoms. She had no idea Oakdale was such a safe-sex-conscious town, considering how many unplanned pregnancies floated just through her own family, not to mention the rest of the community.

She heard a sound.

Katie was aware that the woods were typically full of sounds; birds chirping, owls hooting, flowers blooming, trees budding, the whole kit and caboodle that was nature's great circle of life. She got that. She also got that none of the above sounds included creeping footsteps.

She knew she should probably turn around.

But if she turned around then she would see who it

was. And Katie wasn't sure if she was really ready to see who it was.

And so, instead of turning around, Katie did the opposite. With the most direct path back to her car blocked by her pursuer, she did exactly what every idiot in every horror move ever did (and it was usually the last thing they did, too)— Katie ran. Katie ran as far and as fast as she could away from the approaching footsteps, deeper into the woods. She marveled at how much sound sense such a strategy made when you were the one being pursued, instead of the one sitting comfortably in a movie theater, popcorn on your lap, a Coke by your side, and no killer on your trail.

In Katie's dream, the woods emptied into a clearing within seconds. In Katie's reality, the woods emptied into . . . more woods. She no longer had a clue where she was going or what she intended to do once she got there, outside of whimpering and pleading.

But Katie didn't really need to decide what to do because just then a pair of male hands grabbed her from behind.

Leaving her, once again, with a single option: to scream.

24

But even that didn't work out so well.

One of the hands managed to move from around her waist to clamp over her mouth. She felt herself being lifted off the ground, and so proceeded to kick like crazy in retaliation. She made heel-along-bone contact with what might have been a knee, while her pinned elbows flailed against a chest. Or maybe a shoulder.

"Jesus Christ, Katie, cut it out!"

The sturdy hands both let go at the same time, and Katie slid to the ground. She barely managed to balance upright as she skidded over then off a pile of grimy leaves before turning around and finally coming face to face with . . . Jack Snyder?

"Jack?"

"Didn't you hear me calling you?" he demanded.

"Jack?"

"I yelled for you to stay put—why the heck were you running away?"

"Jack?"

"I think we've established who I am, Katie."

"You? You're my stalker?"

"No, Katie, that was a fictional guy you made up a couple of years ago. During your WOAK days, remember?"

"Why were you chasing me through the woods?"

"Because you wouldn't stop running."

"What are you doing here?"

"Carly told me what you were up to. And she told me your reasons for not going to the police. Lousy reasons, Katie. Very lousy. You might've cost me this whole case."

"You mean you believe me? About Monica and Henry and the syringe?"

"I've got no reason not to believe you. I've certainly got no reason not to at least give the area a once-over. I drove up right behind your car, saw you fishing around in the trees, and tried to catch up before you touched something you weren't supposed to touch."

"But I ran away."

"Yeah. And then you kicked me."

"Sorry."

He winced, rubbed his knee, and moved on. "So did you find it?"

"No. Not yet."

"Good. The last thing I need is your fingerprints making things even more complicated. Look, I'm here now. Why

don't you go back and wait in the car. I'll let you know if I find anything."

"Are you kidding me? This is my case!"

"Really?"

"Yes, really. Well, mine, Carly's, and Maddie's. We're the ones who figured out the evidence about the credit card, and we're the ones who broke the connection between Monica and Henry."

"I understand Maddie accomplished the latter by walking in her own front door."

"More detective work than the Oakdale P.D. did."

"Watch it, Katie."

"No!" It had been a very long day, meaning that Katie's temper was conversely very short. "All your evidence is bunk. You guys hauled Mike to jail on suspicion of killing Gregory, when it was actually his own wife or maybe his daughter or, in any case, not Mike, who did the deed."

"And his prints on the wine bottle?"

"I'm sure there's a logical explanation for that," Katie said, impressed with how easy she found it to defend a position she wasn't even sure she held.

"Fine. We may have made some wrong turns. But if you expect us to bring Monica in, we need evidence. And you, for all I know, just crushed it beneath your feet."

Katie looked down guiltily. Her shoes were covered with an assortment of nature and . . . more. "Oops," she said.

"Just try not to make too much of a mess tromping back to your car."

"I can help you," Katie offered.

Jack pulled on a pair of latex gloves, then extracted a clean

plastic bag from his jacket pocket. "No, thank you, I think I can manage on my own. Go away, Katie."

"Come on. You don't want me stomping all the way back to my car! Think of all the potential evidence I might accidentally destroy. Wouldn't it be better if I just hung around here, where you could guide me on where to stand so I don't get in the way?"

Jack, who'd crouched over to sift through the dirt, looked up. Katie rewarded him with her most beaming, sincere smile.

He asked, "You really expected me to buy that?"

"Actually, I just expected you to lack the energy to fight me."

He sighed and shook his head. And then he mumbled some words under his breath that Katie couldn't quite make out. But got the gist of.

As Jack looked around, Katie made a conscientious point of only stepping in the spaces where his feet had been, to prevent accidentally destroying something. She hoped he appreciated the effort she was making. She also hoped he appreciated her, apropos of nothing, noting, "You know, Jack, you and Carly, you really are an awesome couple."

Jack grunted.

"I'm really inspired by how much Carly loves you. She would do anything for you. You know that, right, Jack?"

With his back to her, Katie couldn't tell how he was reacting to her spontaneous ode. On the one hand, he didn't tell her to shut up. On the other hand, he didn't rush over to his phone to call Carly and tell her how much she meant to him, either.

Still, figuring that no "shut up" was as good as "please, do continue," Katie went on: "I know about Carly and Gregory."

"Yes. Apparently quite a few people do."

"I used to be jealous of Carly and Mike. I hid it well. But then I realized that what they had added up to nothing. She didn't mean anything to him, and he didn't mean anything to her. No guy meant anything to Carly, until you."

"Katie?" Jack turned around so quickly, she almost toppled onto her butt trying to hop back in surprise.

"What?"

"What the hell are you doing? Look, I know that Carly loves me, all right? I know that she would do anything for me, and that the kids and I are the most important things in the world to her. Some bastard she slept with a decade ago? Who cares? I don't and she doesn't. My only interest in Gregory Marron is finding out who killed him so that I don't have to hear his name mentioned every minute of the day by political friends of his daddy's calling to find out how the investigation is going. You got that?"

"I got it."

"Thank God."

"But, Jack . . ."

"What?"

"Maybe you should tell Carly that."

He turned his back on Katie without another word.

And he continued to exercise his right to remain silent until, almost a half hour after they'd had their little misunderstanding about who was stalking whom, Katie heard

him let out a low whistle and then an actual, honest-to-goodness laugh.

"Katie," Jack said, standing up and turning around. In his hand, he held a loose tree branch. Dangling from the end of the branch, carefully picked up by the back end so as not to smear any potential evidence, was a mud-encrusted, plastic syringe. "I think I love you."

His love, unfortunately, did not extend to permitting Katie to accompany him to the police station and hang around until the lab was able to determine whose prints were on the syringe, and whether it also tested positive for cherry laurel toxin.

Jack told her, "Go home, Katie. I'll call you when I have any news, I promise."

"Call Carly first. She's dying to hear from you."

"Yeah, yeah, I think I got that. You were very subtle back there."

"I meant what I said. You guys are an inspiring couple. I only wish Mike and I could somehow get to the same place in our relationship that you two are in yours."

"I don't know if inspiration is precisely what anyone should be getting from Carly and me," Jack managed to look both sheepish and proud at the same time. "But, I'll tell you this, you call Mike and you tell him what you did for him today. You took on an Oakdale P.D. officer—unarmed!"

"Thanks for not arresting me, by the way."

"When he hears about the lengths you were willing to go

to for him—to start with, I think those shoes will never be the same again—I bet you two will be able to straighten everything out. If Carly and I can get through Carly—"

"Being Carly?"

"Exactly. You and Mike should have some serious smooth sailing ahead of you."

Katie ended up taking half of Jack's advice. She did make a phone call. But she called Carly, not Mike. Katie had no intention of calling Mike (and forcing him to take her call) until she had some genuine, confirmable good news along the lines of "Monica and Aurora have finally confessed to everything! You are completely and totally off the hook!"

Instead, she offered Carly a play-by-play of her chat with Jack, including the part where he compared Katie and Mike to himself and Carly—in a good way.

"I'm not sure saying that if he can put up with me being me, Mike can put up with you being you, is necessarily a compliment."

"Well, I've chosen to interpret it as such," Katie stubbornly insisted. "I'm sorry, but I'm feeling optimistic. Do you realize how close we are to closing the book on this nightmare? As soon as the forensic report comes back on the syringe—"

"Did Jack say when he expected that to happen?"

"No. Jack basically gave me a don't-call-us/we'll-call-you. But I intend to be at the station bright and early tomorrow morning. Just in case there's something a grateful Jack wants to share with me. Off the record."

Carly said, "Save me a seat."

"There is nothing that I would like to share with you, off the record," Jack assured both Katie and Carly, in response to their bright-eyed, bushy-tailed, early morning query. "The only thing that I would like to share with you, on the record, is that our forensics lab is analyzing the syringe now. I'll keep you posted."

"I'll wait," Katie said, and she took a seat.

Carly looked from the still bright-eyed and bushy-tailed Katie to the fed-up and overworked Jack. She said, "I think I'll wait, too."

"Suit yourself," Jack shrugged and staggered back to his desk, rubbing the three-day-old stubble on his chin with his palm, while his index finger massaged the lid of his left eye. He needed to cover up a yawn by lifting a file from his desk to face-level, but there was no mistaking the exhausted slump of his shoulders or the practically visible crimp in his neck.

"Jack looks awful," Katie offered.

"I know. This case is killing him."

"At least he realizes that, whatever happens, he'll always have you in his corner. Maybe if I'd been able to convince Mike of that, we wouldn't be in this mess." Katie lowered her voice, realizing that a police station might not be the optimal place to voice her fears about Mike's integrity and character. Nonetheless, she needed to get the doubts off her chest once and for all and she suspected that Carly was the perfect person to enlighten her. "How do you do it, Carly? How do you suspect your husband of murder, and then don't let it bother you? When you thought Jack might have killed Gregory, your first thought was: How do I protect him from getting caught? When I thought Mike might have done it, my first thought was: Oh, God, what if he's not the man I thought he was, what does this say about our relationship, and is he going to try and kill me next?"

"That's technically three thoughts." Carly looked over her shoulder at Jack. Like Katie, she, too, realized that a police station wasn't the optimal setting for a soul-bearing heart-to-heart. Unlike Katie, however, she actually decided to do something about it.

"Come on," Carly said. "I'll buy you a cup of coffee."

"Why can't I be like you? Why can't I trust Mike implicitly?" Katie said, clutching a paper cup of coffee that Carly had bought for her at Al's Diner.

"I don't know, Katie." Sitting across from her in the booth closest to the door, Carly took a sip from her own cup and tossed the question right back. "Why can't you? I've always found him to be a pretty upright guy."

"But he lied to me."

"When?" Carly challenged. "No, really, Katie, when did he lie to you? Did you ever flat out ask him if he killed Gregory? Or even if he stole that car fifteen years ago?"

"I—I asked him to tell me what was going on . . ."

"That's not the same thing. Unless you have concrete

proof that Mike really was trying to kill you when he drove Monica's car off the road, what lies has he told you?"

"You're confusing me."

"I'm trying to make everything more simple. Who are you afraid of, Katie? The Mike that you think you know, or the Mike that you suspect he might be?"

Her head spun. "That last one, I guess."

"There's nothing you can do about that last one. The only Mike you need to care about is the one who's in front of you right now. The Mike he used to be? Who cares? What does that have to do with anything? Jack and I have been together forever, and he still hasn't told me what he did in the FBI while he was working undercover. He hasn't told me the name of the first girl who broke his heart or half the things that nutty mother of his put him through. And you know what, Katie? It doesn't matter. If Jack wants to tell me he will, and if he doesn't, what does that have to do with our life together now?"

It all sounded so logical and grown up. What a shame Katie usually failed at being either. "But what if something from his past has an effect on your future?"

"Then we'll face it when it comes. How does me knowing about the past prevent the future from happening? If, down the road, Mike does something, for whatever reason, that you can't live with, you should deal with it then. You can't forgive a man today for something he might do tomorrow. There's no point in it."

"But I like to know what's coming up tomorrow," Katie insisted. "I *need* to know what's coming up tomorrow."

"Tough luck, Katie. Nobody comes with a guarantee. You

either love the Mike of today, or you don't. That's the only thing that matters. At this point—and I'm talking about things you know, not the things you're feverishly making up as we speak—at this point, has Mike done anything you can't live with?"

"He lied to me."

"No, as I've pointed out earlier, he didn't."

"All right then, he kept secrets from me."

"And you can't live with that? People have a lot of different reasons for keeping secrets, Katie. . . ."

"I know, but . . ."

They kept on talking for close to an hour. About Mike, Jack, men, life, and all the highs and lows that came with them, until Carly's cell phone rang. She checked the Caller I.D. and said, "It's Jack."

Katie scooted her chair over and tilted her head while Carly held the receiver between their ears so Katie could hear what Jack was saying, as well.

"We have a match, ladies. Not only did the syringe test positive for cherry laurel toxin, but it's got Monica Marron's fingerprints all over it. We're bringing her in now."

Monica arrived at the station, like her mother, without a lawyer. But she did have both Henry and Maddie with her. She informed Jack, "This better be important. I was in the middle of a business meeting with my colleagues when your storm troopers burst into my home and demanded my presence at the police station. I warn you, if you're planning to cross-examine me about my mother, expect a standing reply of 'no comment.' I know nothing about her plot to poison Gregory and I have no evidence to contribute."

"Actually, Miss Marron. My questions have more to do with you, a syringe found in Snyder Woods, and your activities the day of your stepfather's death, specifically between the hours of one and two P.M." Jack indicated the open door behind them with his arm. "If you would please step this way, we can have our little chat in private—"

"No!" Monica shook her head, her eyes suddenly flooded with tears where earlier there had been only impatience. "No, I'm sorry, I'm sorry. I can't."

"Are you asking for your lawyer, Miss Marron?"

"I can't keep lying anymore, I'm sorry. You're right. I haven't been honest with you. I should have been, right from the start, but I couldn't. I was trying to be good, I was trying not to—"

"Miss Marron, do you or do you not want a lawyer present for this?"

"I do know who killed my stepfather. I've always known."

"Monica," Henry warned. He stepped forward to take her hand in his, but Monica yanked it out of his grip and pivoted around, pointing in Henry's direction, shaking.

"It was him," she sobbed. "It was Henry Coleman!"

25

Henry froze in his tracks. So did everybody around him. A moment passed when nobody said anything, and then another moment when everyone began shouting at once.

"You're lying!" Maddie was the first to regain her power of speech, followed by Carly scoffing, "Jack, you're not going to buy that, are you?" and Katie asserting, "Then why are your prints on the murder weapon?"

"I'm sorry, Henry, I'm sorry," Monica insisted on repeating. "I know I promised I wouldn't tell but, can't you see, they know everything!"

Henry just kept staring at her, shell-shocked. He had yet to so much as put down his upraised hand.

"Hold it!" Jack's bark split the melee. "Everybody, in here." He pointed to the interrogation room and stood by the door, holding it open with his back, until Monica,

Henry, Katie, Carly, and Maddie were completely inside. He slammed the door shut and, in response to the chorus of objections that instantly started up again, announced, "One at a time. You, Miss Marron, you're up first. Go."

Monica brought her palms up to her face, as if praying. She tucked her thumbs under her chin and closed her eyes, trying to regain her composure.

"Get on with it, Monica," Carly snapped. "My husband hasn't slept in several days, he doesn't need your theatrics."

"I'll handle this, Carly." Jack reached for Monica's wrist and lowered her arms, prompting her to open her eyes, as well. "I'm listening."

"I'm sorry," she said.

"We've all heard that part. Let's move on to what precisely are you sorry for?"

"That I didn't confess sooner. But I didn't put all the pieces together until just now. When you told me about the syringe, suddenly it all made sense. I can't believe I didn't figure it out sooner. I guess I was too naïve to realize what he was doing."

"Who, Miss Marron?"

Monica averted her eyes. "Henry Coleman."

"Wait a minute—now wait a minute," Henry burst out, but was quickly silenced by Jack's threatening glare.

"You'll have your turn, Henry. If there's one thing I promise, it's that everyone in this room will have a chance to speak. Because we're not leaving until I've got the full story. Now Monica. You said Henry poisoned your stepfather. Do you have any evidence you wish to present to that end?"

"You have the evidence. You said you found the syringe."

"We did. But Henry's fingerprints aren't on it. Only yours are."

"See, I knew you were a liar," Maddie said in triumph. "I knew it."

"Maddie!"

"Sorry, Detective Snyder." She shrank back into her assigned spot.

"I figure my fingerprints are the only ones on it," Monica admitted. "Because, you see, Henry wore gloves."

"He wore gloves to do what?"

Monica said, "To poison the wine."

The nuclear-level shock inside the room made their collective silence feel even louder than their yelling a few moments earlier. Only Jack recovered quickly enough to question, "And why would Henry Coleman do that, Miss Marron?"

"He owed my stepfather money. And Gregory was asking for it back."

"Is that true, Henry?" Jack asked.

Five pairs of eyes turned in his direction. Henry merely nodded, unable to speak.

Monica said, "Henry didn't have the money to pay Gregory back. So he came up with this scheme. You know the wine my stepfather loved?"

"Oh, yes, I believe we're all quite familiar with that particular brand of wine." Jack sighed.

"Well, Henry was stealing the real Château Petrus bottles and replacing them with cheap knock-offs, then selling the originals through some shady friends of his, and using the profits to pay Gregory back. He told me all about it. When I caught him."

"Caught him stealing the wine?"

"Caught him injecting the bottle with that syringe," Monica practically whispered. "The day Gregory died. I saw Henry doing it. He told me what he was up to, he told me it was just an additive to make the fake stuff taste real. And then he gave me the syringe and he asked me to do him a favor and toss it in the woods."

"Okay, that's it!" Henry shot out of the corner like a boxer late for his bell. "It's over. I can see clearly now! The rain is gone! My sister was right about you. This was all a scam. You set me up!"

"Henry?" Jack inquired. "Would you like to speak now?"

"You bet!" He was so full of righteous indignation he bounced up and down with every word, finally stretching to his full potential height. "You bet I'd like to speak. This woman, Detective, is a liar."

"So you deny that you've been stealing Mr. Marron's beverage of choice?"

The bouncing stopped while Henry was on the tips of his toes. He awkwardly settled down. He cleared his throat. "Well, I—no. I have been doing that."

"That should make the paperwork easier."

"But it was a victimless crime. Nobody was supposed to get hurt. Mike Kasnoff can vouch for me on that. He knows all about it. He was in on it, too."

Katie gasped. And then, right away, realized, "That's why his fingerprints were on the bottle!"

"And why he had another one stashed at your house,

yeah, we were going to sell that one next. I'm sorry, Bubbles." Henry turned to face her. "I should have come clean earlier. I know it drove you nuts, wondering what the hell his prints were doing there."

Katie demanded to know, "Why in the world would Mike let you get him mixed up in such a dumb scheme?"

"He felt guilty, I think. He knew my money woes began after you two got back together and I had to move out of the cottage. He wanted to help me out. Plus, there was the chance to pull one over on Marron Jr., that didn't exactly hurt his feelings either."

"So that's why Mike refused to explain himself! He was protecting you!"

Carly and Katie's eyes met, and Katie could read, clear and pointed as day, her words from earlier. "*People have a lot of different reasons for keeping secrets.*"

Jack interrupted the wordless communication with several pertinent words. "So you did inject Gregory Marron's wine bottle?"

"No. No, absolutely not, no way, no how, no! I confessed to the wine-switching scam so you'd believe I'm being straight with you about the murder thing."

"And because you knew it would be trivial for us to test whether the red wine left in the bottle was genuine Château Petrus or an imitation."

"That, too. But write this down, Jack: I confessed to stealing. I am not, repeat not, underline, italicize, bold, and cover with the universal symbol for no, not confessing to murder. I have no idea where the poison came from."

"It came from"—Jack held up a plastic evidence bag—"this syringe."

"I have never seen that item before in my life."

"That's not true," Monica insisted. "Henry, why are you doing this? Just tell them the truth."

"Hey, right back-atcha, babe."

Jack asked Henry, "So while Miss Marron can place the syringe in your hand, you technically can't place it in hers?"

"Shouldn't fingerprints speak louder than lies?"

"Were you and Miss Marron together in the car the entire time you were parked there? Or was there a moment when she might have had time to inject the bottle, outside of your view, and then dispose of the syringe?"

"Well . . ." Henry hesitated. "We were together pretty much . . ."

"Condoms!" Katie yelled.

Now the five pairs of eyes were planted squarely on her.

"While your commitment to safe sex is admirable, Katie," Jack observed dryly, "I'm not sure if now is the right time to broadcast your public service announcement."

Katie ignored him to ask Henry, "Did you guys use a condom?"

"Katie . . ." He blushed and jerked his head in Maddie's direction to remind her that children were present.

"Yes or no."

"Well, yes, of course."

"What did you do with it when you were done?"

"Detective Snyder," Monica whined, "she's just trying to embarrass me, I don't get why . . ."

But Jack was nodding thoughtfully. "Don't worry. I think I do. Go on, Katie."

Emboldened to realize Jack also thought her suspicion had merit, Katie repeated, "What did you do with the condom when you were done?"

Henry looked as if he wanted to die. Right here and right now. Or, at the very least, confess to murder, if only to put an end to this conversation.

"We — I — we threw it out."

"Where? Not in the car. You wouldn't have risked leaving it in the car."

"No. Of course not. My boss would've . . . God, I can't even imagine. . . . We threw it in the woods. I know you're not supposed to do that. Littering, right? Hell, how many crimes am I supposed to own up to today, anyway? What's this, you got a bunch of cases to close before lunchtime, Jack?"

"Was it you who threw it out," Katie pressed. "Or Monica?"

And suddenly, Henry got it. As if literally being hit by a lightening bolt anvil from above, Henry sang out, "Monica! It was Monica! She stepped out of the car for a second to throw the condom out!"

"And what were you doing at the time?"

Henry thought about it, mentally retracing his steps. "I was up front. Yeah, I was up front because the dispatcher was calling with my next fare and then he had some billing questions."

"Which means," Jack held up a restraining hand indicating to Katie that he'd be taking it from here, "Miss Marron had ample time alone in the back of the limo to poison the bottle, then step out of the car to get rid of the syringe, without your being any wiser?"

"Oh, believe me, Jack, wise ain't an adjective that should ever be applied to me. I understand that now."

"You have no proof," Monica said. "It's his word against mine."

"You're right," Jack agreed. "Which is why, Monica Marron, Henry Coleman, I am arresting you both for the murder of Gregory Marron Jr."

26

Maddie was the first one to go ballistic.

"You can't do that!" she screamed at Jack. "It isn't fair! Her fingerprints are on the syringe, not Henry's. He's not a killer, he's a stooge."

"I want my lawyer," Monica calmly said. "I'm entitled to a lawyer. I want my lawyer," she kept repeating, over and over again like a mantra.

Henry, on the other hand, had slunk against a wall, head back, staring blankly at the ceiling.

"Henry!" Maddie hysterically tried to snap him out of it, but Jack grabbed her by the shoulder to prevent Maddie from touching him.

"I'm sorry, Maddie," his voice was gentle but intractable. "You, Katie, and Carly are going to have to leave. This is police business now. I can't have you in here."

"But she's lying. Can't you tell she's lying?"

"Maddie." Carly clicked into Mommy-mode. She wrapped her arms around the girl's shoulders and softly shushed her, rubbing Maddie's arms soothingly with both hands and whispering, "It's all right, honey—it'll be okay, this isn't over. We'll fix it. I promise. Just come outside with Katie and me and calm down. Please."

Carly and Jack locked eyes over Maddie's head and Jack smiled sympathetically. Carly, relieved to finally be getting a glimpse of her old, loving, compassionate Jack, nodded reassuringly, indicating that Maddie would be okay, Carly and Katie would look after her. And Carly would be okay, too; not to worry.

Jack smiled. He kissed her gently on the forehead and, for a moment, it was just the two of them again, frozen in time, frozen in space, frozen in sensation. Jack's lips were on Carly's flesh, warm, safe and, most important, familiar. This was Jack. She had her Jack back. Even if it was only for an instant.

They pulled apart reluctantly. Jack helped Carly and Katie lead Maddie out the door, into a private waiting area, and then briefly squeezed Carly's hand before heading back into the interrogation room. Katie noticed the loving gesture and, despite everything else going on around them, winked in Carly's direction. Carly winked back.

But the rest of what they wanted to say would have to wait.

They got Maddie a glass of water and forced her to drink it, even when she swore that she had to get in there, she had to help Henry, this wasn't right, they were going to convict him of killing Gregory when obviously anyone with eyes could see that it was his wife and daughter who wanted him dead. Henry was being set up!

"I know," Katie reassured. "Of course, I know."

"I know it, too," Carly confirmed. "We'll get to the bottom of this, don't worry. We're in this together, right?"

"Are we?" Maddie asked hesitantly. "I thought, now that you know for sure that it wasn't Jack or Mike . . ."

Carly and Katie exchanged looks. The kid was absolutely right. And absolutely wrong, too.

"We're in this together," Katie said. "Just us . . . and our secret weapon."

Katie left Maddie in Carly's capable hands, and drove off to fetch said secret weapon. By the time she returned, the station's front room was occupied not only by Jack, Monica, Henry, Maddie, and Carly (not to mention a handful of uniformed officers who seemed to be doing a combination of crowd control . . . and ducking and covering), but also by the recently arrived Aurora, Gig, and their lawyer, L.B.

Aurora was clinging to L.B.'s arm, listening to him yell at Jack and periodically interjecting with an outrage of her own. Gig, with Monica beside him, had targeted his fury at Henry, who seemed to be doubling over with each verbal blow until he looked like he might be sick on Gig's polished shoes.

Maddie was trying to cut in, shouting back at Gig. Carly

was doing her best to calm Maddie down and keep an eye on Jack and Aurora's clash a few feet away.

Katie tried raising her voice to be heard above the bedlam, but her attempts only prompted everyone else to knock it up a notch.

"Excuse me," Nancy Hughes said politely.

Everyone stopped talking.

"Thank you," Nancy said. She took a step forward and greeted Gig, Aurora, and Monica individually by name. They all dutifully replied.

"Hello, Nancy."

"Hello, Mrs. Hughes."

"Hello, ma'am."

"I understand we have a bit of a problem here," she said.

"These people are trying to frame my brother!" Maddie cried out. Following the disapproving look her outburst provoked from Nancy, she added, "I'll be quiet now."

"Why don't we all have a seat," Nancy suggested.

"This is highly unorthodox." L.B. objected.

"Why, Larry?" Nancy asked pleasantly, as people seated themselves. "I'm just suggesting that we all have a little chat. Nothing official. Right, Detective Snyder? No one here is under oath or on the record, are they?"

"No, ma'am," Jack said, leaning against the edge of a nearby desk. "Mrs. Hughes, you have the floor."

"Before we begin I'd like to say that if any of you think of something relevant to add," she paused and looked directly at Katie, Carly, and Maddie, "you jump right in, all right?"

"Yes, Mrs. Hughes."

"Come on, Nancy," Gig snorted. "This is a bit ridiculous. We're not kidding around. This is serious business. My ladies are under arrest for murder. This is no time to be playing games."

"Gig." Nancy smiled kindly, if somewhat condescendingly. "We are all interested in the same thing, today, aren't we? Finding out who killed your son. I would have thought you'd support such an important endeavor. With your outstanding public record of speaking out against police brutality, the Rockefeller Laws, racial profiling, not to mention our three-strikes-you're-out sentencing requirements, I would have expected you to be on the front lines here, demanding justice for all."

For a moment, something dark flashed in Gig's eyes that made Katie flinch. But then he got control of himself and replied in a voice as pleasant as one could expect under the circumstances, "Well, of course, Nancy, of course I want to know who killed my son."

"Thank you, Gig." Nancy smiled. "To start with," she observed, "there appears to be some question about who actually controls the family's fortune. Gig, would you care to explain to everyone how the Marron trust works?"

Gig looked startled. "Now, what in blazes does that have to do with anything?"

"Just humor me, dear, would you?"

He tugged on his shirt collar then grudgingly explained, "The trust passes down from son to son."

"So, until the father dies, his son can't access any money, is that correct?"

"Well, there are a few loose accounts here and there, but, yes, I suppose in the big picture, that's right."

"So, still staying in that big picture: Your son, Gregory Marron Jr., he didn't really have money of his own, did he?"

"He had what I gave him. Spent it as he saw fit, too. No consulting with me, that's for certain."

Monica cocked her head to one side. "But . . . Gregory always told me that he was in charge of our money. That you just handled the charity, but he was the one in charge of the overall fortune."

"Gregory lied," Aurora snapped. "I know, shocking, isn't it? Gregory loathed having to go to Daddy on bended knee for an allowance, so he put the rest of us in the same uncomfortable situation by making Monica and me grovel for the crumbs he deigned throw our way. Not that they were even his to throw. Those checks he made such a big show of writing us every month? They were drawn from an account Gig set up and Gig managed. Gregory was just the powerless middleman."

"Now, that's interesting," Nancy observed. "Because, correct me if I'm wrong, Aurora, but didn't you tell the police that you might have killed Gregory because you were impatient to inherit his money?"

"Don't answer that," L.B. warned.

"Mrs. Marron's statement to that effect is already on the record," Jack reminded the lawyer.

Aurora shrugged. "I was distraught. Perhaps I didn't know what I was saying."

"That's our story," L.B. told Jack. "And you'll be hearing a lot of it."

"So if inheritance wasn't your motive," Nancy queried. "Pray tell, what was?"

"Well, there's also the minor factor of his being a Class A son of a bitch. . . ."

"Except that he'd been one for quite a while," Carly spoke up.

"Yes," Aurora noted. "You would know all about that."

"So why did you kill him now?" Carly pressed. "Especially since you knew there'd be no inheritance until after Gig passed away—heck, maybe not even then. If money was your motive, you'd have been better off waiting for Gig to die, then suing Gregory for divorce and half his new fortune. The way things are now, Gig can still choose to leave you out of his will completely."

"I guess we're back to my first theory again then, aren't we?"

Carly asked, "Why did you ever marry him in the first place? I know he didn't love you. He would tell that to anyone who listened. It was part of his pickup line."

"My husband, the romantic . . ."

"Is it possible that, in spite of all that, you actually loved him?"

"I was in love," Aurora conceded. She attempted to make her revelation sound flip, a throwaway without much behind it, an ephemeral wisp. And the men in the room may have taken it at face value. But Carly, Nancy, Katie, even Maddie saw the way that she nervously rubbed a palm against her throat. They heard the way her voice dipped and caught between the words *in* and *love*, and, most important, not one of them missed the way her eyes darted, just for a second, to the left. And landed right on Gig Marron, before guiltily darting aside.

"Oh . . ." Nancy, Katie, and Maddie thought.

"Oh . . ." Carly actually said out loud.

And Aurora, glancing from one to the other to the other, understood that her jig was up. She laughed a little. Not a happy laugh, more one of relief. She chuckled at her own stupidity at thinking she could hide forever, and shrugged as she faced Carly. For the first time utterly stripped of defenses.

"Yes," she said. "Exactly."

"I didn't know," Carly said. "Gregory never said a word."

"Of course not. It would have humiliated him. That's why he played the big man for Monica, pretending he was the one keeping her on an allowance. Because he didn't want her to see him for what he was—a puppet. If he cared so much about something so trivial, how do you think he would have reacted if the world knew he'd been forced, well, bribed, really, to marry his wife . . . who was in love with his father?"

Now the men in the room got with the program.

Jack, who'd been listening to both women but keeping his eyes planted on Carly, whipped his head around to stare incredulously at Aurora. Henry practically slipped off the side of the desk and had to scramble to remain upright. L.B. merely looked amused, like he'd either known or suspected the truth all along. While Gig Marron, the man of the moment, looked as if Aurora's revelation was all news to him.

He tried to backpedal. "Now, now, let's not get carried away here. The lady is upset, she's confused, this conversation is highly inappropriate and—"

"Oh, cut it out, Granddad," Monica snapped. "Do you think we're idiots? We've all got eyes. We can see the obvious. My mother is in love with my grandfather. Great. That should add a few extra thousand dollars to the therapy bills."

"You don't understand," Gig pleaded. "It isn't that simple."

"You were sleeping with your son's wife," Carly summarized. "Sounds pretty simple to me, Gig. Anyone else having trouble following along?"

A uniform shake of the head was her reply.

"The only question that remains is, why did you have to force Gregory to marry Aurora? Was it just so you could keep her around? If that's the case, why didn't you just marry her yourself?"

"I couldn't," Gig explained. "It would have looked—"

"Like a sixty-year-old fool shacking up with a girl half his age?" Nancy contributed.

In response to the shocked expressions on people's faces that Nancy Hughes knew such words, much less used them, she merely shrugged innocently.

"Exactly!" Gig leaped on her explanation, not seeming to have noticed Nancy's unflattering terminology. "I would have been a laughingstock. No one would have taken me seriously. I had to weigh the good that my foundation could do in the world at large, versus my own petty needs. I had to think about all the people that I could help as long as I kept up my respected standing in the philanthropic community. This wasn't about my happiness or Aurora's, this was about my life's work. I couldn't sacrifice that. It would have been wrong."

"You're kidding," Carly crossed her arms. "You are seriously using the for-the-good-of-the-planet excuse to justify pawning your girlfriend off on your pathetic son?"

"Yes," Aurora confirmed. "That's exactly what he said."

Carly didn't know whether to laugh or cry, so she settled for clarifying. "And you went along with it! Why?"

"Because." Aurora looked down as she smoothed the edges of her skirt. "Gig told me the easiest way for us to be together was if I was married to Gregory. That way we could live together, travel together, appear in public together, without suspicion. And I believed him. Because that's how much I wanted to be with him. I would have done anything he asked. I still would do anything he asked," she said softly.

"Is that why you killed Gregory?" Carly guessed. "Because Gig asked you to?"

"Now wait a minute, young lady!" Gig jumped out of his chair. "You don't have a shred of evidence that links me to my boy's murder. What kind of man do you think I am? Gregory and I may have had our differences—"

"He was planning to have you declared incompetent," Katie reminded him.

"Oh, that never would have happened. Boy didn't have the nerve, much less the smarts."

"Maybe you wanted to be sure it never happened," Carly hypothesized. "So you and Aurora conspired—"

"That still doesn't explain Monica's fingerprints on the syringe," Maddie butted in. "She had to be involved, too."

"I explained that, you little idiot! That was Henry!" Monica snapped.

"Maybe we're looking at a family-wide conspiracy," Carly suggested. "You all had something to gain from Gregory's death. Gig masterminded the plan, Aurora cooked up the poison, and Monica injected it into his wine. Sounds pretty efficient to me. And cozy. The family that slays together, after all—"

"Oh my God." Monica was staring at Aurora and Gig with horrified eyes. "She's right, isn't she? You were both in on it. And not just you—Henry, too. It all makes sense now. Every last bit of it. You all had your own little deal going. Granddad, you wanted Gregory gone so he wouldn't have you declared incompetent. And Mother, you wanted Gig, so obviously Gregory had to go."

"Now you hold on there a minute, missy," Gig said. "I know you're upset. We're all upset from this circus, I don't blame you for that. But I would not kill my own boy. You hear me? Gregory's my only son, my heir, what man would—"

"With Gregory dead," Monica asked out of the blue, "who inherits your fortune now?"

That got Gig's attention.

He paused and took a deep breath. "Well, to be honest, I'm not sure what the trust says about—"

"Am I your heir now?" she pressed.

Gig blinked, clearly never having given it much consideration. "Well, you're . . . yes . . . I suppose so . . ."

"And if I die, then who? Who inherits the money then?"

"Monica, don't be morbid," Aurora urged.

"That's it, isn't it? That's the final piece. God, how could I have been so blind? My accident. It wasn't an accident, at all."

"No," Katie said. "Your mother was trying to kill me."

"Oh, get over yourself!" Monica was practically shaking with fury. "Why the hell would she want to kill you? You're nothing to her. It was me, wasn't it, Mother? I'm the one you were trying to kill. First Gregory, then me, then Gig, and the money is all yours. That was your master plan all along. All that crap about marrying Gregory to stay close to Gig. You did it to stay close to Gig's money!"

"And your fingerprints?" Maddie, still stinging from the stupid-kid remark, was determined to not let that particular thread drop.

"Oh, yes." Monica seethed. "My fingerprints. The physical evidence that ties me to your grotesque plot. What did they offer you, Henry?" she asked. "Cash? Or was it simply having your debts forgiven? Was seducing me their idea, or did you improvise that part on your own? I loved you. Do you even care? Does anybody care?"

Henry closed his eyes, pained, a tempest of emotions playing out on his face, each struggling for control. He opened his eyes again. He straightened his shoulders and he walked up to Monica.

He took her hands in his and he looked deeply into her eyes. "You, lady, are one, sick, twisted piece of work."

She yanked her hands away as if bitten. "Of course I am! What do you expect? My mother and father are both cold-blooded killers!"

Maddie was the first one to catch that particular slip of the tongue.

And it intrigued her enough to ask, "Your mother and who, now?"

27

Monica's eyes darted around the room. "My mother and grandfather," she said. "I meant my mother and grandfather."

"Oh my God," Aurora gasped. "You know."

"The T-shirt!" Katie exclaimed.

In an afternoon full of non sequiturs, Katie's won the prize for oddest utterance and timing.

Even Jack, who'd managed to remain cool, reserved, and professional throughout the ceaseless back and forths, accusations, allegations, and finger pointing, now had to simply stop in his tracks and demand, "What the hell, Katie?"

But Katie knew what she was saying. And she could see that Aurora did, too.

"I found a picture in Gregory's study," Katie explained. "It was wrinkled and stuffed in a drawer, like he'd been using it as a bookmark. It was a picture of Monica blowing out candles on a birthday cake. And she was wearing a T-shirt with the Marron family crest on it. On the back, somebody— Aurora, I guess—had written 'To Daddy—from Monica.' I thought it was Aurora's way of trying to make Gregory bond with his stepdaughter. But, the candles on the cake, there were only two of them. And Gregory and Aurora didn't get married until you were what? Three?"

"Almost four," Monica replied dully.

"It wasn't Gregory you were trying to make love Monica, was it?" Katie asked Aurora. "It was Gig. You thought seeing his daughter wearing the family crest would just tug on his heartstrings, didn't you?"

Aurora nodded. And then she answered, though no one asked, "It didn't work."

"Oh, damn it all to hell, woman!" Gig had had enough of his life story being mangled by people who just didn't *get* what he was about. "Enough with the poor-sad-little-me number. I took care of you, didn't I? You and Monica both. I paid your expenses, even got Gregory to marry you and adopt the child so she'd get her fair share of the estate. I did right by you. More than any other guy would have done, that's for sure."

Nancy said, "You are truly a prince among men."

"Gregory wasn't using that picture as a bookmark," Monica told Katie. "He stole it from Gig so he could show it to me when he told me who my real father was."

"That son of a bitch," Aurora hissed. "Now I wish I really had killed him."

"Aurora!" Gig admonished.

"Excuse me?" Jack asked. "Is there something you want to say, Mrs. Marron? For the record?"

"Back off, Snyder," L.B. warned.

"I'm happy to do this officially, Mrs. Marron. Your attorney is present, we can go into a private room now, cross our t's and dot our i's."

"No," Aurora said, sounding fatigued. "I have no new statement to make."

"I do," Monica offered. "And I want it on the record."

"Don't do it, Monica," L.B. warned. "If you want to talk, talk to me first. Then—"

"Oh, shut up. Game's over. I want the world to know."

"Fine," Jack said. "Let's do this right, then."

Inside the interrogation room, Jack was seated at one end of the table, while L.B., with Aurora and Monica on either side of him, took the other. Gig initially demanded to be let in as well.

"This is Marron family business, and I'm head of the Marron family, damn it!"

But the dead look in both Aurora's and Monica's eyes made it clear that he wasn't wanted. And so the head of the Marron family was relegated to jostling for space behind the two-way mirror, along with Carly, Katie, Maddie, Nancy, and Henry.

L.B. said, "I would like the record to show that my client is giving her statement voluntarily. She came to you of her own free will."

"Eventually," Jack noted.

"Of her own free will," L.B. repeated.

"Fine. It's duly noted." Jack jotted something on a piece of paper. "All right, your attorney is present, so this is the real deal, ladies. No claiming later that you didn't know what was going on."

"I know what's going on," Monica said. She looked over her shoulder, her glare practically melting through the two-way mirror at Henry, Gig, Maddie, all of them: "Finally, I know precisely what's going on."

"Then go right ahead, Miss Marron. Enlighten the rest of us."

"First," she said, "Henry Coleman had nothing to do with poisoning Gregory."

Behind the glass, Maddie squeaked with delight and flung her arms around her brother's waist, practically tackling him. "Oh, thank God," she murmured.

She let go and grabbed Carly by one hand, Katie by another, squeezing tightly. "Thank you both, thank you, thank you."

Carly and Katie smiled back at her.

Monica confessed, "I put the poison in the wine bottle. I stole a syringe from Gig, and I used it to poison my step-father."

"Who asked you to do that, Monica? Was it your mother? Your grandfather?"

"Have you heard of women's lib, Detective? Girls don't need to be told what to do these days. Sometimes we come up with ideas on our very own."

"Monica, don't," her mother warned.

"But I want to." She said to Jack, "I was the one who ordered the saucepan and cooked up the poison. I charged it on my mother's credit card, just to be safe, but I was the one who ordered it. If you don't believe me, check my signature against the one on the receipt. Bet you'll be in for a surprise!"

Behind the glass, Carly looked over at Katie and shrugged. You win a few, you lose a few. Just as long as the results came out in her favor, she could stand being wrong on the details.

Jack asked Aurora, "You lied about it being your signature?"

"I never said that it was my signature. I simply did not say that it wasn't. I was protecting my daughter. I owed her that much."

"That and a lot more. But we'll get to that," Monica told Jack. "So, yes, it was all my doing. Getting access to the wine was easy enough. I threw myself at Henry. I only had to do it once. By the end, I even had him thinking it was his idea."

Henry mumbled, "One, sick, sick, twisted piece of work."

"I never intended for anybody else to get blamed," Monica went on. "Just having Gregory drop dead in front of all those people—oh, he would have hated looking like a fool—that was reward enough. I didn't need the glory, too. But then, see, your officers found Kasnoff's prints on the bottle and everything just got so damn complicated. First Katie started snooping around, then Maddie. The kid was easier to disarm. I saw her at Fashions, thinking she was being so clever—spare me!"

"What do you know?" Maddie observed to Henry. "Guess gullibility must run in the family."

Monica said, "I hired her to work for me. Figured it would give me a chance to, what's the axiom, keep my friends close and my enemies closer?"

Again, Carly and Katie exchanged looks. Great minds and all that . . .

"Plus," Monica said, "it allowed me to feed her false information when it suited my purposes. Like that cell phone number for Mike she found in Aurora's trash. Honey, we have people cleaning our house every hour of every day, what are the odds that a piece of three-day-old trash would just be lying there for some dumb kid to find?"

Maddie had run out of clever remarks. So, she went ahead and acted like a dumb kid, making faces at Monica.

"Still, that number did work well for throwing Katie off balance. See, I have to backtrack now: When I got the wrong blonde in front of the vet's office, I decided to kill two birds with one stone: Get Katie into my own car and flip it— at best, she gets terminally snuffed, at worst, I permanently wipe the evidence from that first 'accident' off my bumper."

Katie couldn't help it. She shuddered, thinking of how close she'd come to being killed—and feeling guilty that poor Sadie, who had nothing to do with any of this, got caught in the crossfire.

"As an added bonus," Monica continued, "Katie thinks her beloved Mike is responsible. I was actually the one who called him and screamed that Katie was being kidnapped. I did it practically right in front of her face; while we were split up looking for retail space. It was almost too easy. Everyone is always so ready to see whatever they want to see."

"Like me," Aurora mused. "Even when I saw your handwriting on the receipt, I thought, there's got to be an explanation for this. My daughter wouldn't kill a man in cold blood."

"A man, no. Gregory Marron Jr. . . . Come on, Mother, cut the crocodile tears. He treated you worse than he treated me. Carly in there, she's just a drop in the bucket—no offense, Detective Snyder."

Jack raised an eyebrow and continued taking notes.

"I was there, remember, Mother? I was there from day one of your little love match. I got to hear the names he called you, and the way he talked about you to other people, and the way he treated you in public. Maybe you didn't care because you had the noble and sexy Gig around to comfort you—"

"Okay," Katie whispered to Carly, "I never want to hear the words *sexy* and *Gig* in the same sentence again."

"I second the motion," Nancy agreed.

"—but I had to go to school and have my alleged friends show me pictures of my alleged father and his bimbos in the newspaper. I got to be the kid who never had parents on Visiting Day because you and Gregory couldn't be in the same room together and if he refused to go, you refused to go—to make some stupid point. So you won, and I lost. My personal favorite was the way Gregory loved to remind me, time and time again, how he and I didn't have a drop of blood in common. Because he was a Marron, and I was an illegitimate pretender to the throne." She smiled. "Except that last one wasn't exactly true, was it, Mommy? And Gregory knew it. So one day, when he and I were having our biweekly fight— I actually think it was about his plan to have Gig declared incompetent and I was foolishly defending my dear 'granddad' by telling Gregory that Gig was twice the man he'd ever be. That's when my legal daddy decided to smack me around with a bit of truth: The man whom I'd just praised to the skies was actually my biological father."

"I'm sorry," Aurora said. She repeated the phrase over and over again, as if trying to convince her daughter of her remorse. "I thought I was doing what was best for you. I thought Gig would marry me, I really thought he would. But he said he couldn't. I thought when he saw you, he would change his mind. He always said family meant so much to him."

"And what a close family it was," Katie whispered behind the glass.

"When Gig suggested I marry Gregory as a way to ensure your inheritance—"

"Oh, so now it was all for me? A moment ago it was all for Gig."

"I was trying to please everyone! But putting up with Gregory for all these years, I did that for you!"

"Exactly," Monica said. "You put up with Gregory because being one kind of Mrs. Marron was better than being no kind of Mrs. Marron. I don't blame you, Mother. I did the same thing. I'm an adult. I could have moved out at any time. Gotten a job, lived my own life. I didn't. Because I liked the perks that came with being Monica Marron. I liked the charge accounts, and the country-club access, and the servants at my disposal. I even liked the allowances Gregory made me beg for. Among four out of five people surveyed, a little groveling still beats digging ditches—or, frankly, any kind of working for a living. I put up with Gregory's cruelty for precisely the same reason that you did, Mother—I did it for the money."

"Is that what I taught you?" Aurora could barely form the words. "Is this what my life choices taught you to be?"

"Oh, that and much more. You also taught me—by example, naturally; mother-and-daughter talks were never your strong point—you taught me how to be ruthless about getting what I want. That's why I had to kill Gregory. Because he was in the way of me getting what I wanted."

"I slept with that," Henry offered to no one in particular. He pointed at Monica through the glass and observed, "I slept with that girl."

"Oh, Henry," Katie took a step back and rested her head against his arm.

He hugged her back.

Monica said, "It was his fault, though. I would have been perfectly content to let things stay the way they were, just wiling away the days until he dropped dead of natural causes—the way that man ate and drank, not to mention the fine company he kept, surely clogged arteries or a social disease would have gotten him sooner rather than later. But, Gregory's greed got out of control. Can you believe he actually boasted to me about his plan to have Gig committed? He let me know that, once that happened, things were going to change. And he made it very clear the changes wouldn't be to my benefit. He said that once the money was all his, he could do anything he wanted with it. And he could leave it to anyone he wanted when he died. Since I wasn't his biological child, he didn't have to leave me a red penny. Which wasn't really fair, was it? Especially once I knew Gig was my father. I got to thinking: Why should Gregory be Gig's only heir? I have as much right to that money as he does. But if Gig died before Gregory, he'd leave it all to his legitimate son. And his son was adamantly not into sharing with his little half sister. So I thought I'd change the rules of the game. With Gregory gone, Gig would have to leave his fortune to me. He wouldn't have any other option. It's no less than I deserve. Hazard pay for putting up with Stepdaddy Dearest and Mother and dear old Granddad all these years, no?"

L.B. cleared his throat and leaned over to Jack. "Detective Snyder, my client is obviously mentally ill. Perhaps we can talk about a—"

"I'm fine." Monica settled back in her chair. "I know exactly what I'm doing."

"Monica, let L.B. handle—"

"He wants people to think I'm crazy. I'm not crazy. I knew what I was doing every step of the way. I said it before: I was willing to lie low, let the mystery remain unsolved forever. I'm not one of those criminals compelled to return to the scene of the crime or talk about how clever I am. If it weren't for Katie and company, I'd have let this whole thing go. I had what I wanted. Gregory was out of the way. But you all just had to keep pushing and pushing and pushing, and now that the truth is partially out about how screwed up the Marron family tree is, I want the entire English-speaking world to know. That's why I want every word of my confession on the record. I want to tell my story in court! I want to read about it in the newspapers and watch twenty-four/seven coverage on *Court TV*. This all started because Gig was afraid his great humanitarian reputation would be ruined if people found out he knocked up a barely legal chick, then dumped both her and the baby on his lousy son. Well, now let's see how Daddy likes dealing with the fallout from his executive decision."

Gig Marron was out of invectives. He was out of commands. He'd watched Monica's entire presentation without saying a word. Katie felt like they were seeing a man literally age and wither away before their eyes. By the end of Monica's recital he was still physically present, but his mind seemed to be elsewhere.

Katie, Carly, Nancy, Maddie, and Henry filed out of the viewing room quietly when it became clear that Monica's show was over—this episode, anyway. No one doubted that there were many more exciting ones still to come.

Afterward, Nancy went into the interrogation room and walked over to Gig.

Katie hesitated. She watched through the door as they exchanged words. She couldn't hear what they were saying.

All she knew was, by the time Gig left the room, the man looked completely and utterly destroyed.

28

Jack said, "You might as well go home without me, Carly. I've clearly got a ton of loose ends to tie up here."

"And miles to go before you sleep?" Carly asked sympathetically.

"And miles to go before I sleep," he agreed, smiling. It had been a very long time since Jack smiled at her like that. It had been a very long time since he'd even looked at her like that. No doubts, no suspicions, no reservations. Just Jack and Carly, eyes locked on each other, ignoring all the other people in the world.

"That's okay," Carly told him. "I'll stick around. You're worth waiting for."

She kissed her husband, happy to note that he kissed her back—and like he meant it, too—then crossed the room to where Katie was standing with Nancy and Maddie.

"Can you believe we can't just go?" Maddie said. "Henry's

still got all this paperwork to fill out and a statement to sign. This is ridiculous. He's an innocent man. What, am I supposed to pitch a tent here?"

"Maddie, chill," Katie advised. "I can drive you home. I'm taking Mrs. Hughes, and it's on the way."

Maddie looked over to Margo Hughes's desk, where Henry was slumped on a too-small folding chair.

"Nah," she begged off. "I better stay. I think Henry's going to need some serious moral support when this is all over."

"You're right about that," Katie agreed. "Maybe I should stay, too."

"No." Carly placed her hands on Katie's shoulders and pivoted her toward the door. "You, young lady, should get in your car, drive Mrs. Hughes home, then get back in your car again and drive straight to wherever Mike happens to be at the moment."

"And then what, Carly?" Katie inquired.

Carly sighed. "I'm in charge of the big ideas, here. You work out the details."

Katie laughed. "You did have some good ideas, Carly."

"And you worked out some awesome details."

Maddie grinned from one to the other. "We really did it, didn't we? We figured it out and we cracked the case."

"You girls most certainly did," Nancy agreed.

"Well, only with your help." Katie remembered to give credit where credit was due. "You got them all talking, Mrs. Hughes. We just picked up the threads."

"And wound them to their logical conclusion. That's the most important part." Nancy said, "You three make an excellent team. You complement each other. The next time there's wrongdoing in Oakdale, those criminals better watch out."

"Oh, no," Carly said. "No, thank you, I'm out of the amateur detective business."

"And my professional detective business is in the red. Like always."

"On the other hand . . ." Maddie began.

"No other hands. Goodnight, Maddie," Katie said. She laughed, grabbed her coat, and followed Mrs. Hughes to the door.

She opened it and courteously let the older woman through. She paused.

Katie turned around. Her eyes met Maddie's, then Carly's.

The three of them smiled. Maddie mischievously, Carly with bemusement, and Katie, full of possibilities.

"On the other hand . . ." Katie said.

And left it at that.

For now.

"Go take care of your brother, Maddie," Carly urged the teen as soon as Katie had stepped out of sight.

Henry was rising, as if in pain, from the chair that had pinned his body like an especially unsympathetic steel trap.

"Hey." Maddie crossed the bull pen to materialize behind him. "How's it going?"

"Just ducky." Henry shook first one foot, then the other,

wincing at the resulting pins and needles. "I'd say this has been a super swell evening, how about you?"

"Well . . ." Maddie decided to focus on the positive. "The murder charges Jack filed against you have been dropped. That's a pretty good thing, isn't it?"

"Murder charges that would have never been filed, if I'd been thinking with my head instead of my . . ." Henry remembered who he was talking to and went with a mild, "Um . . . manliness."

"Monica played you. She played all of us."

"This is true. But you, Madeline, my darling, are a six-teen-year-old girl, with no life experience outside of the mul-tiplex. . . . I'm correct in assuming that, right? Tell me I'm right, because I don't think my ticker could take another jolt tonight."

"You're absolutely right," she assured him. "Absolutely no experience outside of the multiplex."

"Good." He limped his way over to the door, balancing along the way upon any object—be it a desk, chair, com-puter monitor, or hat stand, that met his height require-ments. "I, on the other hand, am a grown man of a certain age. I should have known better than to fall for the oldest trick in the book. And I definitely should have kept you from getting messed up in it. That nut-job could have killed you!"

"I'm fine, Henry. Look. No harm, no foul."

"But you know what the worst of this is?"

"What?"

"I really liked that girl." The last of Henry's bravado crum-pled, leaving him devoid of quips, clichés, and pop-culture

formally confessed to murdering her stepfather, the case would be more or less closed and the work left to be done, minimal. Boy, was she wrong.

Watching Jack, Margo, Hal, even the new guy, Nick, struggle with the mounds of paperwork that would allow the matter to proceed to Tom at the D.A.'s office, was an eye-opener. It was also incredibly tedious. Somehow, when the policework was done on TV, or even when Jack regaled them with tales from his day around the dinner table, the part that went, "Then I filled out this piece of paper, and then I filled out that piece of paper, and then I stapled them together and took them to another officer to fill out . . ." just didn't come up quite as often.

For two hours, Carly watched her husband shuffle papers, and do it, she was certain, better than any other officer on the force. She watched him check his work, then she watched him go over other people's work. And all the while, Carly knew there was no place else she'd rather be.

"Having fun yet?" Jack asked during a break.

"I am, actually." Carly scooted over, inviting Jack to join her on the faded brown couch on which his fellow cops took turns pulling all-nighters.

Jack sat down, leaned in close, and slipped one arm around Carly's shoulder. He whispered, "Don't you ever scare me like that again."

"Scare you? I scared you?"

"When I saw you in the crowd gathered around Gregory's body, all I could think was: Carly, what have you done?"

"You what?" Carly couldn't believe what she was hearing. "You thought I—"

"What was I supposed to think? You tell me you couldn't survive it if Gregory ever had a chance to tell Parker and Sage some of the things he'd told me about you, you tell me you'd never let that happen, and then, a day later, the guy is murdered and you're standing there at a party you swore you wouldn't be caught dead at."

"But, Jack, no, I—"

"And afterward you were acting so strangely. Stealing my case file . . ."

"You knew about that?"

"Honey, I'm a cop."

"Why didn't you say anything?"

"What could I say? Excuse me, kids, would you leave the room for a second so I can ask your mother if she murdered that nice man from the hospital?"

"Yes!" She practically bounced up and down on the cushions, keeping her voice down but her tone up. "Yes, Jack! That's exactly what you should have done! Because then I would have said, Kids, would you leave the room for a second so I can ask Daddy if he murdered that awful man for me?"

"You thought I killed Gregory?"

"Where were you the afternoon before he died?"

"What?"

"I called the station. Margo said you took the afternoon off for personal reasons. No one knew where you were. You weren't answering your phone. I didn't know what to think."

"Did you think that maybe I just needed some time to clear my head? After my little chat with Gregory, I was having trouble keeping my mind on my work. Plus, there was the minor issue of me losing my temper like that. If it happened again on the job . . . I just needed a couple hours to pull myself together. Especially considering I'd committed to helping Nancy Hughes out later that night. I couldn't afford to have Gregory bait me like that again, especially not in public. So, I'm not proud of it, but, yeah, I went and had a few drinks to help me chill out. Though, I certainly wasn't going to say as much to Margo." He sighed, "You honestly thought I'd killed him?"

"You honestly thought that *I* did?"

Jack said, "It crossed my mind, yes. That's why I made sure I was put in charge of this case. I thought if I found any evidence connecting you to the murder—"

"But that's why I stole your case file! I wanted to see if you'd done it so that I could protect you! Helping Katie and Mike, and Maddie and Henry, yes, that turned out to be great, I'm happy everything worked out for everyone, but from the beginning this case was about one person and one person only for me, Jack. This was about you."

He stared at Carly for a long moment. And then he started to laugh. He laughed so loudly that both Hal and Margo looked up from their desks in curiosity. They saw that he was with Carly and, knowing that Jack was never, ever in his right mind when around his wife, they went on with what they were doing.

Jack said, "My God, Carly. What does it say about our marriage that we both were so quick to believe the other capable of murder?"

"Actually, I think a better question is, what does it say

about our marriage that we both were so quick to jump in and protect each other—no matter what the cost?"

Jack stopped laughing. He looked Carly in the eye and, for the second time that day, the existence of other people in the universe ceased to be a consideration. In a husky voice, he said, "I think it says something pretty good, as a matter of fact."

"Yeah." She kissed him on the chin. She kissed him on the cheek. She kissed him on the forehead and she kissed him, deeply, on the lips. "Me, too."

Carly's edict to Katie had been, "Get in your car and drive straight to wherever Mike happens to be at the moment."

A simple enough edict, but here came the pesky detail: Where in the world was Mike at the moment?

Katie didn't even know where he'd been staying since moving out of the cottage with her. She tried calling the Lakeview Hotel, but he wasn't registered—though Lisa, who was working the front desk, was very eager to gossip about what had gone down with the Marrons, which made Katie wonder how the news had traveled so fast. Did Lisa have spies in the police department?

Katie called Mike's ex-wife, Jennifer, who said she hadn't spoken to Mike in weeks, but she sarcastically wished Katie the very best of luck in tracking him down. Katie called Jack's cousin, Holden, and spoke to Holden's wife, Lily, who was equally at a loss. Then, in a fit of inspiration, Katie called Lily's mother, Lucinda Walsh, figuring if Mike was working on her guest house, Lucinda had to have a number where she could reach him.

"I'm sorry, Katie, I don't," Lucinda told her.

"Oh. Well, thanks anyway, Mrs. Walsh, it was just a thought."

"If I need Mike, I simply lean out my window and call him."

"Excuse me?"

"Connect the dots, dear. He's staying at the guest house while he's working here. Do you need everything spelled out for you?"

Despite the insult, Katie thanked her and hit the gas pedal. Hard. She was at the Walsh estate within fifteen minutes, and at the guest house door thirty seconds later.

Katie knocked loudly, chucking timid in favor of assertive. This was no time to be coy. Apologetic, yes, but not coy. She was here to win Mike Kasnoff back. And their reunion wasn't going to happen if she beat around the bush.

Of course, it wasn't going to happen period, if he never answered the door. So Katie knocked harder. She called Mike's name. She shouted that she wasn't leaving until they'd talked, so he might as well come out wherever he was.

Where he was, it turned out, was in the shower.

Katie knew this because he came to the door dressed only in a white towel around his waist.

She'd wanted to see him face to face. She got him face to chest. It was a very nice chest. Muscular and grooved and rippling in all the right places. It was the kind of chest that could make a girl forget everything she'd intended to say. Or spur her to say it even quicker, so they could get on with things.

"Henry told me everything," Katie said.

Mike stepped aside, gesturing for Katie to come in and closed the door behind her. "Okay."

"I still wish that you'd been the one to tell me, but—"

"I don't rat out my friends," Mike reminded her.

"—But I get it now. I understand why you couldn't explain how your fingerprints got on the bottle."

"That's good for you, Katie."

"I want to apologize."

"Forget about it."

"I'm sorry I didn't trust you."

"I gave you no reason to."

"I should have anyway." Katie tried to get closer to him but, with every step she took, Mike moved farther away. "I should have known you'd never do anything to hurt me."

"Yeah, Katie, you should have."

"It's just that Simon—"

"I don't give a damn about Simon, okay?" Mike erupted. "He was a jerk, he treated you badly, he broke your heart, he lied to you, and he even faked his own death a couple times—you'd think that particular trick would get old after the first go-around but hey, to each his own. . . . Do you know how many times I've heard that song from you, Katie?"

"I was only trying to explain why—"

"I know why. Everybody in town knows why. And guess what, Katie? I don't care anymore. I am tired of everything that I think is about you and me, turning out to be about you and me and Simon."

"That's totally untrue!"

"Oh, yeah? Would you have doubted me if it wasn't for

Simon? Would you have suspected me of hiding a deep, dark, dangerous secret if it wasn't for Simon? Would you have ever, in a million years, believed that I was capable of trying to kill you, if it wasn't for Simon?"

"I made a mistake!"

"Yeah, Katie, you did. And I'm starting to think—so did I."

If he'd slapped her, he couldn't have hurt Katie more than he did at that moment. "You mean . . . me?"

"Yeah." Mike didn't look at her as he said it, but he said it, nonetheless. "I mean you."

She felt her legs weaken and she placed her hand on the wall to steady herself. She couldn't think of anything to say short of "Oh . . ."

"I'm sorry," Mike said.

"I know. I know you are. You're a nice guy, you wouldn't be saying this if—"

"I don't know what else to do. This isn't working, Katie. I mean, it works for a while, everything is going great, we're happy—at least, I think we're happy, everything's cool, and then boom, you get some crazy idea and that's it, the universe is upside-down and the rest of us just better get out of the way."

"I'm something," Katie agreed.

"That you are."

"But that can be a good thing."

"It can," he conceded. "And it can't. I guess it all depends on how you look at the world."

"I want us to look at it the same way. I want us to look at it together. Always."

"And do you know what I want, Katie? I want to quit being your Not Simon."

"My what?"

"That's how you think of me, isn't it? Mike-is-Not Simon."

"I—"

"You have no idea how sick and tired I am of everything I do being judged against that Great Simon Scoreboard in the Sky."

"It's not. I swear it won't be. I love you, Mike."

"I know you do. It's just not enough."

"I'll make it enough."

"Katie . . ."

"No, Mike, I'm serious," Katie vowed. "I am promising you right here, right now, in the eyes of God and Lucinda Walsh next door, I'll make it enough. I'll prove that you and I belong together. I'll prove that I can change. You'll see. You just watch me and see."

Epilogue

❧

Nancy Hughes understood quite well that the town of Oakdale would continue to endure even if she were not around to keep an eye on things.

But why take unnecessary chances?

So as she went about her day, shopping, working, and running errands, Nancy kept her eyes open.

Driving through the park on her way to the hospital, she caught sight of Maddie and Henry Coleman. They did look somewhat unstable, but Nancy chalked that up to the clunky roller-blades strapped to their feet, rather than to any emotional crises that might require a pull-over intervention. Instead, Nancy merely honked her horn and waved.

Maddie and Henry looked up and waved back.

"Looking good, Mrs. H!" Maddie shouted.

"And she means that with all due respect!" Henry hollered.

"Right back at you," Nancy said, without raising her voice. After all, when called upon, she could get down and jiggy with it as well as the next person.

Popping into Al's Diner to pick up an order of doughnuts for her tutoring session with the children of the Earl Mitchell Center for Runaways, Nancy stopped by Jack and Carly's frenetic table. They had both kids with them. Parker was seemingly trying to swallow an entire chili-cheese dog in one ambitious, messy bite, while Sage appeared determined to make her guaranteed unspillable sippy cup of milk spill— all over Parker's lunch. Between them, Jack and Carly looked to be employing five hands as they tucked a napkin under Parker's chin, wiped up his spills, struggled with Sage over the cup, moved their own plates out of harm's way and, in final parental surrender, signaled the waitress for their check.

But, even in the midst of all that, Nancy was happy to note that at least one of Jack's hands remained under the table, gently squeezing Carly's knee the entire time.

Nancy said a quick hello, noting with a playful smile that *they sure did have their hands full, didn't they?* then moved on.

The Snyder family clearly had everything perfectly under control.

Nancy didn't end up seeing Katie and Mike until evening. And she didn't see much. Just the parts of them that were bobbing above the surface as they skinny-dipped in Snyder Pond in the moonlight.

She'd stopped by the farm to visit with Jack's Aunt Emma and, looking out the kitchen window, could just make out

Mike and Katie's sodden heads. Face to face, nose to nose. Lips to lips. Mike was kissing Katie like a man in love.

Katie's hands were on Mike's shoulders, while the tips of his fingers held her up below her arms. Even when they had to briefly shift to regain their balance in the water, their bodies were always touching.

Closing the curtains, Nancy turned her back on the scene—giving Katie and Mike their privacy—and smiled. For today, at least, the world was still turning.

And she expected it to keep doing so for a very long time to come.